# No Direction Home

Norman Spinrad was born in New York in 1940. He was first published in *Analog* in 1963 with 'The Last of Romany' and has followed this up with numerous short stories and novels, including the controversial *Bug Jack Barron* and *The Iron Dream*, an alternate history in which Hitler won the war. The latter novel won the French Prix Apollo in 1974.

D1353460

# No Direction Home

An anthology of science
fiction stories by

## Norman Spinrad

Fontana/Collins

For Terry Champagne
in memory of our season

Copyright © Norman Spinrad 1975
First British edition published by Millington Books 1976
First issued in Fontana 1977

Made and printed in Great Britain by
William Collins Sons & Co. Ltd, Glasgow

# Acknowledgments

'No Direction Home' reprinted from *New Worlds 2*, copyright © 1971 by Michael Moorcock.

'Heirloom' reprinted from the *Los Angeles Staff*, copyright © 1972 by the *Los Angeles Staff*.

'The Big Flash' reprinted from *Orbit 5*, copyright © 1969 by Damon Knight.

'The Conspiracy' reprinted from *New Worlds* Magazine, copyright © 1969 by New Worlds Publishing.

'The Weed of Time' reprinted from *Alchemy & Academe*, copyright © 1970 by Anne McCaffrey.

'A Thing of Beauty' reprinted from *Analog*, copyright © 1972 by Condé Nast Publications, Inc.

'The Lost Continent' reprinted from *Science Against Man*, copyright © 1970 by Avon Books.

'Heroes Die But Once' reprinted from *If* Magazine, copyright © 1969 by Universal Publishing Company.

'The National Pastime' reprinted from *Nova 3*, copyright © 1973 by Harry Harrison.

'In the Eye of the Storm', originally published under the title: 'Eye of the Storm', reprinted from *Galaxy*, copyright © 1974 by Universal Publishing and Distributing Company.

'All the Sounds of the Rainbow' reprinted from *Vertex*, copyright © 1973 by Mankind Publishing, Inc.

# Contents

# No Direction Home

How does it feel
To be on your own?
With no direction home.
Like a complete unknown.
Like a rolling stone.
    – Bob Dylan,
        from 'Like a Rolling Stone'

'But I once *did* succeed in stuffing it all back in Pandora's box,' Richarson said, taking another hit. 'You remember Pandora Deutchman, don't you, Will? Everybody in the biochemistry department stuffed it all in Pandora's box at one time or another. I seem to vaguely remember one party when you did it yourself.'

'Oh, you're a real comedian, Dave,' Goldberg said, stubbing out his roach and jamming a cork into the glass vial which he had been filling from the petcock at the end of the apparatus's run. 'Any day now I expect you to start slipping strychnine into the goods. That'd be pretty good for a yock, too.'

'You know, I never thought of that before. Maybe you got something there. Let a few people go out with a smile, satisfaction guaranteed. Christ, Will, we could tell them exactly what it was and still sell some of the stuff.'

'That's not funny, man,' Goldberg said, handing the vial to Richarson, who carefully snugged it away with the others in the excelsior-packed box. 'It's not funny because it's true.'

'Hey, you're not getting an attack of morals, are you? Don't move, I'll be right back with some methalin – that oughta get your head straight.'

'My head is straight already. Canabinolic acid, our own invention.'

'*Canabinolic acid?* Where did you get that, in a drugstore? We haven't bothered with it for three years.'

Goldberg placed another empty vial in the rack under the petcock and opened the valve. 'Bought it on the street for kicks,' he said. 'Kids are brewing it in their bathtubs now.' He shook his head, almost a random gesture. 'Remember what a bitch the original synthesis was?'

'Science marches on!'

'Too bad we couldn't have patented the stuff,' Goldberg said as he contemplated the thin stream of clear green liquid entering the open mouth of the glass vial. 'We could've retired off the royalties by now.'

'If we had the Mafia to collect for us.'

'That might be arranged.'

'Yeah, well, maybe I should look into it,' Richarson said as Goldberg handed him another full vial. 'We shouldn't be pigs about it, though. Just about ten per cent off the top at the manufacturing end. I don't believe in stifling private enterprise.'

'No, really, Dave,' Goldberg said, 'maybe we made a mistake in not trying to patent the stuff. People *do* patent combo psychedelics, you know.'

'You don't mean *people*, man, you mean outfits like American Marijuana and Psychedelics, Inc. They can afford the lawyers and grease. They can work the FDA's head. We can't.'

Goldberg opened the petcock valve. 'Yeah, well, at least it'll be six months or so before the dope industry or anyone else figures out how to synthesize this new crap, and by that time I think I'll have just about licked the decay problem in the cocanol extraction process. We should be one step ahead of the squares for at least another year.'

'You know what I think, Will?' Richarson said, patting the side of the half-filled box of vials. 'I think we got a holy mission, is what I think. I think we're servants of the evolutionary process: Every time we come up with a new psychedelic, we're advancing the evolution of human consciousness. We develop the stuff and make our bread off it for a while, and then the dope industry comes up with our synthesis and mass-produces it, and then we gotta come up with the next drug out so we can still set our tables in style. If it weren't for the dope industry and the way the drug laws are set up, we could stand still and become bloated plutocrats just by putting out the same old dope year after year. This way, we're doing some good in the world; we're doing something to further human evolution.'

Goldberg handed him another full vial. 'Screw human evolution,' he said. 'What has human evolution ever done for us?'


'As you know, Dr Taller, we're having some unforeseen side effects with eucomorfamine,' General Carlyle said, stuffing his favourite Dunhill with rough-cut burley. Taller took out a pack of Golds, extracted a joint, and lit it with a lighter bearing an air force, rather than a Psychedelics, Inc., insignia. Perhaps this had been a deliberate gesture, perhaps not.

'With a psychedelic as new as eucomorfamine, General,' Taller said, 'no side effects can quite be called "unforeseen". After all, even Project Groundhog itself is an experiment.'

Carlyle lit his pipe and sucked in a mouthful of smoke, which was good and carcinogenic; the general believed that a good soldier should cultivate at least one foolhardy minor vice. 'No word-games, please, Doctor,' he said. 'Eucomorfamine is supposed to help our men in the Groundhog moon-base deal with the claustrophobic conditions; it is not supposed to promote faggotry in the ranks. The reports I've been getting indicate that the drug is doing both. The air force does not want it to do both. Therefore, by definition, eucomorfamine has an undesirable side effect. Therefore, your contract is up for review.'

'General, General, psychedelics are not uniforms, after all. You can't expect us to tailor them to order. You asked for a drug that would combat claustrophobia without impairing alertness or the sleep cycle or attention span or initiative. You think this is easy? Eucomorfamine produces claustrophilia without any side effect but a raising of the level of sexual energy. As such, I consider it one of the minor miracles of psychedelic science.'

'That's all very well, Taller, but surely you can see that we simply cannot tolerate violent homosexual behaviour among our men in the moonbase.'

Taller smiled, perhaps somewhat fatuously. 'But you can't very well tolerate a high rate of claustrophobic breakdown, either,' he said. 'You have only four obvious alternatives, General Carlyle: continue to use eucomorfamine and accept a certain level of homosexual incidents, discontinue eucomorfamine and accept a very high level of claustrophobic break-down, or cancel Project Groundhog. Or . . .'

It dawned upon the general that he had been the object of a rather sophisticated sales pitch. 'Or go to a drug that would cancel out the side effect of eucomorfamine,' he said. 'Your company just wouldn't happen to have such a drug in the works, would it?'

Dr Taller gave him a we're-all-men-of-the-world grin. 'Psychedelics, Inc., *has* been working on a sexual suppressant,' he admitted none too grudgingly. 'Not an easy psychic spec to fill. The problem is that if you actually decrease sexual energy, you tend to get impaired performance in the higher cerebral centres, which is all very well in penal institutions, but hardly acceptable in Project Groundhog's case. The trick is to channel the excess energy elsewhere. We decided that the only viable alternative was to siphon it off into mystical fugue-states. Once we worked it out, the biochemistry became merely a matter of detail. We're about ready to bring the drug we've developed – trade name nadabrin – into the production stage.'

The general's pipe had gone out. He did not bother to relight it. Instead, he took five milligrams of lebemil, which seemed more to the point at the moment. 'This nadabrin,' he said very deliberately, 'it bleeds off the excess sexuality into *what*? Fugue-states? Trances? We certainly don't need a drug that makes our men psychotic.'

'Of course not. About three hundred micrograms of nada-brin will give a man a mystical experience that lasts less than four hours. He won't be much good to you during that time, to be sure, but his sexual energy level will be severely depressed for about a week. Three hundred micrograms to each man on eucomorfamine, say every five days, to be on the safe side.'

General Carlyle relit his pipe and ruminated. Things seemed to be looking up. 'Sounds pretty good,' he finally admitted. 'But what about the content of the mystical experiences? Nothing that would impair devotion to duty?'

Taller snubbed out his roach. 'I've taken nadabrin myself,' he said. 'No problems.'

'What was it like?'

Taller once again put on his fatuous smile. 'That's the best part of nadabrin,' he said. 'I don't remember what it was like. You don't retain any memories of what happens to you under nadabrin. Genuine fugue-state. So you can be sure the mystical experiences don't have any undesirable content, can't you? Or at any rate, you can be sure that the experience can't impair a man's military performance.'

'What the men don't remember can't hurt them, eh?' Carlyle muttered into his pipestem.

'What was that, General?'

'I said I'd recommend that we give it a try.'

They sat together in a corner booth back in the smoke, sizing each other up while the crowd in the joint yammered and swirled around them in some other reality, like a Bavarian

12

merry-go-round.

'What are you on?' he said, noticing that her hair seemed black and seamless like a beetle's carapace, a dark metal helmet framing her pale face in glory. Wow.

'Peyotadrene,' she said, her lips moving like incredibly jewelled and articulated metal flower petals. 'Been up for about three hours. What's your trip?'

'Canabinolic acid,' he said, the distortion of his mouth's movement casting his face into an ideogramic pattern which was barely decipherable to her perception as a foreshadowing of energy release. Maybe they would make it.

'I haven't tried any of that stuff for months,' she said. 'I hardly remember what that reality feels like.' Her skin luminesced from within, a translucent white china mask over a yellow candle-flame. She was a magnificent artifact, a creation of jaded and sophisticated gods.

'It feels good,' he said, his eyebrows forming a set of curves which, when considered as part of a pattern containing the movement of his lips against his teeth, indicated a clear desire to donate energy to the filling of her void. They *would* make it. 'Call me old-fashioned, maybe, but I still think canabinolic acid is groovy stuff.'

'Do you think you could go on a sex trip behind it?' she asked. The folds and wrinkles of her ears had been carved with microprecision out of pink ivory.

'Well, I suppose so, in a peculiar kind of way,' he said, hunching his shoulders forward in a clear gesture of offering, an alignment with the pattern of her movement through space-time that he could clearly perceive as intersecting her trajectory. 'I mean, if you want me to ball you, I think I can make it.'

The tiny gold hairs on her face were a microscopic field of wheat shimmering in a shifting summer breeze as she said, 'That's the most meaningful thing anyone has said to me in hours.'

The convergence of every energy configuration in the entire universe towards complete identity with the standing wave pattern of its maximum ideal structure was brightly mirrored for the world to see in the angle between the curves of her lips as she spoke.

Cardinal McGavin took a peyotadrene-mescamil combo and five milligrams of metadrene an hour and a half before his meeting with Cardinal Rillo; he had decided to try to deal

13

with Rome on a mystical rather than a political level, and that particular prescription made him feel most deeply Christian. And the Good Lord knew that it could become very difficult to feel deeply Christian when dealing with a representative of the Pope.

Cardinal Rillo arrived punctually at three, just as Cardinal McGavin was approaching his mystical peak; the man's punctuality was legend. Cardinal McGavin felt pathos in that: the sadness of a Prince of the Church whose major impact on the souls of his fellows lay in his slavery to the hands of a clock. Because the ascetic-looking old man, with his colourless eyes and pencil-thin lips, was so thoroughly unlovable, Cardinal McGavin found himself cherishing the man for his very existential hopelessness. He sent forth a silent prayer that he, or if not he, then at least someone, might be chosen as an instrument through which this poor, cold creature might be granted a measure of Divine Grace.

Cardinal Rillo accepted the amenities with cold formality, and in the same spirit agreed to share some claret. Cardinal McGavin knew better than to offer a joint; Cardinal Rillo had been in the forefront of the opposition which had caused the Pope to delay his inevitable encyclical on marijuana for long, ludicrous years. That the Pope had chosen such an emissary in this matter was not a good sign.

Cardinal Rillo sipped at his wine in sour silence for long moments while Cardinal McGavin was nearly overcome with sorrow at the thought of the loneliness of the soul of this man, who could not even break the solemnity of his persona to share some Vatican gossip over a little wine with a fellow cardinal. Finally, the papal emissary cleared his throat – a dry, archaic gesture – and got right to the point.

'The Pontiff has instructed me to convey his concern at the addition of psychedelics to the composition of the communion host in the Archdiocese of New York,' he said, the tone of his voice making it perfectly clear that he wished the Holy Father had given him a much less cautious warning to deliver. But if the Pope had learned anything at all from the realities of this schismatic era, it was caution, especially when dealing with the American hierarchy, whose allegiance to Rome was based on nothing firmer than nostalgia and symbolic convenience. The Pope had been the last to be convinced of his own fallibility, but in the last few years events seemed to have finally brought the new refinement of Divine Truth home.

'I acknowledge and respect the Holy Father's concern,'

Cardinal McGavin said. 'I shall pray for divine resolution of his doubt.'

'I didn't say anything about doubt!' Cardinal Rillo snapped, his lips moving with the crispness of pincers. 'How can you impute doubt to the Holy Father?'

Cardinal McGavin's spirit soared over a momentary spark of anger at the man's pigheadedness; he tried to give Cardinal Rillo's soul a portion of peace. 'I stand corrected,' he said. 'I shall pray for the alleviation of the Holy Father's concern.'

But Cardinal Rillo was implacable and inconsolable; his face was a membrane of control over a musculature of rage. 'You can more easily relieve the Holy Father's concern by removing the peyotadrene from your hosts!' he said.

'Are those the words of the Holy Father?' Cardinal McGavin asked, knowing the answer.

'Those are *my* words, Cardinal McGavin,' Cardinal Rillo said, 'and you would do well to heed them. The fate of your immortal soul may be at stake.'

A flash of insight, a sudden small satori, rippled through Cardinal McGavin: Rillo was sincere. For him, the question of a chemically augmented host was not a matter of Church politics, as it probably was to the Pope; it touched on an area of deep religious conviction. Cardinal Rillo was indeed concerned for the state of his soul and it behoved him, both as a cardinal and as a Catholic, to treat the matter seriously on that level. For, after all, chemically augmented communion was a matter of deep religious conviction for him as well. He and Cardinal Rillo faced each other across a gap of existentially meaningful theological disagreement.

'Perhaps the fate of yours as well, Cardinal Rillo,' he said.

'I didn't come here all the way from Rome to seek spiritual guidance from a man who is skating on the edge of heresy, Cardinal McGavin. I came here to deliver the Holy Father's warning that an encyclical may be issued against your position. Need I remind you that if you disobey such an encyclical you may be excommunicated?'

'Would you be genuinely sorry to see that happen?' Cardinal McGavin asked, wondering how much of the threat was Rillo's wishful thinking, and how much the instructions of the Pope. 'Or would you simply feel that the Church had defended itself properly?'

'Both,' Cardinal Rillo said without hesitation.

'I like that answer,' Cardinal McGavin said, tossing down the rest of his glass of claret. It was a good answer – sincere on both counts. Cardinal Rillo feared both for the Church and for the soul of the archbishop of New York, and there was no doubt that he quite properly put the Church first. His sincerity was spiritually refreshing, even though he was thoroughly wrong all around. 'But you see, part of the gift of Grace that comes with a scientifically sound chemical augmentation of communion is a certainty that no one – not even the Pope – can do anything to cut you off from communion with God. In psychedelic communion, one experiences the love of God directly. It's always just a host away; faith is no longer even necessary.'

Cardinal Rillo grew sombre. 'It is my duty to report that to the Pope,' he said. 'I trust you realize that.'

'Who am I talking to, Cardinal Rillo, you or the Pope?'

'You are talking to the Catholic Church, Cardinal McGavin,' Cardinal Rillo said. 'I am an emissary of the Holy Father.' Cardinal McGavin felt an instant pang of guilt: his sharpness had caused Cardinal Rillo to imply an untruth out of anger, for surely his papal mission was far more limited than he had tried to intimate. The Pope was too much of a realist to make the empty threat of excommunication against a Prince of the Church who believed that his power of excommunication was itself meaningless.

But, again, a sudden flash of insight illuminated the cardinal's mind with truth: in the eyes of Cardinal Rillo – in the eyes of an important segment of the Church hierarchy – the threat of excommunication still held real meaning. To accept their position on chemically augmented communion was to accept the notion that the word of the Pope could withdraw a man from Divine Grace. To accept the sanctity and validity of psychedelic communion was to deny the validity of excommunication.

'You know, Cardinal Rillo,' he said, 'I firmly believe that if I am excommunicated by the Pope, it will threaten my soul not one iota.'

'That's merely cheap blasphemy!'

'I'm sorry,' Cardinal McGavin said sincerely. 'I meant to be neither cheap nor blasphemous. All I was trying to do was explain that excommunication can hardly be meaningful when God through the psychedelic sciences has seen fit to grant us a means of certain direct experience of His countenance. I believe with all my heart that this is true. You believe with all your heart that it is not.'

'I believe that what you experience in your psychedelic

16

communion is nothing less than a masterstroke of Satan, Cardinal McGavin. Evil is infinitely subtle; might not it finally masquerade as the ultimate good? The Devil is not known as the Prince of Liars without reason. I believe that you are serving Satan in what you sincerely believe is the service of God. Is there any way that you can be sure that I am wrong?'

'Can you be sure that *I'm* not right?' Cardinal McGavin said. 'If I am, you are attempting to stifle the will of God and wilfully removing yourself from His Grace.'

'We cannot both be right . . .' Cardinal Rillo said.

And the burning glare of a terrible and dark mystical insight filled Cardinal McGavin's soul with terror, a harsh illumination of his existential relationship to the Church and to God: they both couldn't be right, but there was no reason why they both couldn't be wrong. Apart from both God and Satan existed the void.

Dr Braden gave Johnny a pat-on-the-head smile and handed him a mango-flavoured lollipop from the supply of goodies in his lower left desk drawer. Johnny took the lollipop, unwrapped it quickly, popped it into his mouth, leaned back in his chair, and began to suck the sweet avidly, oblivious to the rest of the world. It was a good sign – a preschooler with a proper reaction to a proper basic prescription should focus strongly and completely on the most interesting element in its environment; he should be fond of unusual flavours. In the first four years of its life, a child's sensorium should be tuned to accept the widest possible spectrum of sensual stimulation.

Braden turned his attention to the boy's mother, who sat rather nervously on the edge of her chair, smoking a joint. 'Now, now, Mrs Lindstrom, there's nothing to worry about,' he said. 'Johnny has been responding quite normally to his prescription. His attention span is suitably short for a child of his age; his sensual range slightly exceeds the optimum norm; his sleep pattern is regular and properly deep. And as you requested, he has been given a constant sense of universal love.'

'But then why did the school doctor ask me to have his basic prescription changed, Dr Braden? He said that Johnny's prescription was giving him the wrong personality pattern for a school-age child.'

Dr Braden was rather annoyed, though of course he would never betray it to the nervous young mother. He knew the sort of failed GP who usually occupied a school doctor's

17

position; a faded old fool who knew about as much about psychedelic pediatrics as he did about brain surgery. What he did know was worse than nothing – a smattering of half-assed generalities and pure rubbish that was just enough to convince him that he was an expert – which entitled him to go around frightening the mothers of other people's patients, no doubt.

'I'm . . . ah, certain you misunderstood what the school doctor said, Mrs Lindstrom,' Dr Braden said. 'At least I hope you did, because if you didn't, then the man is mistaken. You see, modern psychedelic pediatrics recognizes that the child needs to have his consciousness focused in different areas at different stages of his development if he is to grow up to be a healthy, maximized individual. A child of Johnny's age is in a transitional stage. In order to prepare him for schooling, I'll simply have to alter his prescription so as to increase his attention span, lower his sensory intensity a shade, and increase his interest in abstractions. Then he'll do fine in school, Mrs Lindstrom.'

Dr Braden gave the young woman a moderately stern admonishing frown. 'You really should have brought Johnny in for a check-up *before* he started school, you know.'

Mrs Lindstrom puffed nervously on her joint while Johnny continued to suck happily on his lollipop. 'Well . . . I was sort of afraid to, Dr Braden,' she admitted. 'I know it sounds silly, but I was afraid that if you changed his prescription to what the school wanted, you'd stop the paxum. I didn't want that – I think it's more important for Johnny to continue to feel universal love than to increase his attention span or any of that stuff. You're not going to stop the paxum, are you?'

'Quite the contrary, Mrs Lindstrom,' Dr Braden said. 'I'm going to increase his dose slightly and give him ten milligrams of orodalamine daily. He'll submit to the necessary authority of his teachers with a sense of trust and love, rather than out of fear.'

For the first time during the visit, Mrs Lindstrom smiled. 'Then it all really *is* all right, isn't it?' She radiated happiness born of relief.

Dr Braden smiled back at her, basking in the sudden surge of good vibrations. This was his peak experience in pediatrics: feeling the genuine gratitude of a worried mother whose fears he had thoroughly relieved. This was what being a doctor was all about. She trusted him. She put the consciousness of her child in his hands, trusting that those hands would not falter or fail. He was proud and grateful to be a psychedelic pediatrician. He was maximizing human happiness.

'Yes, Mrs Lindstrom,' he said soothingly, 'everything is going to be all right.'

In the chair in the corner, Johnny Lindstrom sucked on his lollipop, his face transfigured with boyish bliss.


There were moments when Bill Watney got a soul-deep queasy feeling about psychedelic design, and lately he was getting those bad flashes more and more often. He was glad to have caught Spiegelman alone in the designers' lounge; if anyone could do anything for his head, Lennie was it. 'I dunno,' he said, washing down fifteen milligrams of lebemil with a stiff shot of bourbon, 'I'm really thinking of getting out of this business.'

Leonard Spiegelman lit a Gold with his fourteen-carat-gold lighter – nothing but the best for the best in the business – smiled across the coffee table at Watney, and said quite genially, 'You're out of your mind, Bill.'

Watney sat hunched slightly forward in his easy chair, studying Spiegelman, the best artist Psychedelics, Inc., had, and envying the older man – envying not only his talent, but his attitude towards his work. Lennie Spiegelman was not only certain that what he was doing was right, he enjoyed every minute of it. Watney wished he could be like Spiegelman. Spiegelman was happy; he radiated the contented aura of a man who really did have everything he wanted.

Spiegelman opened his arms in a gesture that seemed to make the whole designers' lounge his personal property. 'We're the world's best-pampered artists,' he said. 'We come up with two or three viable drug designs a year, and we can live like kings. And we're practising the world's ultimate art form: creating realities. We're the luckiest mothers alive! Why would anyone with your talent want out of psychedelic design?'

Watney found it difficult to put into words, which was ridiculous for a psychedelic designer, whose work it was to describe new possibilities in human consciousness well enough for the biochemists to develop psychedelics which would transform his specs into styles of reality. It was humiliating to be at a loss for words in front of Lennie Spiegelman, a man he both envied and admired. 'I'm getting bad flashes lately,' he finally said, 'deep flashes that go through every style of consciousness that I try, flashes that tell me I should be ashamed and disgusted about what I'm doing.'

Oh-oh, Lennie Spiegelman thought, the kid is coming up

with his first case of designer's cafard. He's floundering around with that no-direction-home syndrome and he thinks it's the end of the world. 'I know what's bothering you, Bill,' he said. 'It happens to all of us at one time or another. You feel that designing psychedelic specs is a solipsistic occupation, right? You think there's something morally wrong about designing new styles of consciousness for other people, that we're playing God, that continually altering people's consciousness in ways only we fully understand is a thing that mere mortals have no right to do, like hubris, eh?'

Watney flashed admiration for Spiegelman – his certainty *wasn't* based on a thick ignorance of the existential doubt of their situation. There was hope in that, too. 'How can you understand all that, Lennie,' he said, 'and still dig psychedelic design the way you do?'

'Because it's a load of crap, that's why,' Spiegelman said. 'Look, kid, we're artists – commercial artists at that. We design psychedelics, styles of reality; we don't tell anyone what to think. If people like the realities we design for them, they buy the drugs, and if they don't like our art, they don't. People aren't going to buy food that tastes lousy, music that makes their ears hurt, or drugs that put them in bummer realities. *Somebody* is going to design styles of consciousness for the human race; if not artists like us, then a lot of crummy politicians and power freaks.'

'But what makes us any better than them? Why do we have any more right to play games with the consciousness of the human race than they do?'

The kid is really dense, Spiegelman thought. But then he smiled, remembering that he had been on the same stupid trip when he was Watney's age. 'Because we're artists, and they're not,' he said. 'We're not out to control people. We get our kicks from carving something beautiful out of the void. All we want to do is enrich people's lives. We're creating new styles of consciousness that we think are improved realities, but we're not shoving them down people's throats. We're just laying out our wares for the public – right doesn't even enter into it. We have a compulsion to practise our art. Right and wrong are arbitrary concepts that vary with the style of consciousness, so how on earth can you talk about the right and wrong of psychedelic design? The only way you can judge is by an aesthetic criterion – are we producing good art or bad?'

'Yeah, but doesn't *that* vary with the style of consciousness, too? Who can judge in an absolute sense whether your stuff is artistically pleasing or not?'

'Jesus Christ, Bill, *I* can judge, can't I?' Spiegelman said. 'I know when a set of psychedelic specs is a successful work of art. It either pleases me or it doesn't.'

It finally dawned on Watney that that was precisely what was eating at him. A psychedelic designer altered his own reality with a wide spectrum of drugs and then designed other psychedelics to alter other people's realities. Where was anyone's anchor?

'But don't you see, Lennie?' he said. 'We don't know what the hell we're doing. We're taking the human race on an evolutionary trip, but we don't know where we're going. We're flying blind.'

Spiegelman took a big drag on his joint. The kid was starting to get to him; he was whining too much. Watney didn't want anything out of line – just certainty! 'You want me to tell you there's a way you can know when a design is right or wrong in some absolute evolutionary framework, right?' he said. 'Well, I'm sorry, Bill, there's nothing but us and the void and whatever we carve out of it. We're our own creations; our realities are our own works of art. We're out here all alone.'

Watney was living through one of his flashes of dread, and he saw that Spiegelman's words described its content exactly. 'But that's exactly what's eating at me!' he said. 'Where in hell is our basic reality?'

'There is no basic reality. I thought they taught that in kindergarten these days.'

'But what about the basic state? What about the way our reality was before the art of psychedelic design? What about the consciousness style that evolved naturally over millions of years? Damn it, that was the basic reality, and we've lost it!'

'The hell it was!' Spiegelman said. 'Our pre-psychedelic consciousness evolved on a mindless random basis. What makes that reality superior to any other? Just because it was first? We may be flying blind, but natural evolution was worse – it was an idiot process without an ounce of consciousness behind it.'

'Goddamn it, you're right all the way down the line, Lennie!' Watney cried in anguish. 'But why do you feel so good about it while I feel so rotten? I want to be able to feel the way you do, but I can't.'

'Of course you can, Bill,' Spiegelman said. He abstractedly

remembered that he had felt like Watney years ago, but there was no existential reality behind it. What more could a man want than a random universe that was anything he could make of it and nothing else? Who wouldn't rather have a style of consciousness created by an artist than one that was the result of a lot of stupid evolutionary accidents?

He says it with such certainty, Watney thought. Christ, how I want him to be right! How I'd like to face the uncertainty of it all, the void, with the courage of Lennie Spiegelman! Spiegelman had been in the business for fifteen years; maybe he *had* finally figured it all out.

'I wish I could believe that,' Watney said.

Spiegelman smiled, remembering what a solemn jerk he himself had been ten years ago. 'Ten years ago, I felt just like you feel now,' he said. 'But I got my head together and now here I am, fat and happy and digging what I'm doing.'

'How, Lennie, for Christ's sake, *how*?'

'Fifty mikes of methalin, forty milligrams of lebemil and twenty milligrams of peyotadrene daily,' Spiegelman said. 'It made a new man out of me, and it'll make a new man out of you.'


'How do you feel, man?' Kip said, taking the joint out of his mouth and peering intently into Jonesy's eyes. Jonesy looked really weird – pale, manic, maybe a little crazed. Kip was starting to feel glad that Jonesy hadn't talked him into taking the trip with him.

'Oh, wow,' Jonesy croaked, 'I feel strange, I feel *really* strange, and it doesn't feel so good . . .'

The sun was high in the cloudless blue sky, a golden fountain of radiant energy filling Kip's being. The wood and bark of the tree against which they sat was an organic reality connecting the skin of his back to the bowels of the earth in an unbroken circuit of protoplasmic electricity. He was a flower of his planet, rooted deep in the rich soil, basking in the cosmic nectar of the sunshine.

But behind Jonesy's eyes was some kind of awful grey vortex. Jonesy looked really bad. Jonesy was definitely floating on the edges of a bummer.

'I don't feel good at all,' Jonesy said. 'Man, you know, the ground is covered with all kinds of hard dead things and the grass is filled with mindless insects and the sun is hot, man. I think I'm burning.'

'Take it easy, don't freak. You're on a trip, that's all,' Kip said from some asshole superior viewpoint. He just didn't understand, he didn't understand how heavy this trip was, what it felt like to have your head raw and naked out here. Like cut off from every energy flow in the universe – a construction of fragile matter, protoplasmic ooze is all, isolated in an energy vacuum, existing in relationship to nothing but empty void and horrible mindless matter.

'You don't understand, Kip,' he said. 'This is reality, the way it *really* is, and, man, it's horrible, just a great big ugly machine made up of lots of other machines; you're a machine, I'm a machine – it's all mechanical clockwork. We're just lumps of dead matter run by machinery, kept alive by chemical and electric processes.'

Golden sunlight soaked through Kip's skin and turned the core of his being into a miniature stellar phoenix. The wind, through random blades of grass, made love to the bare soles of his feet. What was all this machinery crap? What the hell was Jonesy gibbering about? Man, who would want to put himself in a bummer reality like that?

'You're just on a bummer, Jonesy,' he said. 'Take it easy. You're not seeing the universe the way it really is, as if that meant anything. Reality is all in your head. You're just freaking out behind nothing.'

'That's it, that's *exactly* it! I'm freaking out behind nothing. Like zero. Like cipher. Like the void. Nothing is where we're *really* at.'

How could he explain it – that reality was really just a lot of empty vacuum that went on to infinity in space and time? The perfect nothingness had minor contaminations of dead matter here and there. A little of this matter had fallen together through a complex series of random accidents to contaminate the universal deadness with trace elements of life, protoplasmic slime, biochemical clockwork. Some of this clockwork was complicated enough to generate thought, consciousness. And that was all there ever was or would ever be anywhere in space and time. Clockwork mechanisms rapidly running down in the cold black void. Everything that wasn't dead matter already would end up that way sooner or later.

'This is the way it really is,' Jonesy said. 'People used to live in this bummer all the time. It's the way it is, and nothing we can do can change it.'

'I can change it,' Kip said, taking his pillbox out of his pocket. 'Just say the word. Let me know when you've had enough and I'll bring you out of it. Lebemil, peyotadrene,

23

mescamil, you name it.'

'You don't understand, man, it's *real*. That's the trip I'm on. I haven't taken anything at all for twelve hours, remember? It's the natural state, it's reality itself, and, man, it's awful. It's a horrible bummer. Christ, why did I have to talk myself into this? I don't want to see the universe this way. Who needs it?'

Kip was starting to get pissed off – Jonesy was becoming a real bring-down. Why did he have to pick a beautiful day like this to take his stupid nothing-trip?

'Then *take* something already,' he said, offering Jonesy the pillbox.

Shakily, Jonesy scooped out a cap of peyotadrene and a fifteen-milligram tab of lebemil and wolfed them down dry. 'How did people *live* before psychedelics?' he said. 'How could they stand it?'

'Who knows?' Kip said, closing his eyes and staring straight at the sun, diffusing his consciousness into the universe of golden orange light encompassed by his eyelids. 'Maybe they had some way of not thinking about it.'


# Heirloom


'So Bornok was your last campaign, Grandpa?' the boy said, settling back on the couch.

'Uh,' said the old man, lighting his blackened pipe, 'Bornok was the end of it.' He seemed content to leave it at that.

'Why?' said the boy, hoping to draw the old man out. His small experience with old men taught him to expect them to ramble on about the past at the slightest provocation, but Grandpa, who had risen to the rank of captain in the defence force, who had been in on the invasion of seven solar systems, was different. Getting him to talk was like pulling teeth.

'You're too young to remember Bornok,' the old man said. 'Happened before you were born. We'd grabbed off twelve solar systems before Bornok, and I was in on six of 'em. The Knockers were the only gooks that beat us.'

'*Beat us*? But we learned in school that we *won* on Bornok. The Draadens grabbed bases on the other two planets in the system, and on the outer moon, and they were all set to invade Bornok itself, so we temporarily –'

24

'Crap!' the old man said.

'It's not true?'

' 'Course not. Lot of rot. First of all, we had a base on the inner moon before the Draadens even showed up. And second ... Tell me, just what do they teach you about the Knockers? *That* oughta be good for a laugh!'

The boy could see that the old man was beginning to warm up. All he seemed to need was something to get mad at.

'Well ... the Bornoks are a very humanoid race inhabiting the only –'

'Yeah, sure!' the old man grunted. '*Very humanoid.* Believe me, it's the gooks that *look* the humanest you gotta watch out for. Never forget that.'

'But –'

'Look, everything they tell you about Bornok is a pack of lies. Not that I blame them. They damn well better keep it a secret ... if it ever got out ...' The skin at the corner of the old man's left eye began to twitch.

'Tell me about it, Grandpa. You were there.'

'I was there, all right,' the old man said. 'Ain't ever likely to forget *that.* But we were told to keep our mouths shut, and for once the brass was right.'

'Grandpa!'

The old man sighed. His pipe had gone out again. He relit it, shaking his head.

'Ah ... aw, hell!' he said. 'Maybe you got a right to know. Some day you may end up on some lousy mudball wondering what the hell's coming off. All right, son, hang on to your illusions ...'

First of all, let's get one thing straight – *we* were in the Bornok system before the Draadens. Survey had cased the planet for future solar expansion. Warm, fertile, ninety-nine and eight-tenths Earthlike, humanoid natives without any technology, an agrarian planet that could be subjugated with no sweat at all.

Don't interrupt! I know how horrible that sounds to your tender young ears. They fill you full of hogwash about how we just *accidentally* ended up controlling twelve inhabited systems in the past hundred years. Rot! We wanted those planets, and we got 'em, one way or another.

And we had a real slick little scheme worked out for Bornok, with the help of the Draadens.

You heard me, the Draadens! Not that the little green

devils helped us out of love. It was strictly *quid pro quo*. We withdrew our claim to Moali in favour of Draada, and in return the Draadens gave us an excuse to seize Bornok.

Oh, it was quite a little gem, it was. We set up a scientific base on the inner moon. A year later, the Draadens set up a scientific base on the outer moon. Our politicians make a few nasty speeches. Then the Draadens set up another 'scientific base' on one of the worthless rocks in the Bornok system, only this time they made it look like a cover for a military base. Now, our politicians can make *threatening* speeches. They proceeded to do so. So then the Draadens set up an overt military base on the third planet. And *their* politicians make threatening speeches.

What was it all for? Use your head, son! All this Mickey-Mousing around sets it up for us to invade Bornok on the pretext of protecting our 'humanoid brothers' from the 'in-human reptilian Draadens'. We get Bornok, Draada gets Moali. *Quid pro quo*, and everyone's happy but the local gooks.

So we set up an invasion of Bornok. No big deal, nothing fancy – remember, the Knockers were strictly hayseeds, no technology, not even an army. Not even a government you could shake a gun at. The defence force command figured we could pull it off with twenty divisions of mechanized light infantry, and, by every rule in the book, they should've been right.

Only they were wrong.

Who knows where it first happened? Could've been any-where on Bornok. Maybe it was in a little village near a small river about fifty miles from a range of mountains which was scheduled to be occupied by a company of light infantry. Maybe it started somewhere else. It doesn't really matter.

The company wasn't very heavily armed – heat rifles, hand guns, three personnel-carrier tanks. And even that was an awful lot of hardware to haul into a village where the most dangerous weapon was a pickaxe. Bornok had no governments, planet-wide or local; hence, not even the beginnings of a primitive army. Not even a warrior caste.

There was some kind of council that met whenever there was something really important to consider, which was about once every three hundred years, according to what passed as the local historians. The council had met, had passed a resolution to the effect that Bornok did not recognize the right of Sol to occupy the planet, and had gone home without being stupid enough to make hollow threats. A piece of cake.

Or so we thought.

It was a nothing little village: clusters of sod-and-thatch huts around a dirt village square, corrals, scrubby vegetable gardens, and three big wooden longhouses on three sides of the square. A sleepy little village on a sleepy little planet . . .

The captain ordered his three PCTs into the square. Because they were riding PCTs, the soldiers knew that the brass expected no trouble. If you ever end up in the defence force, you'll find out that whenever there's a real fight and PCTs'd do the most good, they make you walk. When they let you ride, it's a sure sign they expect you to get off with a whole hide.

So the whole company was feeling loose and easy as they got out of the PCTs. It was the usual mix of sappy eager kids and old pros, and the pros were maybe a little happier than the kids, knowing there would be no fight.

The captain jumped down from the lead PCT and signalled to his driver, who hit the klaxon button. You can bet that klaxon was the loudest thing the local gooks had ever heard. Still, they just kind of drifted into the square real slowly, milled around a bit, looking the soldiers over without even getting sullen about it.

Good-looking gooks, those Bornoks. Tall as humans on the average, mostly red-haired. Hard to tell 'em from humans, if not for the light green skin. And the women looked good and seemed to know how to smile. That always makes for an easy occupation.

When the square was more or less full, the captain began his little speech, in hypno-learned Bornok.

'We . . . soldiers of Sol . . . greet you. We are your protectors. We promise that as long as we are on Bornok the scaly Draadens . . .' Blah, blah, et cetera. The standard baloney. The Bornoks didn't seem very interested, even when the young captain got to the kicker: 'Naturally, we will need to set up a security system. For that purpose, we have been assigned to this village. All citizens of this village will be issued identity cards which they are to carry on their person at all times. You will now line up in front of the machine on your left for –'

Suddenly an old man at the rear of the crowd shouted something in gook. He must've been the mayor or the medicine man or something, because just as calm as you please the Knockers started walking out of the square.

27

'Stop!' the captain yelled. 'Stop! Form a single line in front of the machine to your left!'

But the damned Knockers kept on walking. They didn't even look back.

'Stop! I order you to stop!'

The gooks kept on walking, silently.

'Stop, or I shoot!' the captain shouted. He had expected *some* kind of minor trouble, maybe even a riot, but this . . .

'Fire a volley over their heads,' he ordered in English.

A hum of heat beams and the crack of bullets.

The gooks kept on walking. They didn't look back.

The captain was turning beet-red. He had seen plenty, but he had never seen anything like this. His blue eyes narrowed.

'Stop!' he shouted in Bornok. 'Stop, or I shoot your . . . your chief . . .' He pointed at the old man. The soldiers tensed. Guns were recocked, aimed lower. The three PCT turrets swivelled to bear on the slowly retreating Bornoks.

The captain drew his pistol. It was an antique, non-reg forty-five, a regular hand-cannon. The old gun gave the captain a sense of continuity with the past, and he loved it. And he was a crack shot.

He sighted along the barrel. 'Last chance!' he yelled, and then gritted his teeth. It looked like these people would have to be taught a lesson. The captain was not used to teaching unarmed civilians lessons.

The Bornoks kept on walking.

There was a loud crack and the old man's head flew apart like a mashed watermelon.

A few of the more nervous and less experienced soldiers, expecting the Bornoks to turn and charge, began firing. A few Knockers fell in the dusty square.

But the rest kept on walking. They did not look back.

And in a minute or two, the soldiers were alone, in the dusty square, in the waning afternoon sun.

The puzzled and shaken captain deployed his men around the village, posted sentries around the PCTs, and sent out patrols along the nearby roads.

That evening, a Bornok led his animal, laden with wicker baskets, down a road from his fields to the village.

An old sergeant, fat and grizzled, and two young privates were posted on the road just around a bend from the village.

'Halt for inspection,' the sergeant grunted as the Bornok and his animal approached the bend.

The Bornok and his animal continued on their way; the Knocker seemed to be looking right through the sergeant and his men.

'I said *halt*!' roared the sergeant, raising his heat rifle.

The Bornok kept on walking.

The sergeant trained his rifle on the Bornok, now no more than five feet from him. The Bornok seemed not to notice.

'Halt, damn you!' the sergeant screamed shrilly. 'Last chance!'

The Bornok walked past the soldiers. The sergeant cursed and fired. The Bornok's body flamed, crisped, and fell. The animal kept on walking.

The soldiers were alone, on the road, in the red twilight.

For a week it went on, in silence. Not a word was spoken by the Bornoks to the soldiers. Fields were burned in retribution; the Bornoks stood idly by. If they were struck, they might bleed, nothing more. When their food was seized, they said nothing.

The captain didn't know what to do. He was young, but he was experienced; nevertheless, neither experience nor The Book covered *this* situation. His men were restless; morale was shot. The women would not speak to them.

There were rapes; the women neither responded nor resisted. Their men stood by and pretended not to see. There were attempts to start fights; the Bornoks would not fight back.

The soldiers began to fight among themselves, as soldiers will.

On the seventh night the captain, accompanied by two sergeants, entered one of the longhouses. It was a kind of primitive tavern. One wall was lined with kegs of wine; in front of the kegs was a long, narrow, wooden table with several score clay mugs on it. A Bornok stood behind the table, mopping it with a dirty rag. In the far corner a Knocker was playing a ten-stringed lutelike instrument and a woman was singing softly. Several Bornoks stood in front of the rude bar, drinking wine out of the clay mugs and talking loudly.

There was no stir when the soldiers walked in. The musician kept playing, the woman kept singing, the Bornoks kept talking.

The tavern keeper mopped the table with his dirty rag.

The captain walked up to the long, narrow table.

'Wine,' he said in Bornok.

The tavern keeper continued mopping the bar.

'*Wine!*'

The tavern keeper did not look up.

The captain's face grew red. He drew his gun and shoved its muzzle in the tavern keeper's face.

'Wine, goddamn you, wine!' he roared.

The tavern keeper ignored him.

Savagely, the captain smashed his gun into the tavern keeper's face. The tavern keeper drooled blood.

He continued mopping the bar.

The captain could not support his rage, not against someone who simply refused to acknowledge his existence. Dazedly, in retreat, he strode out of the longhouse, the two sergeants following silently in his wake.

The captain dismissed the sergeants. He stood alone, in the empty square, in the moonlight.

The captain's world was thoroughly shaken. He was experienced, he was a professional, he had learned the ins and outs of invasion and occupation on six other planets. The Book had ways of dealing with insurrections, guerrillas, even the most subtle techniques of passive resistance, but this . . . this . . . It didn't even have a name.

The captain sighed. He walked moodily towards the PCTs parked in the centre of the square, troubled, confused, staring at his feet . . .

A small figure darted out of the dark and bumped against him.

The captain, startled out of his reverie, whirled, his gun already in his hand.

A young Bornok girl lay sprawled at his feet. Instinctively, he reached down and helped her to her feet. His face had softened.

'Why?' he asked almost plaintively. 'What . . .? What are you doing to us?'

It might have been because she was very young. It might have been because the captain was not unhandsome when he was not being The Captain. Or it might have been . . . planned. He would wonder about it many times in the years to come and he would never know.

'You can kill us,' the girl said, staring at a point three feet to the right of the captain's head. 'All of us. You can do anything you want to to us; the power is yours. But nothing you can do will ever make us acknowledge your existence on

Bornok. *Nothing*. To us, you do not exist.'

Then, more softly, 'I'm sorry.'

She darted away, and the captain was alone, terribly alone, in the empty square.

The soldiers stayed for another two days; while the captain spoke with the colonel, and the colonel spoke with the general, and the general spoke with the commander of operations; while the reports filtered upwards, and then the orders came.

On the third day, the soldiers piled their equipment and their bodies into the PCTs and left. The village took no note of their passing.

By the end of the week, the entire twenty divisions had been evacuated. The solar government agreed to take over the Draaden bases in lieu of Bornok and reluctantly let Draada keep Moali. At least the appearance of victory had been maintained.

But since then, no Solarian ship has ever set down on Bornok.

The old man emptied the grey ashes from his pipe.

'I don't understand,' said the boy.

The old man sighed. 'Of course you don't,' he said. 'You're too young. Maybe we're all too young.'

'*You're* too young, Grandpa?'

The old man laughed shortly. 'Maybe I've just grown up,' he said. He reached into a pocket and pulled out a key chain. He detached a charm and placed it in the boy's palm.

'Here,' he said. 'That's for you.'

The boy stared happily at the tarnished captain's bars in his hand.

# The Big Flash

*T minus 200 days . . . and counting . . .*

They came on freaky for my taste – but that's the name of the game: freaky means a draw in the rock business. And if the Mandala was going to survive in L.A., competing with a network-owned joint like the American Dream, I'd just have to hold my nose and out-freak the opposition. So after I had dug the Four Horsemen for about an hour, I took them into my office to talk turkey.

I sat down behind my Salvation Army desk (the Mandala is the world's most expensive shoestring operation) and the Horsemen sat down on the bridge chairs sequentially, establishing the group's pecking order.

First the head honcho, lead guitar and singer, Stony Clarke – blond shoulder-length hair, eyes like something in a morgue when he took off his steel-rimmed shades, a reputation as a heavy acid-head, and the look of a speed-freak behind it. Then Hair, the drummer, dressed like a Hell's Angel, swastikas and all, a junkie, with fanatic eyes that were a little too close together, making me wonder whether he wore swastikas because he grooved behind the Angel thing or made like an Angel because it let him groove behind the swastika in public. Number three was a cat who called himself Super Spade and wasn't kidding – he wore earrings, natural hair, a Stokeley Carmichael sweatshirt, and on a thong around his neck a shrunken head that had been whitened with liquid shoe polish. He was the utility infielder: sitar, bass, organ, flute, whatever. Number four, who called himself Mr Jones, was about the creepiest cat I had ever seen in a rock group, and that is saying something. He was their visuals, synthesizer and electronics man. He was at least forty, wore early-hippie clothes that looked like they had been made by Sy Devore, and was rumoured to be some kind of Rand Corporation dropout. There's no business like show business.

'Okay, boys,' I said, 'you're strange, but you're my kind of strange. Where you worked before?'

'We ain't, baby,' Clarke said. 'We're the New Thing. I've been dealing crystal and acid in the Haight. Hair was drummer for some plastic group in New York. The Super Spade claims it's the reincarnation of Bird and it don't pay to argue. Mr Jones, he don't talk too much. Maybe he's a Martian. We just started putting our thing together.'

One thing about this business, the groups that don't have square managers, you can get cheap. They talk too much.

'Groovy,' I said. 'I'm happy to give you guys your start. Nobody knows you, but I think you got something going. So I'll take a chance and give you a week's booking. One a.m. to closing, which is two, Tuesday through Sunday, four hundred a week.'

'Are you Jewish?' asked Hair.

'What?'

'Cool it,' Clarke ordered. Hair cooled it. 'What it means,'

Clarke told me, 'is that four hundred sounds like pretty light bread.'

'We don't sign if there's an option clause,' Mr Jones said.

'The Jones-thing has a good point,' Clarke said. 'We do the first week for four hundred, but after that it's a whole new scene, dig?'

I didn't feature that. If they hit it big, I could end up not being able to afford them. But, on the other hand, four hundred dollars was light bread, and I needed a cheap closing act pretty bad.

'Okay,' I said. 'But a verbal agreement that I get first crack at you when you finish the gig.'

'Word of honour,' said Stony Clarke.

That's this business – the word of honour of an ex-dealer and speed-freak.


*T minus 199 days . . . and counting . . .*

Being unconcerned with ends, the military mind can be easily manipulated, easily controlled, and easily confused. Ends are defined as those goals set by civilian authority. Ends are the conceded province of civilians; means are the province of the military, whose duty it is to achieve the ends set for it by the most advantageous application of the means at its command.

Thus the confusion over the war in Asia among my uniformed clients at the Pentagon. The end has been duly set: eradication of the guerrillas. But the civilians have overstepped their bounds and meddled in means. The generals regard this as unfair, a breach of contract, as it were. The generals (or the faction among them most inclined to paranoia) are beginning to see the conduct of the war, the political limitation on means, as a ploy of the civilians for performing a putsch against their time-honoured prerogatives.

This aspect of the situation would bode ill for the country, were it not for the fact that the growing paranoia among the generals has enabled me to manipulate them into presenting both my scenarios to the President. The President has authorized implementation of the major scenario, provided that the minor scenario is successful in properly moulding public opinion.

My major scenario is simple and direct. Knowing that the poor flying weather makes our conventional air power, with its dependency on relative accuracy, ineffectual, the enemy has fallen into the pattern of grouping his forces into larger units and launching punishing annual offensives during the monsoon season. However, these larger units are highly vulnerable to tactical nuclear weapons, which do not depend upon accuracy for effect. Secure in the knowledge that domestic political considerations preclude the use of nuclear weapons, the enemy will once again form into division-sized units or larger during the next monsoon season. A parsimonious use of tactical nuclear weapons, even as few as twenty one-hundred-kiloton bombs, employed simultaneously and in an advantageous pattern, will destroy a minimum of two hundred thousand enemy troops, or nearly two-thirds of his total force, in a twenty-four-hour period. The blow will be crushing.

The minor scenario, upon whose success the implementation of the major scenario depends, is far more sophisticated, due to its subtler goal: public acceptance of, or, optimally, even public clamour for, the use of tactical nuclear weapons. The task is difficult, but my scenario is quite sound, if somewhat exotic, and with the full, if to some extent clandestine, support of the upper military hierarchy, certain civil government circles and the decision-makers in key aerospace corporations, the means now at my command would seem adequate. The risks, while statistically significant, do not exceed an acceptable level.

*T minus 189 days . . . and counting . . .*

The way I see it, the network deserved the shafting I gave them. They shafted me, didn't they? Four successful series I produce for those bastards, and two bomb out after thirteen weeks and they send me to the salt mines! A discotheque, can you imagine they make me producer at a lousy discotheque! A remittance man they make me, those schlockmeisters. Oh, those schnorrers made the American Dream sound like a kosher deal – twenty per cent of the net, they say. And you got access to all our sets and contract players; it'll make you a rich man, Herm. And like a yuk, I sign, being broke at the time, without reading the fine print. I should know they've set up the American Dream as a tax loss? I should know that I've *gotta* use their lousy sets and stiff contract players and have it written off against my gross? I should know their shtick is to run the American Dream at a loss and then do a network TV show out of the joint from which I don't see a penny? So I end up running the place for them at a paper loss, living on salary, while the network rakes it in off the TV show that I end up paying for out of my end.

Don't bums like that deserve to be shafted? It isn't enough they use me as a tax-loss patsy; they gotta tell me who to book! 'Go sign the Four Horsemen, the group that's packing them in at the Mandala,' they say. 'We want them on "A Night with the American Dream". They're hot.'

'Yeah, they're hot,' I say, 'which means they'll cost a mint. I can't afford it.'

They show me more fine print – next time I read the contract with a microscope. I *gotta* book whoever they tell me to and I gotta absorb the cost on my books! It's enough to make a Litvak turn anti-Semitic.

So I had to go to the Mandala to sign up these hippies. I made sure I didn't get there till twelve-thirty so I wouldn't have to stay in that nuthouse any longer than necessary. Such a dive! What Bernstein did was take a bankrupt Hollywood-Hollywood club on the Strip, knock down all the interior walls, and put up this monster tent inside the shell. Just thin white screening over two-by-fours. Real shlock. Outside the tent, he's got projectors, lights, speakers, all the electronic mumbo-jumbo, and inside is like being surrounded by movie screens. Just the tent and the bare floor, not even a real stage, just a platform on wheels they shlepp in and out of the tent when they change groups.

So you can imagine he doesn't draw exactly a class crowd. Not with the American Dream up the street being run as a network tax loss. What they get is the smelly, hard-core hippies I don't let in the door and the kind of j.d. high-school kids that think it's smart to hang around putzes like that. A lot of dope-pushing goes on. The cops don't like the place and the rousts draw professional troublemakers.

A real den of iniquity – I felt like I was walking on to a Casbah set. The last group had gone off and the Horsemen hadn't come on yet. So what you had was this crazy tent filled with hippies, half of them on acid or pot or amphetamine, or, for all I know, Ajax, high-school would-be hippies, also mostly stoned and getting ugly, and a few crazy schwartzes looking to fight cops. All of them standing around waiting for something to happen, and about ready to make it happen. I stood near the door, just in case. As they say, 'The vibes were making me uptight.'

All of a sudden the house lights go out and it's black as a network executive's heart. I hold my hand on my wallet – in this crowd, tell me there are no pickpockets. Just the pitch black and dead silence for what, ten beats, and then I start feeling something, I don't know, like something crawling along my bones, but I know it's some kind of subsonic effect and not my imagination, because all the hippies are standing still and you don't hear a sound.

Then from monster speakers so loud you feel it in your teeth, a heartbeat, but heavy, slow, half-time, like maybe a whale's heart. The thing crawling along my bones seems to be synchronized with the heartbeat and I feel almost like I am that big dumb heart beating there in the darkness.

Then a dark red spot – so faint it's almost infra-red – hits the stage which they have wheeled out. On the stage are four uglies in crazy black robes – you know, like the Grim Reaper wears – with that ugly red light all over them like blood. Creepy. Boom-ba-boom. Boom-ba-boom. The heartbeat still going, still that subsonic bone-crawl, and the hippies are staring at the Four Horsemen like mesmerized chickens.

The bass player, a regular jungle bunny, picks up the rhythm of the heartbeat. Dum-da-dum. Dum-da-dum. The drummer beats it out with earsplitting rim shots. Then the electric guitar, tuned like a strangling cat, makes with horrible, heavy chords. Whang-ka-whang. Whang-ka-whang.

It's just awful, I feel it in my guts, my bones; my eardrums are just like some great big throbbing vein. Everybody is swaying to it; I'm swaying to it. Boom-ba-boom. Boom-ba-boom.

Then the guitarist starts to chant in rhythm with the heartbeat, in a hoarse, shrill voice like somebody dying: 'The big flash . . . the big flash . . .'

And the guy at the visuals console diddles around and rings of light start to climb the walls of the tent, blue at the bottom becoming green as they get higher, then yellow, orange, and, finally as they become a circle on the ceiling, eye-killing neon-red. Each circle takes exactly one heartbeat to climb the walls.

Boy, what an awful feeling! Like I was a tube of toothpaste being squeezed in rhythm till the top of my head felt like it was gonna squirt up with those circles of light through the ceiling.

And then they start to speed it up gradually. The same heartbeat, the same rim shots, same chords, same circles of light, same 'The big flash . . . the big flash . . .' Same bass, same subsonic bone-crawl, but just a little faster . . . Then faster! Faster!

Thought I would die! Knew I would die! Heart beating like a lunatic. Rim shots like a machine-gun. Circles of light sucking me up the walls, into that red neon hole.

*Oy*, incredible! Over and over, faster, faster, till the voice was a scream and the heartbeat a boom and the rim shots a whine and the guitar howled feedback and my bones were jumping out of my body –

Every spot in the place came on and I went blind from the sudden light –

An awful explosion sound came over every speaker, so loud it rocked me on my feet –

I felt myself squirting out of the top of my head and loved it.

Then:

The explosion became a rumble –

The light seemed to run together into a circle on the ceiling, leaving everything else black.

And the circle became a fireball.

The fireball became a slow-motion film of an atomic-bomb cloud as the rumbling died away. Then the picture faded into a moment of total darkness and the house lights came on.

What a number!

*Gevalt*, what an act!

So, after the show, when I got them alone and found out they had no manager, not even an option to the Mandala, I thought faster than I ever had in my life.

To make a long story short and sweet, I gave the network the royal screw. I signed the Horsemen to a contract that made me their manager and gave me twenty per cent of their take. Then I booked them into the American Dream at ten thousand a week, wrote a cheque as proprietor of the American Dream, handed the cheque to myself as manager of the Four Horsemen, then resigned as a network flunky, leaving them with a ten-thousand-dollar bag and me with twenty per cent of the hottest group since the Beatles.

What the hell, he who lives by the fine print shall perish by the fine print.

*T minus 148 days . . . and counting . . .*

'You haven't seen the tape yet, have you, B.D.?' Jake said. He was nervous as hell. When you reach my level in the network structure, you're used to making subordinates nervous, but Jake Pitkin was head of network continuity, not some office boy, and certainly should be used to dealing with executives at my level. Was the rumour really true?

We were alone in the screening room. It was doubtful that

37

the projectionist could hear us.

'No, I haven't seen it yet,' I said. 'But I've heard some strange stories.'

Jake looked positively deathly. 'About the tape?' he said.

'About you, Jake,' I said, deprecating the rumour with an easy smile. 'That you don't want to air the show.'

'It's true, B.D.,' Jake said quietly.

'Do you realize what you're saying? Whatever our personal tastes – and I personally think there's something unhealthy about them – the Four Horsemen are the hottest thing in the country right now and that dirty little thief Herm Gellman held us up for a quarter of a million for an hour show. It cost another two hundred thousand to make it. We've spent another hundred thousand on promotion. We're getting top dollar from the sponsors. There's over a million dollars one way or the other riding on that show. That's how much we blow if we don't air it.'

'I know that, B.D.,' Jake said. 'I also know this could cost me my job. Think about that. Because knowing all that, I'm still against airing the tape. I'm going to run the closing segment for you. I'm sure enough that you'll agree with me to stake my job on it.'

I had a terrible feeling in my stomach. I have superiors too and The Word was that 'A Trip with the Four Horsemen' would be aired, period. No matter what. Something funny was going on. The price we were getting for commercial time was a precedent and the sponsor was a big aerospace company which had never bought network time before. What really bothered me was that Jake Pitkin had no reputation for courage; yet here he was laying his job on the line. He must be pretty sure I would come around to his way of thinking or he wouldn't dare. And though I couldn't tell Jake, I had no choice in the matter whatsoever.

'Okay, roll it,' Jake said into the intercom mike. 'What you're going to see,' he said as the screening-room lights went out, 'is the last number.'

On the screen: a shot of empty blue sky, with soft, lazy electric guitar chords behind it. The camera pans across a few clouds to an extremely long shot on the sun. As the sun, no more than a tiny circle of light, moves into the centre of the screen, a sitar-drone comes in behind the guitar.

Very slowly, the camera begins to zoom in on the sun. As the image of the sun expands, the sitar gets louder and the guitar begins to fade and a drum starts to give the sitar a

38

beat. The sitar gets louder, the beat gets more pronounced and begins to speed up as the sun continues to expand. Finally, the whole screen is filled with unbearably bright light behind which the sitar and drum are in a frenzy.

Then over this, drowning out the sitar and drum, a voice like a sick thing in heat: '*Brighter . . . than a thousand suns . . .*'

The light dissolves into a closeup of a beautiful dark-haired girl with huge eyes and moist lips, and suddenly there is nothing on the sound track but soft guitar and voices crooning low: '*Brighter . . . oh, God, it's brighter . . . brighter . . . than a thousand suns . . .*'

The girl's face dissolves into a full shot of the Four Horsemen in their Grim Reaper robes and the same melody that had played behind the girl's face shifts into a minor key, picks up whining, reverberating electric guitar chords and a sitar-drone and becomes a dirge: '*Darker . . . the world grows darker . . .*'

And a series of cuts in time to the dirge:

A burning village in Asia strewn with bodies —

'*Darker . . . the world grows darker . . .*'

The corpse heap at Auschwitz —

'*Until it gets so dark . . .*'

A gigantic auto graveyard with gaunt Negro children dwarfed in the foreground —

'*I think I'll die . . .*'

A Washington ghetto in flames with the Capitol misty in the background —

'*. . . before the daylight comes . . .*'

A jump-cut to an extreme closeup on the lead singer of the Horsemen, his face twisted into a mask of desperation and ecstasy. And the sitar is playing double-time, the guitar is wailing and he is screaming at the top of his lungs: '*But before I die, let me make that trip before the nothing comes . . .*'

The girl's face again, but transparent, with a blinding yellow light shining through it. The sitar beat gets faster and faster with the guitar whining behind it and the voice is working itself up into a howling frenzy: '*. . . the last big flash to light my sky . . .*'

Nothing but the blinding light now —

'*. . . and zap! the world is done . . .*'

An utterly black screen for a beat that becomes black, fading to blue at a horizon —

'. . . *but before we die let's dig that high that frees us from our binds . . . that blows all cool that ego-drool and burns us from our mind . . . the last big flash, mankind's last gas, the trip we can't take twice . . .*'

Suddenly, the music stops dead for half a beat. Then:

The screen is lit up by an enormous fireball—

A shattering rumble—

The fireball coalesces into a mushroom-pillar cloud as the roar goes on. As the roar begins to die out, fire is visible inside the monstrous nuclear cloud. And the girl's face is faintly visible, superimposed over the cloud.

A soft voice, amplified over the roar, obscenely reverential now: '*Brighter . . . great God, it's brighter . . . brighter than a thousand suns . . .*'

And the screen went blank and the lights came on.

I looked at Jake. Jake looked at me.

'That's sick,' I said. 'That's *really* sick.'

'You don't want to run a thing like that, do you, B.D.?' Jake said softly.

I made some rapid mental calculations. The loathsome thing ran something under five minutes . . . it could be done . . .

'You're right, Jake,' I said. 'We won't run a thing like that. We'll cut it out of the tape and squeeze in another commercial at each break. That should cover the time.'

'You don't understand,' Jake said. 'The contract Herm rammed down our throats doesn't allow us to edit. The show's a package—all or nothing. Besides, the whole show's like that.'

'All like that? What do you mean, all like that?'

Jake squirmed in his seat. 'Those guys are . . . well, perverts, B.D.,' he said.

'*Perverts?*'

'They're . . . well, they're in love with the atom bomb or something. Every number leads up to the same thing.'

'You mean . . . they're *all* like that?'

'You got the picture, B.D.,' Jake said. 'We run an hour of *that*, or we run nothing at all.'

'Jesus.'

I knew what I wanted to say. Burn the tape and write off the million dollars. But I also knew it would cost me my job. And I knew that five minutes after I was out the door, they would have someone in my job who would see things their way. Even my superiors seemed to be just handing down The Word from higher up. I had no choice. There was no choice.

'I'm sorry, Jake,' I said. 'We run it.'

'I resign,' said Jake Pitkin, who had no reputation for courage.

*T minus 10 days . . . and counting . . .*

'It's a clear violation of the Test-Ban Treaty,' I said.

The Under Secretary looked as dazed as I felt. 'We'll call it a peaceful use of atomic energy, and let the Russians scream,' he said.

'It's insane.'

'Perhaps,' the Under Secretary said. 'But you have your orders, General Carson, and I have mine. From higher up. At exactly eight fifty-eight p.m. local time on July fourth, you will drop a fifty-kiloton atomic bomb on the designated ground zero at Yucca Flats.'

'But the people . . . the television crews . . .'

'Will be at least two miles outside the danger zone. Surely, SAC can manage that kind of accuracy under "laboratory conditions".'

I stiffened. 'I do not question the competence of any bomber crew under my command to perform this mission,' I said. 'I question the reason for the mission. I question the sanity of the orders.'

The Under Secretary shrugged, and smiled wanly. 'Welcome to the club.'

'You mean you don't know what this is all about either?'

'All I know is what was transmitted to me by the Secretary of Defence, and I got the feeling he doesn't know everything, either. You know that the Pentagon has been screaming for the use of tactical nuclear weapons to end the war in Asia – you SAC boys have been screaming the loudest. Well, several months ago, the President conditionally approved a plan for the use of tactical nuclear weapons during the next monsoon season.'

I whistled. The civilians were finally coming to their senses. Or were they?

'But what does that have to do with – ?'

'Public opinion,' the Under Secretary said. 'It was conditional upon a drastic change in public opinion. At the time the plan was approved, the polls showed that seventy-eight point eight per cent of the population opposed the use of tactical nuclear weapons, nine point eight per cent favoured their use and the rest were undecided or had no opinion. The President agreed to authorize the use of tactical nuclear weapons by a date, several months from now, which is still top secret, provided that by that date at least sixty-five per cent of the population approved their use and no more than twenty per cent actively opposed it.'

'I see . . . just a ploy to keep the Joint Chiefs quiet.'

'General Carson,' the Under Secretary said, 'apparently you are out of touch with the national mood. After the first Four Horsemen show, the polls showed that twenty-five per cent of the population approved the use of nuclear weapons. After the second show, the figure was forty-one per cent. It is now forty-eight per cent. Only thirty-two per cent are now actively opposed.'

'You're trying to tell me that a rock group –'

'A rock group and the cult around it, General. It's become a national hysteria. There are imitators. Haven't you seen those buttons?'

'The ones with a mushroom cloud on them that say "Do it"?'

The Under Secretary nodded. 'Your guess is as good as mine whether the National Security Council just decided that the Horsemen hysteria could be used to mould public opinion, or whether the Four Horsemen were their creatures to begin with. But the results are the same either way – the Horsemen and the cult around them have won over precisely that element of the population which was most adamantly opposed to nuclear weapons: hippies, students, dropouts, draft-age youth. Demonstrations against the war and against nuclear weapons have died down. We're pretty close to that sixty-five per cent. Someone – perhaps the President himself – has decided that one more big Four Horseman show will put us over the top.'

'The President is behind this?'

'No one else can authorize the detonation of an atomic bomb, after all,' the Under Secretary said. 'We're letting them do the show live from Yucca Flats. It's being sponsored by an aerospace company heavily dependent on defence contracts. We're letting them truck in a live audience. Of course the government is behind it.'

'And SAC drops an A-bomb as the show-stopper?'

'Exactly.'

'I saw one of those shows,' I said. 'My kids were watching it. I got the strangest feeling . . . I almost wanted that red telephone to ring . . .'

'I know what you mean,' the Under Secretary said. 'Sometimes I get the feeling that whoever's behind this has got caught up in the hysteria themselves . . . that the Horsemen are now using whoever was using them . . . a closed circle. But I've been tired lately. The war's making us all so tired. If only we could get it all over with . . .'

'We'd all like to get it over with one way or the other,' I said.

*T minus 60 minutes . . . and counting . . .*

I had orders to muster *Backfish*'s crew for the live satellite relay on 'The Four Horsemen's Fourth'. Superficially, it might seem strange to order the whole Polaris fleet to watch a television show, but the morale factor involved was quite significant.

Polaris subs are frustrating duty. Only top sailors are chosen and a good sailor craves action. Yet if we are ever called upon to act, our mission will have been a failure. We spend most of our time honing skills that must never be used. Deterrence is a sound strategy but a terrible drain on the men of the deterrent forces – a drain exacerbated in the past by the negative attitude of our countrymen towards our mission. Men who, in the service of their country, polish their skills to a razor edge and then must refrain from exercising them have a right to resent being treated as pariahs.

Therefore the positive change in the public attitude towards us that seems to be associated with the Four Horsemen has made them mascots of a kind to the Polaris fleet. In their strange way they seem to speak for us and to us.

I chose to watch the show in the missile control centre, where a full crew must always be ready to launch the missiles on five-minute notice. I have always felt a sense of communion with the duty watch in the missile control centre that I cannot share with the other men under my command. Here we are not captain and crew, but mind and hand. Should the order come, the will to fire the missiles will be mine and the act will be theirs. At such a moment, it will be good not to feel alone.

All eyes were on the television set mounted above the main console as the show came on and . . .

The screen was filled with a whirling spiral pattern, metallic yellow on metallic blue. There was a droning sound that seemed part sitar and part electronic and I had the feeling that the sound was somehow coming from inside my head and the spiral seemed etched directly on my retinas. It hurt mildly, yet nothing in the world could have made me turn away.

Then came two voices, chanting against each other:]

'Let it all come in . . .'

*'Let it all come out . . .'*

'In . . . *out* . . . in . . . *out* . . . in . . . *out* . . .'

My head seemed to be pulsing – in-*out*, in-*out*, in-*out* – and the spiral pattern began to pulse colour changes with the words: yellow-on-blue (in) . . . green-on-red (*out*) . . . In-*out*-in-*out*-in-*out*-in-*out* . . .

In the screen . . . *out* my head . . . I seemed to be beating against some kind of invisible membrane between myself and the screen as if something were trying to embrace my mind and I were fighting it . . . But why was I fighting it?

The pulsing, the chanting, got faster and faster till *in* could not be told from *out* and negative spiral after-images formed in my eyes faster than they could adjust to the changes, piled up on each other faster and faster till it seemed my head would explode –

The chanting and the droning broke and there were the Four Horsemen, in their robes, playing on some stage against a backdrop of clear blue sky. And a single voice, soothing now: 'You are in . . .'

Then the view was directly above the Horsemen and I could see that they were on some kind of circular platform. The view moved slowly and smoothly up and away and I saw that the circular stage was atop a tall tower; around the tower and completely encircling it was a huge crowd seated on desert sands that stretched away to an empty infinity.

'And we are in and they are in . . .'

I was down among the crowd now; they seemed to melt and flow like plastic, pouring from the television screen to enfold me . . .

'And we are all in here together . . .'

A strange and beautiful feeling . . . the music got faster and wilder, ecstatic . . . the hull of the *Backfish* seemed unreal . . . the crowd was swaying to it around me . . . the distance between myself and the crowd seemed to dissolve . . . I was there . . . they were here . . . We were transfixed . . .

'Oh, yeah, we are all in here together . . . together . . .'

*T minus 45 minutes . . . and counting . . .*

Jeremy and I sat staring at the television screen, ignoring each other and everything around us. Even with the short watches and the short tours of duty, you can get to feeling pretty strange down here in a hole in the ground under tons of concrete, just you and the guy with the other key, with nothing to do but think dark thoughts and get on each other's nerves. We're all supposed to be as stable as men can be, or so they tell us, and they must be right because the world's still here. I mean, it wouldn't take much – just two guys on the same watch over the same three Minutemen flipping out at the same time, turning their keys in the dual lock, pressing the three buttons . . . Pow! World War III!

A bad thought, the kind we're not supposed to think or I'll start watching Jeremy and he'll start watching me and we'll get a panaroia feedback going . . . But that can't happen; we're too stable, too responsible. As long as we remember that it's healthy to feel a little spooky down here, we'll be all right.

But the television set is a good idea. It keeps us in contact with the outside world, keeps it real. It'd be too easy to start thinking that the missile control centre down here is the only real world and that nothing that happens up there really matters . . . Bad thought!

The Four Horsemen . . . somehow these guys help you get it all out. I mean that feeling that it might be better to release all that tension, get it all over with. Watching the Four Horsemen, you're able to go with it without doing any harm, let it wash over you and then through you. I suppose they are crazy; they're all the human craziness in ourselves that we've got to keep very careful watch over down here. Letting it all come out watching the Horsemen makes it surer that none of it will come out down here. I guess that's why a lot of us have taken to wearing those 'Do It' buttons off duty. The brass doesn't mind; they seem to understand that it's the kind of inside sick joke we need to keep us functioning.

Now that spiral thing they had started the show with – and the droning – came back on. Zap! I was right back in the screen again, as if the commercial hadn't happened.

'We are all in here together . . .'

And then a closeup of the lead singer, looking straight at me, as close as Jeremy and somehow more real. A mean-looking guy with something behind his eyes that told me he knew where everything lousy and rotten was at.

A bass began to thrum behind him and some kind of electronic hum that set my teeth on edge. He began playing his guitar, mean and low-down. And singing in that kind of drop-dead tone of voice that starts brawls in bars:

*'I stabbed my mother and I mugged my paw . . .'*

A riff of heavy guitar chords echoed the words mockingly as a huge swastika (red-on-black, black-on-red) pulsed like a naked vein on the screen —

The face of the Horseman, leering —

*'Nailed my sister to the toilet door . . .'*

Guitar behind the pulsing swastika —

*'Drowned a puppy in a ce-ment machine . . . Burned a kitten just to hear it scream . . .'*

On the screen, just a big fire burning in slow-motion, and the voice became a slow, shrill, agonized wail:

*'Oh, God, I've got this red-hot fire burning in the marrow of my brain . . .*

*'Oh, yes, I got this fire burning . . . in the stinking marrow of my brain . . .*

*'Gotta get me a blowtorch . . . and set some naked flesh on flame . . .'*

The fire dissolved into the face of a screaming Oriental woman, who ran through a burning village clawing at the napalm on her back.

*'I got this message . . . boiling in the bubbles of my blood . . . A man ain't nothing but a fire burning . . . in a dirty glob of mud . . .'*

A film clip of a Nuremberg rally: a revolving swastika of marching men waving torches —

Then the leader of the Horsemen superimposed over the twisted flaming cross:

*'Don't you hate me, baby, can't you feel somethin' screaming in your mind?*

*'Don't you hate me, baby, feel me drowning you in slime!'*

Just the face of the Horseman howling hate —

*'Oh yes, I'm a monster, mother . . .'*

A long view of the crowd around the platform, on their feet, waving arms, screaming soundlessly. Then a quick zoom in and a kaleidoscope of faces, eyes feverish, mouths open and howling —

*'Just call me —'*

The face of the Horseman superimposed over the crazed faces of the crowd —

*'Mankind!'*

I looked at Jeremy. He was toying with the key on the chain around his neck. He was sweating. I suddenly realized that I was sweating, too, and that my own key was throbbing in my hand alive . . .

*T minus 13 minutes . . . and counting . . .*
A funny feeling, the captain watching the Four Horsemen here in the *Backfish*'s missile control centre with us. Sitting in front of my console watching the television set with the captain kind of breathing down my neck. I got the feeling he knew what was going through me and I couldn't know what was going through him . . . and it gave the fire inside me a kind of greasy feel I didn't like . . .

Then the commercial was over and that spiral-thing came on again and – whoosh! – it sucked me right back into the television set and I stopped worrying about the captain or anything like that . . .

Just the spiral going yellow-blue, red-green, and then starting to whirl and whirl, faster and faster, changing colours and whirling, whirling, whirling . . . And the sound of a kind of Coney Island carousel tinkling behind it, faster and faster and faster, whirling and whirling and whirling, flashing red-green, yellow-blue, and whirling, whirling, whirling . . .

And this big hum filling my body and whirling, whirling, whirling . . . my muscles relaxing, going limp, whirling, whirling, whirling, all limp, whirling, whirling, whirling, oh so nice, just whirling, whirling . . .

And in the centre of the flashing spiralling colours, a bright dot of colourless light, right at the centre, not moving, not changing, while the whole world went whirling and whirling in colours around it, and the humming was coming from the dot the way the carousel music was coming from the spinning colours and the dot was humming its song to me . . .

The dot was a light way down at the end of a long, whirling, whirling tunnel. The humming started to get a little louder. The bright dot started to get a little bigger. I was drifting down the tunnel towards it, whirling, whirling, whirling . . .

*T minus 11 minutes . . . and counting . . .*
Whirling, whirling, whirling down a long, long tunnel of pulsing colours, whirling, whirling, towards the circle of light way down at the end of the tunnel . . . How nice it would be to finally get there and soak up the beautiful hum filling my body and then I could forget that I was down here in this hole in the ground with a hard brass key in my hand, just Duke and me, down here in a cave under the ground that was a spiral of flashing colours, whirling, whirling towards the

friendly light at the end of the tunnel, whirling, whirling . . .

*T minus 10 minutes . . . and counting . . .*
The circle of light at the end of the whirling tunnel was getting bigger and bigger and the humming was getting louder and louder and I was feeling better and better and the *Back-fish*'s missile control centre was getting dimmer and dimmer as the awful weight of command got lighter and lighter, whirling, whirling, and I felt so good I wanted to cry, whirling, whirling . . .

*T minus 9 minutes . . . and counting . . .*
Whirling, whirling . . . I was whirling, Jeremy was whirling, the hole in the ground was whirling, and the circle of light at the end of the tunnel whirled closer and closer and – I was through! A place filled with yellow light. Pale metal-yellow light. Then pale metallic blue. Yellow. Blue. Yellow. Blue. Yellow-blue-yellow-blue-yellow-blue-yellow . . .

Pure light pulsing . . . and pure sound droning. And just the *feeling* of letters I couldn't read between the pulses – not-yellow and not-blue – too quick and too faint to be visible, but important, very important . . .

And then came a voice that seemed to be singing from inside my head, almost as if it were my own:
'*Oh, oh, oh . . . don't I really wanna know . . . Oh, oh, oh . . . don't I really wanna know . . .*'

The world pulsing, flashing around those words I couldn't read, couldn't quite read, had to read, could *almost* read . . .
'*Oh, oh, oh . . . great God, I really wanna know . . .*'

Strange amorphous shapes clouding the blue-yellow-blue flickering universe, hiding the words I had to read . . . Damn it, why wouldn't they get out of the way so I could find out what I had to know!
'*Tell me tell me tell me tell me tell me . . . Gotta know gotta know gotta know gotta know . . .*'

*T minus 7 minutes . . . and counting . . .*
Couldn't read the words! Why wouldn't the captain let me read the words?

And that voice inside me: '*Gotta know . . . gotta know . . . gotta know why it hurts me so . . .*' Why wouldn't it shut up and let me read the words? Why wouldn't the words hold still? Or just slow down a little? If they'd slow down a little, I could read them and then I'd know what I had to do . . .

48

*T minus 6 minutes . . . and counting . . .*

I felt the sweaty key in the palm of my hand . . . I saw Duke stroking his own key. Had to know! Now – through the pulsing blue-yellow-blue light and the unreadable words that were building up an awful pressure in the back of my brain – I could see the Four Horsemen. They were on their knees, crying, looking up at something and begging: *'Tell me tell me tell me tell me . . .'*

Then soft billows of rich red-and-orange fire filled the world and a huge voice was trying to speak. But it couldn't form the words. It stuttered and moaned –

The yellow-blue-yellow flashing around the words I couldn't read – the same words, I suddenly sensed, that the voice of the fire was trying so hard to form – and the Four Horsemen on their knees begging: *'Tell me tell me tell me . . .'*

The friendly warm fire trying so hard to speak –

*'Tell me tell me tell me tell me . . .'*

*T minus 4 minutes . . . and counting . . .*

What were the words? What was the order? I could sense my men silently imploring me to tell them. After all, I was their captain, it was my duty to tell them. It was my duty to find out!

*'Tell me tell me tell me . . .'* the robed figures on their knees implored through the flickering pulse in my brain and I could almost make out the words . . . almost . . .

*'Tell me tell me tell me . . .'* I whispered to the warm orange fire that was trying so hard but couldn't quite form the words. The men were whispering it, too: *'Tell me tell me . . .'*

*T minus 3 minutes . . . and counting . . .*

The question burning blue and yellow in my brain: What was the fire trying to tell me? What were the words I couldn't read?

Had to unlock the words! Had to find the key!

A key . . . *The* key? THE KEY! And there was the lock that imprisoned the words, right in front of me! Put the key in the lock . . . I looked at Jeremy. Wasn't there some reason, long ago and far away, why Jeremy might try to stop me from putting the key in the lock?

But Jeremy didn't move as I fitted the key into the lock . . .

*T minus 2 minutes . . . and counting . . .*

Why wouldn't the captain tell me what the order was? The

fire knew, but it couldn't tell. My head ached from the pulsing, but I couldn't read the words.

'Tell me tell me tell me . . .' I begged.

Then I realized that the captain was asking, too.

*T minus 90 seconds . . . and counting . . .*

'*Tell me tell me tell me . . .*' the Horsemen begged. And the words I couldn't read were a fire in my brain.

Duke's key was in the lock in front of us. From very far away, he said: 'We have to do it together.'

Of course . . . our keys . . . our keys would unlock the words!

I put my key into the lock. One, two, three, we turned our keys together. A lid on the console popped open. Under the lid were three red buttons. Three signs on the console lit up in red letters: ARMED.

*T minus 60 seconds . . . and counting . . .*

The men were waiting for me to give some order. I didn't know what the order was. A magnificent orange fire was trying to tell me but it couldn't get the words out . . . Robed figures were praying to the fire . . .

Then, through the yellow-blue flicker that hid the words I had to read, I saw a vast crowd encircling a tower. The crowd was on its feet begging silently –

The tower in the centre of the crowd became the orange fire that was trying to tell me what the words were –

Became a great mushroom of billowing smoke and blinding orange-red glare . . .

*T minus 30 seconds . . . and counting . . .*

The huge pillar of fire was trying to tell Jeremy and me what the words were, what we had to do. The crowd was screaming at the cloud of flame. The yellow-blue flicker was getting faster and faster behind the mushroom cloud. I could almost read the words! I could see that there were two of them!

*T minus 20 seconds . . . and counting . . .*

Why didn't the captain tell us? I could almost see the words!

Then I heard the crowd around the beautiful mushroom cloud shouting: 'DO IT! DO IT! DO IT! DO IT! DO IT!'

*T minus 10 seconds . . . and counting . . .*
  'DO IT! DO IT! DO IT! DO IT! DO IT! DO IT! DO IT!'
  What did they want me to do? Did Duke know?

## 9

  The men were waiting! What was the order? They hunched
over the firing controls, waiting . . . The firing controls . . .?.
  'DO IT! DO IT! DO IT! DO IT! DO IT!'

## 8

  'DO IT! DO IT! DO IT! DO IT! DO IT!': the crowd screaming.
  'Jeremy!' I shouted. 'I can read the words!'

## 7

  My hands hovered over my bank of firing buttons . . .
  'DO IT! DO IT! DO IT! DO IT!' the words said.
  Didn't the captain understand?

## 6

  'What do they want us to do, Jeremy?'

## 5

  Why didn't the mushroom cloud give the order? My men
were waiting! A good sailor craves action.
  Then a great voice spoke from the pillar of fire: 'DO IT . . .
DO IT . . . DO IT . . .'

## 4

  'There's only one thing we can do down here, Duke.'

## 3

  'The order, men! Action! Fire!'

## 2

  Yes, yes, yes! Jeremy—

I reached for my bank of firing buttons. All along the console, the men reached for their buttons. But I was too fast for them! I would be first!

## THE BIG FLASH

# The Conspiracy

### PLANNED OBSOLESCENCE

*In an obscure hotel room in Geneva, Switzerland, the Grand High Wizard of the United Ku Klux Klan concluded a secret non-aggression pact with the Warlord of the Blackstone Rangers and the Foreign Minister of the Black Panther Party.*

### OVERKILL RATIO

Did Howard Hughes buy Nevada?

### DEFOLIATION

(Press Conference of the Soul)
UPI: 'Do you favour the admission of mainland China to the United Nations?'
A: 'I am in favour of admitting mainland China to the United Nations on condition that the chinks apply for admission under the official title of "Red China" and on condition that Mao Tse-tung must officially state beforehand that communism sucks.'

### VICTOR CHARLIE

Was J. Edgar Hoover turned on to acid by Timothy Leary?

### MEGA-DEATH ESTIMATE

*After being disembarked by submarine under cover of night*

*on the coast of Nova Scotia, L. Ron Hubbard was placed in
a sealed train bound for Los Angeles, California.*

## FUCK COMMUNISM

Could retired Air Force General Curtis LeMay be found
in a Haight-Ashbury crash-pad bombed back into the Stone
Age?

## YOUTH AGAINST WAR AND FASCISM

(Press Conference of the Soul)

Reuters: 'Do you believe that the withdrawal of France
has seriously weakened NATO?'

A: 'I say we're better off without those frogs and their
filthy unAmerican sex practices.'

## WHITE POWER STRUCTURE

Was J. Paul Getty turned on to acid by Hugh Hefner?

## DISTANT EARLY-WARNING LINE

*In Croton, New York, a man caught by police in the act
of emptying a gallon jug of fluid into the reservoir admitted
membership in the International Communist Conspiracy. The
fluid in the jug, when analysed, proved to be a supersaturated
solution of sodium fluoride.*

## LIMITED PRE-EMPTIVE THERMONUCLEAR WAR

Will Earl Warren assassinate Mark Lane in the men's room
of a Washington, DC, YMCA?

## THE ALLIANCE FOR PROGRESS

(Press Conference of the Soul)

*The New York Times*: 'What is your programme for dealing with the black militants?'

A: 'Unlike certain commie-faggot-creeps infesting our
federal government, I want to assure the American people
that I know the best way to handle uppity niggers.'

# THE MOST UNFORGETTABLE CHARACTER
## I EVER MET

Did Howard Hughes buy controlling interest in the National Liberation Front?

## ANTI-DEFAMATION LEAGUE
## OF B'NAI B'RITH

*Partisans freed a gorilla from the world-famous Bronx Zoo. The gorilla made its way, unnoticed, by subway, to New York's Central Park where it was brutally beaten to death by muggers.*

## PEACE AND FREEDOM PARTY

Did J. Paul Getty buy controlling interest in the Mafia, or vice versa?

## PACIFICATION

(Press Conference of the Soul)

AP: 'Do you believe that we should escalate the war on poverty?'

A: 'Not unless absolutely necessary. I have confidence that we can win the war on poverty without resorting to tactical nuclear weapons.'

## CREATIVE FEDERALISM

Was Spiro T. Agnew turned on to acid by J. Edgar Hoover?

## PEPSI GENERATION

*Escaped Nazi war criminal Martin Bormann was kidnapped by Israeli agents in Chicago, Illinois, where he had been living under an assumed name for twenty years. Mr Bormann, at the time of his abduction, was slated for imminent retirement from the Chicago police force.*

## MAKE LOVE, NOT WAR

Was Eldridge Cleaver turned on to acid by William F. Buckley, Jr?

## PSEUDO-INTELLECTUALS

(Press Conference of the Soul)

*Newsweek*: 'What steps have been taken to reverse the gold drain?'

A: 'A three-part plan to increase the flow of gold into Fort Knox has been implemented. The army will confiscate the fillings of all POWs; the Department of Health, Education and Welfare will confiscate the fillings of all welfare recipients, and the Veterans' Administration will replace the stars of all gold-star mothers with lifelike plastic facsimiles.'

## AMERICAN NAZI PARTY

Did H. L. Hunt buy Howard Hughes, or vice versa?

## STUDENTS FOR A DEMOCRATIC SOCIETY

*The Hollywood trade papers reported that Fidel Castro has signed a contract with a major studio to do a minimum of thirteen cameo appearances during the first season of the forthcoming network TV series,* Che.

## DISCOVER AMERICA

Did General Motors buy controlling interest in the Red Guard or vice versa?

## NEW ULTRA-BRITE GIVES YOUR MOUTH
## SEX APPEAL

(Press Conference of the Soul)

*St Louis Post-Dispatch*: 'It has been reported that the Soviet Union is constructing a doomsday machine. Should the United States enter the doomsday race?'

A: 'Definitely! We must not allow the Russians to destroy the world before we can. American prestige is at stake! Do you want the world to think Americans are faggots?'

AP: 'Thank you, Mr President.'

## GOD, APPLE PIE, AND MOTHERHOOD

# The Weed of Time

I, me, the spark of mind that is my consciousness, dwells in a locus that is neither place nor time. The objective duration of my lifespan is one hundred and ten years, but from my own locus of consciousness, I am immortal – my awareness of my own awareness can never cease to be. I am an infant am a child am a youth am an old, old man dying on clean white sheets. I am all these mes, have always been all these mes, will always be all these mes in the place where my mind dwells in an eternal moment divorced from time . . .

A century and a tenth is my eternity. My life is like a biography in a book: immutable, invariant, fixed in length, limitless in duration. On 3 April 2040 I am born. On 2 December 2150 I die. The events in between take place in a single instant. Say that I range up and down them at will, experiencing each of them again and again eternally. Even this is not really true; I experience all moments in my century and a tenth simultaneously, once and for ever . . . How can I tell my story? How can I make you understand? The language we have in common is based on concepts of time which we do not share.

For me, time as you think of it does not exist. I do not move from moment to moment sequentially like a blind man groping his way through a tunnel. I am at all points in the tunnel simultaneously, and my eyes are open wide. Time is to me, in a sense, what space is to you, a field over which I move in more directions than one.

How can I tell you? How can I make you understand? We are all of us men born of women, but in a way you have less in common with me than you do with an ape or an amoeba. Yet I *must* tell you, somehow. It is too late for me, will be too late, has been too late. I am trapped in this eternal hell and I can never escape, not even into death. My life is immutable, invariant, for I have eaten of Temp, the Weed of Time. But you must not! You must listen! You must understand! Shun the Weed of Time! I must try to tell you in my own way. It is pointless to try to start at the beginning. There is no beginning. There is no end. Only significant time-loci. Let me describe these loci. Perhaps I can make you understand . . .

8 September 2050. I am ten years old. I am in the office of Dr Phipps, who is the director of the mental hospital in which I have been for the past eight years. On 12 June 2053 they will finally understand that I am not insane. It is all they will understand, but it will be enough for them to release me. But on 8 September 2050 I am in a mental hospital.

8 September 2050 is the day the first expedition returns from Tau Ceti. The arrival is to be televised, and that is why I am in Dr Phipps's office watching television with the director. The Tau Ceti expedition is the reason I am in the hospital. I have been babbling about it for the previous ten years. I have been demanding that the ship be quarantined, that the plant samples it will bring back be destroyed, not allowed to grow in the soil of Earth. For most of my life this has been regarded as an obvious symptom of schizophrenia – after all, before 12 July 2048 the ship has not left for Tau Ceti, and until today it has not returned.

But on 8 September 2050 they wonder. This is the day I have been babbling about since I emerged from my mother's womb, and now it is happening. So now I am alone with Dr Phipps as the image of the ship on the television set lands on the image of a wide concrete apron . . .

'Make them understand!' I shout, knowing that it is futile. 'Stop them, Dr Phipps, stop them!'

Dr Phipps stares at me uneasily. His small blue eyes show a mixture of pity, confusion, and fright. He is all too familiar with my case. Sharing his desk-top with the portable television set is a heavy oaktag folder filled with my case history, filled with hundreds of therapy session records. In each of these records, this day is mentioned: 8 September 2050. I have repeated the same story over and over and over again. The ship will leave for Tau Ceti on 12 July 2048. It will return on 8 September 2050. The expedition will report that Tau Ceti has twelve planets . . . The fifth alone is Earthlike and bears plant and animal life . . . The expedition will bring back samples and seeds of a small Cetan plant with broad green leaves and small purple flowers . . . The plant will be named *tempis ceti* . . . It will become known as Temp . . . Before the properties of the plant are fully understood, seeds will somehow become scattered and Temp will flourish in the soil of Earth . . . Somewhere, somehow, people will begin to eat the leaves of the Temp plant. They will become changed. They will babble of the future, and they will be considered mad – until the future events of which they speak begin to come to pass . . .

Then the plant will be outlawed as a dangerous narcotic. Eating Temp will become a crime . . . But as with all forbidden fruit, Temp will continue to be eaten . . . And, finally; Temp addicts will become the most sought-after criminals in the world. The governments of the Earth will attempt to milk the secrets of the future from their tortured minds . . .

All this is in my case history, with which Dr Phipps is familiar. For eight years, this has been considered only a remarkably consistent psychotic delusion.

But now it is 8 September 2050. As I have predicted, the ship has returned from Tau Ceti. Dr Phipps stares at me woodenly as the gangplank is erected and the crew begins to disembark. I can see his jaw tense as the reporters gather around the captain, a tall, lean man carrying a small sack.

The captain shakes his head in confusion as the reporters besiege him. 'Let me make a short statement first,' he says crisply. 'Save wear and tear on all of us.'

The captain's thin, hard, pale face fills the television screen. 'The expedition is a success,' he says. 'The Tau Ceti system was found to have twelve planets, and the fifth is Earthlike and bears plant and simple animal life – very peculiar animal life . . .'

'What do you mean, "peculiar"?' a reporter shouts.

The captain frowns and shrugs his wide shoulders. 'Well, for one thing, they all seem to be herbivores and they seem to live off one species of plant which dominates the planetary flora. No predators. And it's not hard to see why. I don't quite know how to explain this, but all the critters seem to know what the other animals will do before they do it. And what we were going to do, too. We had one hell of a time taking specimens. We think it has something to do with the plant. Does something strange to their time sense.'

'What makes you say that?' a reporter asks.

'Well, we fed some of the stuff to our lab animals. Same thing seemed to happen. It became virtually impossible to lay a hand on 'em. They seemed to be living a moment in the future, or something. That's why Dr Lominov has called the plant *tempis ceti.*'

'What's this *tempis* look like?' a reporter says.

'Well, it's sort of . . .' the captain begins. 'Wait a minute,' he says, 'I've got a sample right here.'

He reaches into the small sack and pulls something out. The camera zooms in on the captain's hand.

He is holding a small plant. The plant has broad green leaves and small purple blossoms.

Dr Phipps's hands begin to tremble uncontrollably. He stares at me. He stares and stares and stares . . .

12 May 2062. I am in a small room. Think of it as a hospital room, think of it as a laboratory, think of it as a cell; it is all three. I have been here for three months.

I am seated on a comfortable lounge chair. Across a table from me sits a man from an unnamed government intelligence bureau. On the table is a tape recorder. It is running. The man seated opposite is frowning in exasperation.

'The subject is December 2081,' he says. 'You will tell me all you know of the events of December 2081.'

I stare at him silently, sullenly. I am tired of all the men from intelligence sections, economic councils and scientific bureaux, with their endless, futile demands.

'Look,' the man snaps, 'we know better than to appeal to your non-existent sense of patriotism. We are all too well aware that you don't give a damn about what the knowledge you have can mean to your country. But just remember this: you're a convicted criminal. Your sentence is indeterminate. Co-operate, and you'll be released in two years. Clam up, and we'll hold you here till you rot or until you get it through your head that the only way for you to get out is to talk. The subject is the month of December in the year 2081. Now, give!'

I sigh. I know that it is no use trying to tell any of them that knowledge of the future is useless, that the future cannot be changed because it was not changed because it will not be changed. They will not accept the fact that choice is an illusion caused by the fact that future time-loci are hidden from those who advance sequentially along the timestream one moment after the other in blissful ignorance. They refuse to understand that moments of future time are no different from moments of past or present time: fixed, immutable, invariant. They live in the illusion of sequential time.

So I begin to speak of the month of December in the year 2081. I know they will not be satisfied until I have told them all I know of the years between this time-locus and 2 December 2150. I know they will not be satisfied because they are not satisfied, have not been satisfied, will not be satisfied . . .

So I tell them of that terrible December nineteen years in their future . . .

2 December 2150. I am old, old, a hundred and ten years old. My age-ruined body lies on the clean white sheets of a hospital bed, lungs, heart, blood vessels and organs all failing. Only my mind is for ever untouched, the mind of an infant-child-youth-man-ancient. I am, in a sense, dying. Beyond this day, 2 December 2150, my body no longer exists as a living organism. Time to me forward of this date is as blank to me as time beyond 3 April 2040 is in the other temporal direction.

In a sense, I am dying. But in another sense, I am immortal. The spark of my consciousness will not go out. My mind will not come to an end, for it has neither end nor beginning. I exist in one moment that lasts for ever and spans one hundred and ten years.

Think of my life as a chapter in a book, the book of eternity, a book with no first page and no last. The chapter that is my lifespan is one hundred and ten pages long. It has a starting point and an ending point, but the chapter exists as long as the book exists, the infinite book of eternity . . .

Or, think of my life as a ruler one hundred and ten inches long. The ruler 'begins' at one and 'ends' at one hundred and ten, but 'begins' and 'ends' refer to length, not duration.

I am dying. I experience dying always, but I never experience death. Death is the absence of experience. It can never come for me.

2 December 2150 is but a significant time-locus for me, a dark wall, an endpoint beyond which I cannot see. The other wall has the time-locus 3 April 2040 . . .

3 April 2040. Nothingness abruptly ends, non-nothingness abruptly begins. I am born.

What is it like for me to be born? How can I tell you? How can I make you understand? My life, my whole lifespan of one hundred and ten years, comes into being at once, in an instant. At the 'moment' of my birth I am at the moment of my death and all moments in between. I emerge from my mother's womb and I see my life as one sees a painting, a painting of some complicated landscape: all at once, whole, a complete gestalt. I see my strange, strange infancy, the incomprehension as I emerge from the womb speaking perfect English, marred only by my undeveloped vocal apparatus, as I emerge from my mother's womb demanding that the ship from Tau Ceti in the time-locus of 8 September 2050 be quarantined, knowing that my demand will be futile because it was futile, will be futile, is futile, knowing that at the moment of my birth I am have been will be all that I ever was/am/will be and that I cannot change a moment of it.

I emerge from my mother's womb and I am dying in clean white sheets and I am in the office of Dr Phipps watching the ship land and I am in the government cell for two years babbling of the future and I am in a clearing in some woods where a plant with broad green leaves and small purple flowers grows and I am picking the plant and eating it as I know I will do have done am doing . . .

I emerge from my mother's womb and I see the gestalt painting of my lifespan, a pattern of immutable events painted on the stationary and eternal canvas of time . . .

But I do not merely *see* the 'painting', I *am* the 'painting' and I am the painter and I am also outside the painting viewing the whole and I am none of these.

And I see the immutable time-locus that determines all the rest – 4 March 2060. Change that and the painting dissolves and I live in time like any other man, moment after blessed moment, freed from this all-knowing hell. But change itself is illusion.

4 March 2060 in a wood not too far from where I was born. But knowledge of the horror that day brings, has brought, will bring, can change nothing. I will do as I am doing will do did because I did it will do it am doing it . . .

3 April 2040 and I emerge from my mother's womb, an infant-child-youth-man-ancient, in a government cell in a mental hospital dying in clean white sheets . . .


4 March 2060. I am twenty. I am in a clearing in the woods. Before me grows a small plant with broad green leaves and purple blossoms – Temp, the Weed of Time, which has haunted, haunts, will haunt my never-ending life. I know what I am doing will do have done because I will do have done am doing it.

How can I explain? How can I make you understand that this moment is unavoidable, invariant, that though I have known, do know, will know its dreadful consequences, I can do nothing to alter it?

The language is inadequate. What I have told you is an unavoidable half-truth. All actions I perform in my one-hundred-and-ten-year lifespan occur simultaneously. But even that statement only hints around the truth, for 'simultaneously' means 'at the same time', and 'time' as you understand the word has no relevance to my life. But let me approximate: let me say that all actions I have ever performed, will perform, do perform, occur simultaneously. Thus no knowledge inherent in any particular time-locus can affect any action performed at any other locus in time. Let me construct another useful lie. Let me say that, for me, action and perception are totally independent of each other. At the moment of my birth, I did everything I ever would do in my life, instantly, blindly, in one total gestalt. Only in the next 'moment' do I perceive the results of all those myriad actions, the horror that 4 March 2060 will make has made is making of my life.

Or . . . they say that at the moment of death, one's entire life flashes instantaneously before one's eyes. At the moment of my birth, my whole life flashed before me, not merely before my eyes, but in reality. I cannot change any of it because change is something that exists only as a function of the relationship between different moments in time, and for me life is one eternal moment that is one hundred and ten years long . . .

So this awful moment is invariant, inescapable.

4 March 2060. I reach down, pluck the Temp plant. I pull off a broad green leaf, put it in my mouth. It tastes bitter-sweet, woody, unpleasant. I chew it, bolt it down.

The Temp travels to my stomach, is digested, passes into my bloodstream, reaches my brain. There changes occur which better men than I are powerless, will be powerless, to understand, at least up till 2 December 2150, beyond which is blankness. My body remains in the objective timestream, to age, grow old, decay, die. But my mind is abstracted out of time to experience all moments as one.

It is like a déjà vu. Because this happened on 4 March 2060 I have already experienced it in the twenty years since my birth. Yet this is the beginning point for my Temp-consciousness in the objective timestream. But the objective timestream has no relevance to what happens . . .

The language, the very thought patterns, are inadequate. Another useful lie: in the objective timestream I was a normal human being until this dire 4 March, experiencing each moment of the previous twenty years sequentially, in order, moment after moment after moment . . .

Now on 4 March 2060 my consciousness expands in two directions in the timestream to fill my entire lifespan: forward to 2 December 2150 and my death, backward to 3 April 2040 and my birth. As this time-locus of 4 March 'changes' my future, so, too, it 'changes' my past, expanding my Temp-consciousness to both extremes of my lifespan.

But once the past is changed, the previous past has never existed and I emerge from my mother's womb an infant-child-youth-man-ancient in a government cell a mental hospital dying in clean white sheets . . . And –

*I, me, the spark of mind that is my consciousness, dwells in a locus that is neither place nor time. The objective duration of my lifespan is one hundred and ten years, but from my own locus of consciousness, I am immortal – my awareness of my own awareness can never cease to be. I am an infant am a child am a youth am an old, old man dying on clean white sheets. I am all these mes, have always been all these mes will always be all these mes in the place where my mind dwells in an eternal moment divorced from time . . .*

# A Thing of Beauty

'There's a gentleman by the name of Mr Shiburo Ito to see you,' my intercom said. 'He is interested in the purchase of an historic artifact of some significance.'

While I waited for him to enter my private office, I had computcentral display his specs on the screen discreetly built into the back of my desk. My Mr Ito was none other than Ito of Ito Freight Boosters of Osaka; there was no need to purchase a readout from Dun & Bradstreet's private banks. If Shiburo Ito of Ito Boosters wrote a cheque for anything short of the national debt, it could be relied upon not to bounce.

The slight, balding man who glided into my office wore a red silk kimono with a richly brocaded black obi, Mendocino needlepoint by the look of it. No doubt, back in the miasmic smog of Osaka he bonged the peons with the latest skins from Savile Row. Everything about him was *just so*; he purchased confidently on that razor-edge between class and ostentation that only the Japanese can handle with such grace, and then only when they have millions of hard yen to back them up. Mr Ito would be no sucker. He would want whatever he wanted for precise reasons all his own, and he would not be budgable from the centre of his desires. The typical heavyweight Japanese businessman, a prime example of the breed that's pushed us out of the centre of the international arena.

Mr Ito bowed almost imperceptibly as he handed me his card. I countered by merely bobbing my head in his direction and remaining seated. These face and posture games may seem ridiculous, but you can't do business with the Japanese without playing them.

As he took a seat before me, Ito drew a black cylinder from the sleeve of his kimono and ceremoniously placed it on the desk before me.

'I have been given to understand that you are a connoisseur of Fillmore posters of the early-to-mid-1960s period, Mr Harris,' he said. 'The repute of your collection has penetrated even to the environs of Osaka and Kyoto, where I make my habitation. Please permit me to make this minor addition. The thought that a contribution of mine may repose in such illustrious surroundings will afford me much pleasure and place me for ever in your debt.'

My hands trembled as I unwrapped the poster. With his financial resources, Ito's polite little gift could be almost anything but disappointing. My daddy loved to brag about the old expense-account days when American businessmen ran things, but you had to admit that the fringe benefits of business Japanese-style had plenty to recommend them.

But when I got the gift open, it took a real effort not to lose points by whistling out loud. For what I was holding was nothing less than a mint example of the very first Grateful Dead poster in subtle black and grey, a super-rare item, not available for any amount of sheer purchasing power. I dared not enquire as to how Mr Ito had acquired it. We simply shared a long, silent moment contemplating the poster, its beauty and historicity transcending whatever questionable events might have transpired to bring us together in its presence.

How could I not like Mr Ito now? Who can say that the Japanese occupy their present international position by economic might alone?

'I hope I may be afforded the opportunity to please your

sensibilities as you have pleased mine, Mr Ito,' I finally said. That was the way to phrase it; you didn't thank them for a gift like this, and you brought them around to business as obliquely as possible.

Ito suddenly became obviously embarrassed, even furtive. 'Forgive me my boldness, Mr Harris, but I have hopes that you may be able to assist me in resolving a domestic matter of some delicacy.'

'A domestic matter?'

'Just so. I realize that this is an embarrassing intrusion, but you are obviously a man of refinement and infinite discretion, so if you will forgive my forwardness . . .'

His composure seemed to totally evaporate, as if he was going to ask me to pimp for some disgusting perversion he had. I had the feeling that the power had suddenly taken a quantum jump in my direction, that a large financial opportunity was about to present itself.

'Please feel free, Mr Ito . . .'

Ito smiled nervously. 'My wife comes from a family of extreme artistic attainment,' he said. 'In fact, both her parents have attained the exalted status of National Cultural Treasures, a distinction of which they never tire of reminding me. While I have achieved a large measure of financial success in the freight booster enterprise, they regard me as *nikulturi*, a mere merchant, severely lacking in aesthetic refinement as compared to their own illustrious selves. You understand the situation, Mr Harris?'

I nodded as sympathetically as I could. These Japs certainly have a genius for making life difficult for themselves! Here was a major Japanese industrialist shrinking into low posture at the very thought of his sponging in-laws, who he could probably buy and sell out of petty cash. At the same time, he was obviously out to cream the sons-of-bitches in some crazy way that would only make sense to a Japanese. Seems to me the Japanese are better at running the world than they are at running their lives.

'Mr Harris, I wish to acquire a major American artifact for the gardens of my Kyoto estate. Frankly, it must be of sufficient magnitude so as to remind the parents of my wife of my success in the material realm every time they should chance to gaze upon it, and I shall display it in a manner which will assure that they gaze upon it often. But, of course, it must be of sufficient beauty and historicity so as to prove to them that my taste is no less elevated than their own. Thus shall I gain respect in their eyes and re-establish tranquillity in my household. I have been given to understand that you are a valued counsellor in such matters, and I am eager to inspect whatever such objects you may deem appropriate.'

So that was it! He wanted to buy something big enough to bong the minds of his artsy-fartsy relatives, but he really didn't trust his own taste; he wanted me to show him something he would want to see. And he was swimming like a goldfish in a sea of yen! I could hardly believe my good luck. How much could I take him for?

'Ah . . . what size artifact did you have in mind, Mr Ito?' I asked as casually as I could.

'I wish to acquire a major piece of American monumental architecture so that I may convert the gardens of my estate into a shrine to its beauty and historicity. Therefore, a piece of classical proportions is required. Of course, it must be worthy of enshrinement; otherwise, an embarrassing loss of esteem will surely ensue.'

'Of course.'

This was not going to be just another Howard Johnson or gas-station sale; even something like an old Hilton or the Cooperstown Baseball Hall of Fame I unloaded last year was thinking too small. In his own way, Ito was telling me that price was no object – the sky was the limit. This was the dream of a lifetime! A sucker with a bottomless bank account placing himself trustingly in my tender hands!

'Should it please you, Mr Ito,' I said, 'we can inspect several possibilities here in New York immediately. My jumper is on the roof.'

'Most gracious of you to interrupt your most busy schedule on my behalf, Mr Harris. I would be delighted.'

I lifted the jumper off the roof, floated her to a thousand feet then took a Mach one point five jump south over the decayed concrete jungles at the tip of Manhattan. The curve brought us back to float about a mile north of Bedloe's Island. I took her down to three hundred and brought her in towards the Statue of Liberty at a slow drift, losing altitude imperceptibly as we crept up on the Headless Lady, so that by the time we were just offshore we were right down on the deck. It was a nice touch to make the goods look more impressive – manipulating the perspectives so that the huge, green, headless statue, with its patina of firebomb soot, seemed to rise up out of the bay like a ruined colossus as we floated towards it.

Mr Ito betrayed no sign of emotion. He stared straight ahead out of the bubble without so much as a word or a flicker of gesture.

'As you are no doubt aware, this is the famous Statue of Liberty,' I said. 'Like most such artifacts, it is available to any buyer who will display it with proper dignity. Of course, I would have no trouble convincing the Bureau of National Antiquities that your intentions are exemplary in this regard.'

I set the autopilot to circle the island at fifty yards offshore so that Ito could get a fully rounded view and see how well the statue would look from any angle, how eminently suitable it was for enshrinement. But he still sat there with less expression on his face than the average C-grade servitor.

'You can see that nothing has been touched since the insurrectionists blew the statue's head off,' I said, trying to drum up his interest with a pitch. 'Thus the statue has picked up yet another level of historical significance to enhance its already formidable venerability. Originally a gift from France, it has historical significance as an emblem of kinship between the American and French revolutions. Situated as it is in the mouth of New York Harbour, it became a symbol of America itself to generations of immigrants. And the damage the insurrectionists did only serves as a reminder of how lucky we were to come through that mess as lightly as we did. Also, it adds a certain melancholy atmosphere, don't you think? Emotion, intrinsic beauty and historicity combined in one elegant piece of monumental statuary. And the asking price is a good deal less than you might suppose.'

Mr Ito seemed embarrassed when he finally spoke. 'I trust you will forgive my saying so, Mr Harris, since the emotion is engendered by the highest regard for the noble past of your great nation, but I find this particular artifact somewhat depressing.'

'How so, Mr Ito?'

The jumper completed a circle of the Statue of Liberty and began another as Mr Ito lowered his eyes and stared at the oily waters of the bay as he answered.

'The symbolism of this broken statue is quite saddening, representing as it does a decline from your nation's past greatness. For me to enshrine such an artifact in Kyoto would be an ignoble act, an insult to the memory of your nation's greatness. It would be a statement of overweening pride.'

Can you beat that? *He* was offended because he felt that displaying the statue in Japan would be insulting the United

States, and, therefore, I was implying he was *nikulturi* by offering it to him. All that the damned thing was to any American was one more piece of old junk left over from the glory days that the Japanese, who were nuts for such rubbish, might be persuaded to pay through the nose for the dubious privilege of carting away. These Japs could drive you crazy – who else could you offend by suggesting they do something that they thought would offend you, but you thought was just fine in the first place?

'I hope I haven't offended you, Mr Ito,' I blurted out. I could have bitten my tongue off the moment I said it, because it was exactly the wrong thing to say. I *had* offended him, and it was only further offence to put him in a position where politeness demanded that he deny it.

'I'm sure that could not have been farther from your intention, Mr Harris,' Ito said with convincing sincerity. 'A pang of sadness at the perishability of greatness, nothing more. In fact, as such, the experience might be said to be healthful to the soul. But making such an artifact a permament part of one's surroundings would be more than I could bear.'

Was this his true feeling, or just smooth Japanese politeness? Who could tell what these people really felt? Sometimes I think they don't even know what they feel themselves. But, at any rate, I had to show him something that would change his mood, and fast. Hmmmm . . .

'Tell me, Mr Ito, are you fond of baseball?'

His eyes lit up like satellite beacons and the heavy mood evaporated in the warm, almost childish, glow of his sudden smile. 'Ah, yes!' he said. 'I retain a box at Osaka Stadium, though I must confess I secretly retain a partiality for the Giants. How strange it is that this profound game has so declined in the country of its origin.'

'Perhaps. But that very fact has placed something on the market which I'm sure you'll find most congenial. Shall we go?'

'By all means,' Mr Ito said. 'I find our present environs somewhat overbearing.'

I floated the jumper to five hundred feet and programmed a Mach two point five jump curve to the north that quickly put the great hunk of mouldering, dirty copper far behind. It's amazing how much sickening emotion the Japanese are able to attach to almost any piece of old junk. *Our* old junk at that, as if Japan didn't have enough useless old clutter of its own. But I certainly shouldn't complain about it; it makes me a pretty good living. Everyone knows the old saying about a fool and his money.

The jumper's trajectory put us at float over the confluence of the Harlem and East Rivers at a thousand feet. Without dropping any lower, I whipped the jumper north-east over the Bronx at three hundred miles per hour. This area had been covered by tenements before the insurrection, and had been thoroughly razed by firebombs, high explosives and napalm. No one had ever found an economic reason for clearing away the miles of rubble, and now the scarred earth and ruined buildings were covered with tall grass, poison sumac, tangled scrub growth, and scattered thickets of trees which might merge to form a forest in another generation or two. Because of the crazy, jagged, overgrown topography, this land was utterly useless, and no one lived here except some pathetic remnants of old hippie tribes that kept to themselves and weren't worth hunting down. Their occasional huts and patchwork tents were the only signs of human habitation in the area. This was *really* depressing territory and I wanted to get Mr Ito over it high and fast.

Fortunately, we didn't have far to go, and in a couple of minutes I had the jumper floating at five hundred feet over our objective, the only really intact structure in the area. Mr Ito's stone face lit up with such boyish pleasure that I knew I had it made; I had figured right when I figured he couldn't resist something like this.

'So!' he cried in delight. 'Yankee Stadium!'

The ancient ballpark had come through the insurrection with nothing more than some atmospheric blackening and cratering of its concrete exterior walls. Everything around it had been pretty well demolished except for a short section of old elevated subway line which still stood beside it, a soft, rusty-red skeleton covered with vines and moss. The surrounding ruins were thoroughly overgrown, huge piles of rubble, truncated buildings, rusted-out tanks, forming tangled man-made jungled foothills around the high point of the stadium, which itself had creepers and vines growing all over it, partially blending it into the wild, overgrown landscape.

The Bureau of National Antiquities had circled the stadium with a high, electrified, barbed-wire fence to keep out the hippies who roamed the badlands. A lone guard armed with a Japanese-made slicer patrolled the fence in endless circles at fifteen feet on a one-man skimmer. I brought the jumper down to fifty feet and orbited the stadium five times, giving the enthralled Ito a good, long, contemplative look at how lovely it would look as the centrepiece of his gardens instead of hidden away in these crummy ruins. The guard waved to us each time our paths crossed – must be a lonely, boring job out here with nothing but old junk and crazy wandering hippies for company.

'May we go inside?' Ito said in absolutely reverent tones. Man, was he hooked! He glowed like a little kid about to inherit a candy store.

'Certainly, Mr Ito,' I said, taking the jumper out of its circling pattern and floating it gently up over the lip of the old ballpark, putting it on hover at roof-level over what had once been short centre field. Very slowly, I brought the jumper down towards the tangle of tall grass, shrubbery and occasional stunted trees that covered what had once been the playing field.

It was like descending into some immense, ruined, roofless cathedral. As we dropped, the cavernous triple-decked grandstands – rotted wooden seats rich with moss and fungi, great overhanging rafters concealing flocks of chattering birds in their deep, glowering shadows – rose to encircle the jumper in a weird, lost grandeur.

By the time we touched down, Ito seemed to be floating in his seat with rapture. 'So beautiful!' he sighed. 'Such a sense of history and venerability. Ah, Mr Harris, what noble deeds were done in this Yankee Stadium in bygone days! May we set foot on this historic playing field?'

'Of course, Mr Ito.' It was beautiful. I didn't have to say a word; he was doing a better job of selling the mouldy, useless heap of junk to himself than I ever could.

We got out of the jumper and tramped around through the tangled vegetation while scruffy pigeons wheeled overhead and the immensity of the empty stadium gave the place an illusion of mystical significance, as if it were some Greek ruin or Stonehenge, instead of just a ruined old baseball park. The grandstands seemed choked with ghosts; the echoes of great events that never were filled the deeply shadowed cavernous spaces.

Mr Ito, it turned out, knew more about Yankee Stadium than I did, or ever wanted to. He led me around at a measured, reverent pace, boring my ass off with a kind of historical grand tour.

'Here Al Gionfrido made his famous World Series catch

of a potential home run by the great DiMaggio,' he said, as we reached the high crumbling black wall that ran around the bleachers. Faded numerals said '405'. We followed this curving overgrown wall around to the 467 sign in left centre field. Here there were three stone markers jutting up out of the old playing field like so many tombstones, and five copper plaques on the wall behind them, so green with decay as to be illegible. They really must've taken this stuff seriously in the old days, as seriously as the Japanese take it now.

'Memorials to the great heroes of the New York Yankees,' Ito said. 'The legendary Ruth, Gehrig, DiMaggio, Mantle . . . Over this very spot, Mickey Mantle drove a ball into the bleachers, a feat which had been regarded as impossible for nearly half a century. Ah . . .'

And so on. Ito tramped all through the underbrush of the playing field and seemed to have a piece of trivia of vast historical significance to himself for almost every square foot of Yankee Stadium. At this spot, Babe Ruth had achieved his sixtieth home run; here Roger Maris had finally surpassed that feat; over there Mantle had almost driven a ball over the high roof of the venerable Stadium. It was staggering how much trivia he knew, and how much importance it all had in his eyes. The tour seemed to go on for ever. I would've gone crazy with boredom if it wasn't so wonderfully obvious how thoroughly sold he was on the place. While Ito conducted his love affair with Yankee Stadium, I passed the time by counting yen in my head. I figured I could probably get ten million out of him, which meant that my commission would be a cool million. Thinking about that much money about to drop into my hands was enough to keep me smiling for the two hours that Ito babbled on about home runs, no-hitters and triple plays.

It was late afternoon by the time he had finally saturated himself and allowed me to lead him back to the jumper. I felt it was time to talk business, while he was still under the spell of the stadium, and his resistance was at low ebb.

'It pleasures me greatly to observe the depths of your feeling for this beautiful and venerable stadium, Mr Ito,' I said. 'I stand ready to facilitate the speedy transfer of title at your convenience.'

Ito started as if suddenly roused from some pleasant dream. He cast his eyes downward, and bowed almost imperceptibly.

'Alas,' he said sadly, 'while it would pleasure me beyond all reason to enshrine the noble Yankee Stadium upon my grounds, such a self-indulgence would only exacerbate my domestic difficulties. The parents of my wife ignorantly consider the noble sport of baseball an imported American barbarity. My wife unfortunately shares in this opinion and frequently berates me for my enthusiasm for the game. Should I purchase the Yankee Stadium, I would become a laughing stock in my own household, and my life would become quite unbearable.'

Can you beat that? The arrogant little son-of-a-bitch wasted two hours of my time dragging around this stupid heap of junk, babbling all that garbage and driving me half-crazy, and he knew he wasn't going to buy it all the time! I felt like knocking his low-posture teeth down his unworthy throat. But I thought of all those yen I still had a fighting chance at and made the proper response: a rueful little smile of sympathy, a shared sigh of wistful regret, a murmured 'Alas'.

'However,' Ito added brightly, 'the memory of this visit is something I shall treasure always. I am deeply in your debt for granting me this experience, Mr Harris. For this alone, the trip from Kyoto has been made more than worthwhile.'

Now, that really made my day.

I was in real trouble. I was very close to blowing the biggest deal I've ever had a shot at. I'd shown Ito the two best items in my territory, and, if he didn't find what he wanted in the north-east, there were plenty of first-rate pieces still left in the rest of the country – top stuff like the St Louis Gateway Arch, the Disneyland Matterhorn, the Salt Lake City Mormon Tabernacle – and plenty of other brokers to collect that big fat commission.

I figured I had only one more good try before Ito started thinking of looking elsewhere: the United Nations building complex. The UN had fallen into a complicated legal limbo. The United Nations had retained title to the buildings when they moved their headquarters out of New York, but when the UN folded, New York State, New York City, and the federal government had all laid claim to them, along with the UN's foreign creditors. The Bureau of National Antiquities didn't have clear title, but they did administer the estate for the federal government. If I could palm the damned thing off on Ito, the Bureau of National Antiquities would be only too happy to take his cheque and let everyone else try to pry the money out of them. And once he moved it to Kyoto, the Japanese government would not be about to let anyone repossess something that one of their heavyweight citizens had shelled out hard yen for.

So I jumped her at Mach one point seven to a hover at three hundred feet over the greasy waters of the East River due east of the UN complex at Forty-Second Street. At this time of day and from this angle, the UN buildings presented what I hoped was a romantic Japanese-style vista. The Secretariat was a giant glass tombstone dramatically silhouetted by the late afternoon sun as it loomed massively before us out of the perpetual grey haze hanging over Manhattan; beside it, the slow sweeping curve of the General Assembly gave the grouping a balanced caligraphic outline. The total effect seemed similar to that of one of those ancient Japanese Torii gates rising out of the foggy sunset, only done on a far grander scale.

The insurrection had left the UN untouched – the rebels had had some crazy attachment for it – and from the river, you couldn't see much of the grubby open-air market that had been allowed to spring up in the plaza, or the honky-tonk bars along First Avenue. Fortunately, the Bureau of National Antiquities made a big point of keeping the buildings themselves in good shape, figuring that the federal government's claim would be weakened if anyone could yell that the bureau was letting them fall apart.

I floated her slowly in off the river, keeping at the three-hundred-foot level, and started my pitch. 'Before you, Mr Ito, are the United Nations buildings, melancholy symbol of one of the noblest dreams of man, now unfortunately empty and abandoned, a monument to the tragedy of the UN's unfortunate demise.'

Flashes of sunlight, reflected off the river, then on to the hundreds of windows that formed the face of the Secretariat, scintillated intermittently across the glass monolith as I set the jumper to circling the building. When we came around to the western face, the great glass façade was a curtain of orange fire.

'The Secretariat could be set in your gardens so as to catch both the sunrise and sunset, Mr Ito,' I pointed out. 'It's considered one of the finest examples of twentieth-century utilitarian in the world, and you'll note that it's in excellent repair.'

Ito said nothing. His eyes did not so much as flicker. Even the muscles of his face seemed unnaturally wooden. The jumper passed behind the Secretariat again, which eclipsed both the sun and its giant reflection; below us was the sweeping grey concrete roof of the General Assembly.

'And, of course, the historic significance of the UN buildings is beyond measure, if somewhat tragic –'

Abruptly, Mr Ito interrupted, in a cold, clipped voice. 'Please forgive my crudity in interjecting a political opinion into this situation, Mr Harris, but I believe such frankness will save you much wasted time and effort and myself considerable discomfort.'

All at once, he was Shiburo Ito of Ito Freight Boosters of Osaka, a mover and shaper of the economy of the most powerful nation on earth, and he was letting me know it. 'I fully respect your sentimental esteem for the late United Nations, but it is a sentiment I do not share. I remind you that the United Nations was born as an alliance of the nations which humiliated Japan in a most unfortunate war, and expired as a shrill and contentious assembly of pauperized beggar-states united only in the dishonourable determination to extract international alms from more progressive, advanced, self-sustaining and virtuous states, chief among them Japan. I must therefore regretfully point out that the sight of these buildings fills me with nothing but disgust, though they may have a certain intrinsic beauty as abstract objects.'

His face had become a shiny mask and he seemed a million miles away. He had come as close to outright anger as I had ever heard one of these heavyweight Japs get; he must be really steaming inside. Damn it, how was I supposed to know that the UN had all those awful political meanings for him? As far as I've ever heard, the UN hasn't meant anything to anyone for years, except an idealistic, sappy idea that got taken over by Third Worlders and went broke. Just my rotten luck to run into one of the few people in the world who were still fighting that one!

'You are no doubt fatigued, Mr Harris,' Ito said coldly. 'I shall trouble you no longer. It would be best to return to your office now. Should you have further objects to show me, we can arrange another appointment at some mutually convenient time.'

What could I say to that? I had offended him deeply, and, besides, I couldn't think of anything else to show him. I took the jumper to five hundred and headed downtown over the river at a slow one hundred, hoping against hope that I'd somehow think of something to salvage this blown million-yen deal with before we reached my office and I lost this giant goldfish for ever.

As we headed downtown, Ito stared impassively out the bubble at the bleak ranks of high-rise apartment buildings that lined the Manhattan shore below us, not deigning to speak or take further notice of my miserable existence. The deep orange light streaming in through the bubble turned his round face into a rising sun, straight off the Japanese flag. It seemed appropriate. The crazy bastard was just like his country: a politically touchy, politely arrogant economic overlord, with infinitely refined aesthetic sensibilities inexplicably combined with a packrat lust for the silliest of our old junk. One minute Ito seemed so superior in every way, and the next he was a stupid, childish sucker. I've been doing business with the Japanese for years, and I still don't really understand them. The best I can do is guess around the edges as to whatever their inner reality actually is, and hope I hit what works. And this time out, with a million yen or more dangled in front of me, I had guessed wrong three times and now I was dragging my tail home with a dissatisfied customer whose very posture seemed designed to let me know that I was a crass, second-rate boob, and that he was one of the lords of creation!

'Mr Harris! Mr Harris! Over there! That magnificent structure!' Ito was suddenly almost shouting; his eyes were bright with excitement, and he was actually smiling.

He was pointing due south along the East River. The Manhattan bank was choked with the ugliest public housing projects imaginable, and the Brooklyn shore was worse: one of those huge, sprawling, so-called industrial parks, low, windowless buildings, geodesic warehouses, wharves, a few freight-booster launching pads. Only one structure stood out; there was only one thing Ito could've meant: the structure linking the housing project on the Manhattan side with the industrial park on the Brooklyn shore.

Mr Ito was pointing to the Brooklyn Bridge.

'The . . . ah . . . bridge, Mr Ito?' I managed to say with a straight face. As far as I knew, the Brooklyn Bridge had only one claim to historicity: it was the butt of a series of jokes so ancient that they weren't funny any more. The Brooklyn Bridge was what old comic con-men traditionally sold to sucker tourists – greenhorns or hicks they used to call them – along with phony uranium stocks and gold-painted bricks.

So I couldn't resist the line: 'You want to buy the Brooklyn Bridge, Mr Ito?' It was so beautiful; he had put me through such hassles, and had finally got so damned high and mighty with me, and now I was in effect calling him an idiot to his face and he didn't know it.

In fact, he nodded eagerly in answer like a straight man out of some old joke and said, 'I do believe so. Is it for sale?'

I slowed the jumper to forty, brought her down to a hundred feet, and swallowed my giggles as we approached the crumbling old monstrosity. Two massive and squat stone towers supported the rusty cables from which the bed of the bridge was suspended. The jumper had made the bridge useless years ago; no one had bothered to maintain it and no one had bothered to tear it down. Where the big blocks of dark grey stone met the water, they were encrusted with putrid-looking green slime. Above the waterline, the towers were whitened with about a century's worth of bird shit.

It was hard to believe that Ito was serious. The bridge was a filthy, decayed, reeking old monstrosity. In short, it was just what Ito deserved to have sold to him.

'Why, yes, Mr Ito,' I said, 'I think I might be able to sell you the Brooklyn Bridge.'

I put the jumper on hover about a hundred feet from one of the filthy old stone towers. Where the stones weren't caked with seagull guano, they were covered with about an inch of black soot. The roadbed was cracked and pitted and thickly paved with garbage, old shells and more bird shit; the bridge must've been a seagull rookery for decades. I was mighty glad that the jumper was air-tight; the stink must've been terrific.

'Excellent!' Mr Ito exclaimed. 'Quite lovely, is it not? I am determined to be the man to purchase the Brooklyn Bridge, Mr Harris.'

'I can think of no one more worthy of that honour than your esteemed self, Mr Ito,' I said with total sincerity.

About four months after the last section of the Brooklyn Bridge was boosted to Kyoto, I received two packages from Mr Shiburo Ito. One was a mailing envelope containing a mini-cassette and a holo slide; the other was a heavy package about the size of a shoebox wrapped in blue rice paper.

Feeling a lot more mellow towards the memory of Ito

these days with a million of his yen in my bank account, I dropped the mini into my playback and was hardly surprised to hear his voice.

'Salutations, Mr Harris, and once again my profoundest thanks for expediting the transfer of the Brooklyn Bridge to my estate. It has now been permanently enshrined and affords us all much aesthetic enjoyment and has enhanced the tranquillity of my household immeasurably. I am enclosing a holo of the shrine for your pleasure. I have also sent you a small token of my appreciation, which I hope you will take in the spirit in which it is given. Sayonara.'

My curiosity aroused, I got right up and put the holo slide in my wall viewer. Before me was a heavily wooded mountain which rose into twin peaks of austere, dark grey rock. A tall waterfall plunged gracefully down the long gorge between the two pinnacles to a shallow lake at the foot of the mountain, where it smashed on to a table of flat rock, generating perpetual billows of soft mist which turned the landscape into something straight out of a Chinese painting. Spanning the gorge between the two peaks like a spiderweb directly over the great falls, its stone towers anchored to islands of rock on the very lip of the precipice, was the Brooklyn Bridge, its ponderous bulk rendered slim and graceful by the massive scale of the landscape. The stone had been cleaned and glistened with moisture; the cables and roadbed were overgrown with lush green ivy. The holo had been taken just as the sun was setting between the towers of the bridge, outlining it in rich orange fire, turning the rising mists coppery, and sparkling in brilliant sheets off the falling water.

It was very beautiful.

It was quite a while before I tore myself away from the scene, remembering Mr Ito's other package.

Beneath the blue paper wrapping was a single gold-painted brick. I gaped. I laughed. I looked again.

The object looked superficially like an old brick covered with gold paint. But it wasn't. It was a solid brick of soft, pure gold, a replica of the original item, perfect in every detail.

I knew that Mr Ito was trying to tell me something, but I still can't quite make out what.

# The Lost Continent

I felt a peculiar mixture of excitement and depression as my Pan African jet from Accra came down through the interlocking fringes of the East Coast and Central American smog banks above Milford International Airport, made a slightly bumpy landing on the east-west runway, and taxied through the thin blue haze towards a low, tarnished-looking aluminium dome that appeared to be the main international arrivals terminal.

Although American history *is* my field, there was something about actually being in the United States for the first time that filled me with sadness, awe, and perhaps a little dread. Ironically, I believe that what saddened me about being in America was the same thing that makes that country so popular with tourists, like the people who filled most of the seats around me. There is nothing that tourists like better than truly servile natives, and there are no natives quite so servile as those living off the ruins of a civilization built by ancestors they can never hope to surpass.

For my part – perhaps because I am a professor of history and can appreciate the parallels and ironies – I not only feel personally diminished at the thought of lording it over the remnants of a once-great people, but it also reminds me of our own civilization's inevitable mortality. Was not Africa a continent of so-called 'underdeveloped nations' not two centuries ago when Americans were striding to the moon like gods?

Have we in Africa *really* preserved the technical and scientific heritage of Space-Age America intact, as we like to pretend? We may claim that we have not repeated the American feat of going to the moon because it was part of the overdevelopment that destroyed Space-Age civilization, but few reputable scientists would seriously contend that we could go to the moon if we so chose. Even the jet in which I had crossed the Atlantic was not quite up to the airliners the Americans had flown two centuries ago.

Of course, the modern Americans are still less capable than we of re-creating twentieth-century American technology. As our plane reached the terminal, an atmosphere-sealed extension ramp reached out creakily from the building for its airlock. Milford International was the port of entry for the entire north-eastern United States; yet, the best it had was recently obsolescent African equipment. Milford itself, one of the largest modern American towns, would be lost next to even a city like Brazzaville. Yes, African science and technology are certainly now the most advanced on the planet, and some day perhaps we will build a civilization that can truly claim to be the highest the world has yet seen, but we only delude ourselves when we imagine that we have such a civilization now. As of the middle of the twenty-second century, Space-Age America still stands as the pinnacle of man's fight to master his environment. Twentieth-century American man had a level of scientific knowledge and technological sophistication that we may not fully attain for another century. What a pity he had so little deep understanding of his relationship to his environment or of himself.

The ramp linked up with the plane's airlock, and after a minimal amount of confusion we disembarked directly into a Customs control office, which consisted of a drab, dun-coloured, medium-sized room divided by a line of twelve booths across its width. The Customs officers in the booths were very polite, hardly glanced at our passports, and managed to process nearly a hundred passengers in less than ten minutes. The American government was apparently justly famous for doing all it could to smooth the way for African tourists.

Beyond the Customs control office was a small auditorium in which we were speedily seated by courteous uniformed Customs agents. A pale, sallow, well-built young lady in a trim blue Customs uniform entered the room after us and walked rapidly through the centre aisle and up on to the little low stage. She was wearing face-fitting atmosphere goggles, even though the terminal had a full seal.

She began to recite a little speech; I believe its actual wording is written into the American tourist-control laws.

'Good afternoon, ladies and gentlemen, and welcome to the United States of America. We hope you'll enjoy your stay in our country, and we'd like to take just a few moments of your time to give you some reminders that will help make your visit a safe and pleasurable one.'

She put her hand to her nose and extracted two small transparent cylinders filled with grey gossamer. 'These are government-approved atmosphere filters,' she said, displaying them for us. 'You will be given complimentary sets as you leave this room. You are advised to buy only filters with the official United States Government Seal of Approval. Change your filters regularly each morning, and your stay here should in no way impair your health. However, it is understood that all visitors to the United States travel at their own risk. You are advised not to remove your filters, except inside buildings or conveyances displaying a green circle containing the words FULL ATMOSPHERE SEAL.'

She took off her goggles, revealing a light red mask of welted skin that their seal had made around her eyes. 'These are self-sealing atmosphere goggles,' she said. 'If you have not yet purchased a pair, you may do so in the main lobby. You are advised to secure goggles before leaving this terminal and to wear them whenever you venture out into the open atmosphere. Purchase only goggles bearing the Government Seal of Approval, and always take care that the seal is air-tight.

'If you use your filters and goggles properly, your stay in the United States should be a safe and pleasant one. The government and people of the United States wish you a good day, and we welcome you to our country.'

We were then handed our filters and guided to the baggage area, where our luggage was already unloaded and waiting for us. A sealed bus from the Milford International Inn was already waiting for those of us who had booked rooms there, and porters loaded the luggage on the bus while a representative from the hotel handed out complimentary atmosphere goggles. The Americans were most efficient and most courteous; there was something almost unpleasant about the way we moved so smoothly from the plane to seats on a bus headed through the almost empty streets of Milford towards the faded white plastic block that was the Milford International Inn, by far the largest building in a town that seemed to be mostly small houses, much like an African residential village. Perhaps what disturbed me was the knowledge that Americans were so good at this sort of thing strictly out of necessity. Thirty per cent of the total American Gross National Product comes from the tourist industry.

I keep telling my wife I gotta get out of this tourist business. In the good old days, our ancestors would've given these African brothers nothing but about eight feet of rope. They'd've shot off a nuclear missile and blasted all those black brothers to atoms! If the damned brothers didn't have so

80

much loose money, I'd be for riding every one of them back to Africa on a rail, just like the Space-Agers did with their black brothers before the Panic.

And I bet we could do it, too. I hear there's all kinds of Space-Age weapons sitting around in the ruins out West. If we could only get ourselves together and dig them out, we'd show those Africans whose ancestors went to the moon while they were still eating each other.

But, instead, I found myself waiting with my copter bright and early at the International Inn for the next load of customers of Little Old New York Tours, as usual. And I've got to admit that I'm doing pretty well off of it. Ten years ago, I just barely had the dollars to make a down-payment on a used ten-seat helicopter, and now the thing is all paid off, and I'm shovelling dollars into my stash on every day-tour. If the copter holds up another ten years – and this is a genuine Space-Age American Air Force helicopter restored and converted to energy cells in Aspen, not a cheap piece of African junk – I'll be able to take my bundle and split to South America, just like a tycoon out of the good old days. They say they've got places in South America where there's nothing but wild country as far as you can see. Imagine that! And you can buy this land. You can buy jungle filled with animals and birds. You can buy rivers full of fish. You can buy air that doesn't choke your lungs and give you cancer and taste like fried turds even through a brand-new set of filters.

Yeah, that's why I suck up to Africans! That's worth spending four or five hours a day in that New York hole, even worth looking at subway dwellers. Every full day-tour I take in there is maybe twenty thousand dollars net towards South America. You can buy ten acres of prime Amazon swampland for only fifty-six million dollars. I'll still be young ten years from now. I'll only be forty. I take good care of myself, I change my filters every day just like they tell you to, and I don't use nothing but Key West Supremes, no matter how much the damned things cost. I'll have at least ten good years left; why, I could even live to be fifty-five! And I'm gonna spend at least ten of those fifty-five years some place where I can walk around without filters shoved up my nose, where I don't need goggles to keep my eyes from rotting, where I can finally die from something better than lung cancer.

I picture South America every time I feel the urge to tell off those brothers and get out of this business. For ten years with Karen in that Amazon swampland, I can take their superior-civilization crap and eat it and smile back at 'em afterwards.

With filters wadded up my nose and goggle seals bruising the tender skin under my eyes, I found myself walking through the blue haze of the open American atmosphere, away from the second-class twenty-second-century comforts of the International Inn, and towards the large and apparently ancient tour helicopter. As I walked along with the other tourists, I wondered just what it was that had drawn me here.

Of course, Space-Age America is my speciality, and I had reached the point where my academic career virtually required a visit to America, but, aside from that, I felt a personal motivation that I could not quite grasp. No doubt, I know more about Space-Age America than all but a handful of modern Americans, but the reality of Space-Age civilization seems illusive to me. I am an enlightened modern African, five generations removed from the bush; yet I have seen films — the obscure ghost town of Las Vegas sitting in the middle of a terrible desert clogged with vast mechanized temples to the God of Chance; Mount Rushmore, where the Americans carved an entire landscape into the likenesses of their national heroes; the Cape Kennedy National Shrine, where rockets of incredible size are preserved almost intact – which have made me feel like an ignorant primitive trying to understand the minds of gods. One cannot contemplate the Space Age without concluding that the Space-Agers possessed a kind of sophistication which we modern men have lost. Yet they destroyed themselves.

Yes, perhaps the resolution of this paradox was what I hoped to find here, aside from academic merit. Certainly, true understanding of the Space-Age mind cannot be gained from study of artifacts and records – if it could, I would have it. A true scholar, it has always seemed to me, must seek to understand, not merely to accumulate knowledge. No doubt, it was understanding that I sought here . . .

Up close, the Little Old New York Tours helicopter was truly impressive – an antique ten-seater built during the Space Age for the military by the look of it, and lovingly restored. But the American atmosphere had still been breathable even in the cities when it was built, so I was certain that this copter had only a filter system of questionable quality, no doubt installed by the contemporary natives in modern times.

I did not want anything as flimsy as all that between my eyes and lungs and the American atmosphere, so I ignored the FULL ATMOSPHERE SEAL sign and kept my filters in and my goggles on as I boarded. I noticed that the other tourists were doing the same.

Mike Ryan, the native guide and pilot, had been recommended to me by a colleague from the University of Nairobi. A professor's funds are quite limited, of course – especially one who has not attained significant academic stature as yet – and the air fares ate into my already meagre budget to the point where all I could afford was three days in Milford, four in Aspen, three in Needles, five in Eureka, and a final three at Cape Kennedy on the way home. Aside from the Cape Kennedy National Shrine, none of these modern American towns actually contained Space-Age ruins of significance. Since it is virtually impossible, and, at any rate, prohibitively dangerous, to visit major Space-Age ruins without a helicopter and a native guide, and since a private copter and guide would be far beyond my means, my only alternative was to take a day-tour like everyone else.

My Kenyan friend had told me that Ryan was the best guide to Old New York that he had had in his three visits. Unlike most of the other guides, he actually took his tours into a subway station to see live subway dwellers. There are reportedly only a thousand or two subway dwellers left; they are nearing extinction. It seemed like an opportunity I should not miss. At any rate, Ryan's charge was only about five hundred dollars above the average guide's.

Ryan stood outside the helicopter in goggles, helping us aboard. His appearance gave me something of a surprise. My Kenyan informant had told me that Ryan had been in the tour business for ten years; most guides who had been around that long were in terrible shape. No filters could entirely protect a man from that kind of prolonged exposure to saturation smog; by the time they're thirty, most guides already have chronic emphysema, and their lung-cancer rate at age thirty-five is over fifty per cent. But Ryan, who could not be under thirty, had the general appearance of a forty-year-old Boer; physiologically, he should have looked a good deal older. Instead, he was short, squat, had only slightly greying black hair, and looked quite alert, even powerful. But, of course, he had the typical American greyish-white pimply pallor.

There were eight other people taking the tour, a full copter. A prosperous-looking Kenyan who quickly introduced himself as Roger Koyinka, travelling with his wife; a rather strange-looking Ghanaian in very rich-looking old-fashioned robes and his similarly clad wife and young son; two rather willowy and modishly dressed young men who appeared to be Luthuli-ville dandies, and the only other person in the tour who was travelling alone, an intense young man whose great bush of hair, stylized dashiki and gold earring proclaimed that he was an Amero-African.

I drew a seat next to the Amero-African, who identified himself as Michael Lumumba rather diffidently when I introduced myself. Ryan gave us a few moments to get acquainted – I learned that the Ghanaian was named Kulongo, that Koyinka was a department store executive from Nairobi, that the two young men were named Ojubu and Ruala – while he checked out the helicopter, and then seated himself in the pilot's seat, back towards us, goggles still in place, and addressed us without looking back through an internal public-address system.

'Hallo, ladies and gentlemen, and welcome to your Little Old New York Tour. I'm Mike Ryan, your guide to the wonders of Old New York, Space-Age America's greatest city. Today you're going to see such sights as the Fuller Dome, the Empire State Building, Rockefeller Centre, and, as a grand finale, a subway station still inhabited by the direct descendants of the Space-Age inhabitants of the city. So don't just think of this as a guided tour, ladies and gentlemen. You are about to take part in the experience of a lifetime – an exploration of the ruins of the greatest city built by the greatest civilization ever to stand on the face of the earth.'

'Stupid arrogant honkie!' the young man beside me snarled aloud. There was a terrible moment of shocked, shamed embarrassment in the cabin, as all of us squirmed in our seats. Of course, the Amero-Africans are famous for this sort of tastelessness, but to be actually confronted with this sort of blatant racism made one for a moment ashamed to be black.

Ryan swivelled very slowly in his seat. His face displayed the characteristic red flush of the angered Caucasian, but his voice was strangely cold, almost polite: 'You're in the *United States* now, *Mr* Lumumba, not in Africa. I'd watch what I said if I were you. If you don't like me or my country, you can have your lousy money back. There's a plane leaving for Conakry in the morning.'

'You're not getting off that easy, honkie,' Lumumba said. 'I paid my money, and you're not getting me off this heli-

84

copter. You try, and I go straight to the tourist board, and there goes your licence.'

Ryan stared at Lumumba for a moment. Then the flush began to fade from his face, and he turned his back on us again, muttering, 'Suit yourself, pal. I promise you an interesting ride.'

A muscle twitched in Lumumba's temple; he seemed about to speak again. 'Look here, Mr Lumumba,' I whispered at him sharply, 'we're guests in this country, and you're making us look like boorish louts in front of the natives. If you have no respect for your own dignity, have some respect for ours.'

'You stick to your pleasures, and I'll stick to mine,' he told me, speaking more calmly, but obviously savouring his own bitterness. 'I'm here for the pleasure of seeing the descendants of the stinking honkies who kicked my ancestors out grovel in the putrid mess they made for themselves. And I intend to get my money's worth.'

I started to reply, but then restrained myself. I would have to remain on civil terms with this horrid young man for hours. I don't think I'll ever understand these Amero-Africans and their pointless blood-feud. I doubt if I want to.

I started the engines, lifted her off the pad, and headed east into the smog bank trying hard not to think of that black brother Lumumba. No wonder so many of his ancestors were lynched by the Space-Agers! Some time during the next few hours, that crud was going to get his . . .

Through my cabin monitor (this Air Force Iron was just loaded with real Space-Age stuff) I watched the stupid looks on their flat faces as we headed for what looked like a solid wall of smoke at about one hundred miles per hour. From the fringes, a major smog bank looks like that – solid as a steel slab – but once you're inside there's nothing but a blue haze that anyone with a half-way decent set of goggles can see right through.

'We are now entering the East Coast smog bank, ladies and gentlemen,' I told them. 'This smog bank extends roughly from Bangor, Maine, in the north to Jacksonville, Florida, in the south, and from the Atlantic coastline in the east to the slopes of the Alleghenies in the west. It is the third largest smog bank in the United States.'

Getting used to the way things look inside the smog always holds 'em for a while. Inside a smog bank, the colour of everything is a kind of washed-out, greyed, and blued. The air is something you can see, a mist that doesn't move; it almost sparkles at you. For some reason, these Africans always seem to be knocked out by it. Imagine thinking stuff like that is beautiful, crap that would kill you horribly and slowly in a couple of days if you were stupid or unlucky enough to breathe it without filters.

Yeah, they sure were a bunch of brothers! Some executive from Nairobi who acted like just being in the same copter with an American might give him and his wife lung cancer. Two rich young fruits from Luthuliville who seemed to be travelling together so they could congratulate themselves on how smart they both were for picking such rich parents. Some professor named Balewa who had never been to the States before, but probably was sure he knew what it was all about. A backwoods jungle-bunny named Kulongo who had struck it rich off uranium or something, taking his wife and kid on the grand tour. And, of course, that creep, Lumumba. The usual load of African tourists. Man, in the good old days, these niggers wouldn't have been good enough to shine our shoes!

Now we were flying over the old state of New Jersey. The Space-Agers did things in New Jersey that not even the African professors have figured out. It was weird country we were crossing: endless patterns of box-houses, all of them the same, all bleached blue-grey by two centuries of smog; big old freeways jammed with the wreckage of cars from the Panic of the Century; a few twisted grey trees and a patch of dry grass here and there that somehow managed to survive in the smog.

And this was western Jersey; this was nothing. Farther east, it was like an alien planet or something. The view from the Jersey Turnpike was a sure tourist-pleaser. It really told them just where they were. It let them know that the Space-Agers could do things they couldn't hope to do. Or want to.

Yeah, the Jersey lowlands are spectacular, all right, but why in hell did our ancestors want to do a thing like that? It really makes you think. You look at the Jersey lowlands and you know that the Space-Agers could do about anything they wanted to . . .

But why in hell did they want to do some of the things they did?

There was something about actually standing in the open American atmosphere that seemed to act directly on the consciousness, like kif. Perhaps it was the visual effect. Ryan had landed the helicopter on a shattered arch of six-lane freeway that soared like the frozen contrail of an ascending jet over a surreal metallic jungle of amorphous Space-Age rubble on a giant's scale – all crumbling rusted storage tanks, ruined factories, fantastic mazes of decayed valving and piping – filling the world from horizon to horizon. As we stepped out on to the cracked and pitted concrete, the spectrum of reality changed, as if we were suddenly on the surface of a planet circling a bluer and greyer sun. The entire grotesque panorama appeared as if through a blue-grey filter. But we were inside the filter; the filter was the open American smog and it shone in drab sparkles all around us. Strangest of all, the air seemed to remain completely transparent while possessing tangible visible substance. Yes, the visual effects of the American atmosphere alone are enough to affect you like some hallucinogenic drug: distorting your consciousness by warping your visual perception of your environment.

Of course, the exact biochemical effects of breathing saturation smog through filters are still unknown. We know that the American atmosphere is loaded with hydrocarbons and nitrous oxides that would kill a man in a matter of days if he breathed them directly. We know that the atmosphere filters developed towards the end by the Space-Agers enable a man to breathe the American atmosphere for up to three months without permanent damage to his health and enable the modern Americans – who have to breathe variations of this filtered poison every moment of their lives – to often live to be fifty. We know how to duplicate the Space-Age atmosphere filters, and we more or less know how their complex catalytic fibres work, but the reactions that the filters must put the American atmosphere through to make it breathable are so complex that the only thing we can say for sure of what comes out the other side is that it usually takes about four decades to kill you.

Perhaps that strange feeling that came over me was a combination of both effects. But, for whatever reasons, I saw that weird landscape as if in a dream or a state of intoxication: everything faded and misty and somehow unreal, vaguely supernatural.

Beside me, staring silently and with a strange dignity at the totally artificial vista of monstrous rusted ruins, stood the Ghanaian, Kulongo. When he finally spoke, his wife and son seemed to hang on his words, as if he were one of the old chiefs dispensing tribal wisdom.

'I have never seen such a place as this,' Kulongo said. 'In this place, there once lived a race of demons or witch-doctors or gods. There are those who would call me an ignorant savage for saying this thing, but only a fool doubts what he sees with his eyes or his heart. The men who made these things were not human beings like us. Their souls were not as our souls.'

Although he was putting it in naïve and primitive terms, there was the weight of essential truth in Kulongo's words. The broken arch of freeway on which we stood reared like the head of a snake whose body was a six-lane road clogged with the rusted corpses of what had been a regionwide traffic-jam during the Panic of the Century. The freeway led south, off into the fuzzy horizon of the smog bank, through a ruined landscape in which nothing could be seen that was not the decayed work of man; that was not metal or concrete or asphalt or plastic or Space-Age synthetic. It was like being perched above some vast ruined machine the size of a city, a city never meant for man. The scale of the machinery and the way it encompassed the visual universe made it very clear to me that the reality of America was something that no one could put into a book or a film.

I was in America with a vengeance. I was overwhelmed by the totality with which the Space-Agers had transformed their environment, and by the essential incomprehensibility – despite our sophisticated sociological and psycho-historical explanations – of why they had done such a thing and of how they themselves had seen it. 'Their souls were not as our souls' was as good a way to put it as any.

'Well, it's certainly spectacular enough,' Ruala said to his friend, the rapt look on his face making a mockery of his sarcastic tone.

'So it is,' Ojubu said softly. Then, more harshly: 'It's probably the largest junk heap in the world.'

The two of them made a half-hearted attempt at laughter, which withered almost immediately under the contemptuous look that the Kulongos gave them; the timeless look that the people of the bush have given the people of the towns for centuries, the look that said only cowardly fools attempt to hide their fears behind a false curtain of contempt, that only those who truly fear magic need to openly mock it.

And again, in their naïve way, the Kulongos were right. Ojubu and Ruala were just a shade too shrill, and, even while they played at diffidence, their eyes remained fixed on that totally surreal metal landscape. One would have to be a lot worse than a mere fool not to feel the essential strangeness of that place.

Even Lumumba, standing a few yards from the rest of us, could not tear his eyes away.

Just behind us, Ryan stood leaning against the helicopter. There was a strange power, perhaps a sarcasm as well, in his words as he delivered what surely must have been his routine guide's speech about this place.

'Ladies and gentlemen, we are now standing on the New Jersey Turnpike, one of the great highways that linked some of the mighty cities of Space-Age America. Below you are the Jersey lowlands, which served as a great manufacturing, storage, power-producing, and petroleum refining and distribution centre for the greatest and largest of the Space-Age cities, Old New York. As you look across these incredible ruins – larger than most modern African cities – think of this: all of this was nothing to the Space-Age Americans but a minor industrial area to be driven through at a hundred miles an hour without even noticing. You're not looking at one of the famous wonders of Old New York, but merely at an unimportant fringe of the greatest city ever built by man. Ladies and gentlemen, you're looking at a very minor work of Space-Age man!'

'Crazy damned honkies . . .' Lumumba muttered. But there was little vehemence or real meaning in his voice, and, like the rest of us, he could not tear his eyes away. It was not hard to understand what was going through his mind. Here was a man raised in the Amero-African enclaves on an irrational mixture of hate for the fallen Space-Agers, contempt for their vanished culture, fear of their former power, and perhaps a kind of twisted blend of envy and identification that only an Amero-African could fully understand. He had come to revel in the sight of the ruins of the civilization that had banished his ancestors, and now he was confronted with the inescapable reality that the 'honkies' whose memory he both hated and feared had indeed possessed power and knowledge not only beyond his comprehension, but applied to ends which his mind was not equipped to understand.

It must have been a humbling moment for Michael Lumumba. He had come to sneer and had been forced instead to gape.

I tore my gaze away from that awesome vista to look at

Ryan; there was a grim smile on his pale, unhealthy face as he drank in our reactions. Clearly, he had meant this sight to humble us, and, just as clearly, it had.

Ryan stared back at me through his goggles as he noticed me watching him. I couldn't read the expression in his watery eyes through the distortion of the goggle lenses. All I understood was that somehow some subtle change had occurred in the pattern of the group's interrelationships. No longer was Ryan merely a native guide, a functionary, a man without dignity. He had proved that he could show us sights beyond the limits of the modern world. He had reminded us of just where we were, and who and what his ancestors had been. He had suddenly gained second-hand stature from the incredible ruins around him, because, in a very real way, they were *his* ruins. Certainly they were not ours.

'I've got to admit they were great engineers,' Koyinka, the Kenyan executive, said.

'So were the ancient Egyptians,' Lumumba said, recovering some of his bitterness. 'And what did it get *them*? A fancy collection of old junk over their graves – exactly what it got these honkies.'

'If you keep it up, pal,' Ryan said coldly, 'you may get a chance to see something that'll impress you a bit more than these ruins.'

'Is that a threat or a promise, Ryan?'

'Depends on whether you're a man . . . or a *boy*, Mr Lumumba.'

Lumumba had nothing to say to that, whatever it all had meant. Ryan appeared to have won a round in some contest between them.

And when we followed Ryan back into the helicopter, I think we were all aware that for the next few hours, this pale, unhealthy American would be something more than a mere convenient functionary. We were the tourists; he was the guide.

But as we looked over our shoulders at the vast and overwhelming heritage that had been created and then squandered by his ancestors, the relationship that those words described took on a new meaning. The ancestral ruins off which he lived were a greater thing in some absolute sense than the totality of our entire living civilization. He had convinced us of that, and he knew it.

That view across the Jersey lowlands always seems to shut

them up for a while. Even that crud, Lumumba. God knows why. Sure it's spectacular, bigger than anything these Africans could ever have seen where they come from, but when you come right down to it, you gotta admit that Ojubu was right – the Jersey lowlands are nothing but a giant pile of junk. Crap. Space-Age garbage. Sometimes looking at a place like that can piss me off. I mean, we had *some* ancestors. They built the greatest civilization the world ever saw, but what did they leave for us? The most spectacular junk piles in the world, air that does you in sooner or later even through filters, and a continent where seeing something alive that people didn't put there is a big deal. Our ancestors went to the moon, they were a great people, the greatest in history, but sometimes I get the feeling they were maybe just a little out of their minds. Like that crazy 'Merge with the Cosmic All' thing I found that time in Grand Central – still working after two centuries or so; it must do *something* besides kill people, but *what*? I dunno, maybe our ancestors went a little over the edge, sometimes . . .

Not that I'd ever admit a thing like that to any black brothers! The Space-Agers may have been a little bit nuts, but who are these Africans to say so, who are they to decide whether a civilization that had them beat up and down the line was sane or not? Sane according to whom? Them, or the Space-Agers? For that matter, who am I to think a thing like that? An ant or a rat living off their garbage. Who are nobodies like us and the Africans to judge people who could go to the moon?

Like I keep telling Karen, this damned tourist business is getting to me. I'm around these Africans too much. Sometimes, if I don't watch myself, I catch myself thinking like them. Maybe it's the lousy smog this far into the smog bank – but hell, that's another crazy African idea!

That's what being around these Africans does to me, and looking at subway dwellers five times a week sure doesn't help, either. Let's face it, stuff like the subways and the lowlands is really depressing. It tells a man he's a nothing. Worse, it tells him that people who were better than he is still managed to screw things up. It's just not good for your mind.

But as the copter crested the lip of the Palisades ridge and we looked out across that wide Hudson River at Manhattan, I was reminded again that this crummy job had its compensations. If you haven't seen Manhattan from a copter crossing the Hudson from the Jersey side, you haven't seen nothing, pal. That Fuller Dome socks you right in the eye. It's ten miles in diameter. It has facets that make it glitter like a giant blue diamond floating over the middle of the island. Yeah, that's right, it floats. It's made of some Space-Age plastic that's been turned blue and hazy by a couple of centuries of smog, it's ten miles wide at the base, and the god-damned thing floats over the middle of Manhattan a few hundred feet off the ground at its rim like a cloud or a hover or something. No motors, no nothing. It's just a hemisphere made of plastic panels and alloy tubing and it floats over the middle of Manhattan like half a giant diamond all by itself. Now, *that's* what I call a real piece of Space-Age hardware!

I could hear them suck in their breath behind me. Yeah, it really does it to you. I almost forgot to give them the spiel. I mean, who wants to? What can you really say to someone while he's looking at the Fuller Dome for the first time?

'Ladies and gentlemen, you are now looking at the world-famous Fuller Dome, the largest architectural structure ever built by the human race. It is ten miles in diameter. It encloses the centre of Manhattan Island, the heart of Old New York. It has no motors, no power source, and no moving parts. But it floats in the air like a cloud. It is considered the First Wonder of the World.'

What else is there to say?


We came in low across the river towards that incredible floating blue diamond, the Fuller Dome, parallel to the ruins of a great suspension bridge which had collapsed and now hung in fantastic rusted tatters half in and half out of the water. Aside from Ryan's short guidebook speech, no one said a word as we crossed the water to Manhattan.

Like the moon landing, the Fuller Dome was one of the peak achievements of the Space Age, a feat beyond the power of modern African civilization. As I understood it, the Dome held itself aloft by convection currents created by its own greenhouse effect, though this has always seemed to me the logical equivalent of a man lifting himself by his own shoulders. No one quite knows exactly how a dome this size was built, but the records show that it required a fleet of two hundred helicopters. It took six weeks to complete. It was named after Buckminster Fuller, one of the architectural geniuses of the early Space Age, but it was not built till after his death, though it is considered his monument. But it was more than that; it was staggeringly, overwhelmingly beautiful.

We crossed the river and headed towards the rim of the Fuller Dome at about two hundred feet, over a shoreline of crumbling docks and the half-sunken hulks of rusted-out ships; then over a wide strip of elevated highway filled with the usual wrecked cars; and finally we slipped under the rim of the Dome itself, an incredibly thin metal hoop floating in the air from which the Dome seemed to blossom like a soap bubble from a child's bubble pipe.

And we were flying inside the Fuller Dome. It was an incredible sensation – the world inside the Dome existed in blue crystal. Our helicopter seemed like a buzzing fly that had intruded into an enormous room. The room was a mile high and ten miles wide. The facets of the Fuller Dome had been designed to admit natural sunlight and thus preserve the sense of being outdoors, but they had been weathered to a bluish hue by the saturation smog. As a result, the interior of the Dome was a room on a superhuman scale, a room filled with a pale blue light – and a room containing a major portion of a giant city.

Towering before us were the famous skyscrapers of Old New York, a forest of rectangular monoliths hundreds of feet high, in some cases well over a thousand feet tall. Some of them stood almost intact, empty concrete boxes transformed into giant sombre tombstones by the eerie blue light that permeated everything. Others had been ripped apart by explosions and were jagged piles of girders and concrete. Some had had walls almost entirely of glass; most of these were now airy mazes of framework and concrete platforms, where the blue light here and there flashed off intact patches of glass. And far above the tops of the tallest buildings was the blue stained-glass faceted sky of the Fuller Dome.

Ryan took the helicopter up to the five-hundred-foot level and headed for the giant necropolis, a city of monuments built on a scale that would have caused the pharaohs to whimper, packed casually together like family houses in an African residential village. And all of it was bathed in a sparkly blue-grey light which seemed to enclose a universe – here in the very core of the East Coast smog bank, where everything seemed to twinkle and shimmer.

We all gasped as Ryan headed at one hundred miles per hour for a thin canyon that was the gap between two rows of buildings which faced each other across a not-very-wide street hundreds of feet below.

For a moment, we seemed to be a stone dropping towards

a narrow shaft between two immense cliffs – then, suddenly, the copter's engines screamed, and the copter seemed to somehow skid and slide through the air to a dead hover no more than a hundred feet from the sheer face of a huge grey skyscaper.

Ryan's laugh sounded unreal, partially drowned out by the descending whine of the copter's relaxing engines. 'Don't worry, folks,' he said over the public-address system, 'I'm in control of this aircraft at all times. I just thought I'd give you a little thrill. Kind of wake up those of you who might be sleeping, because you wouldn't want to miss what comes next: a helicopter tour of what the Space-Agers called "The Sidewalks of New York".'

And we inched forward at the pace of a running man; we seemed to drift into a canyon between two parallel lines of huge buildings that went on for miles.

Man, no matter how many times I come here, I still feel weird inside the Fuller Dome. It's another world in there. New York seems like it's built for people fifty feet tall; it makes you feel so small, like you're inside a giant's room. But when you look up at the inside of the Dome, the buildings that seemed so big seem so small; you can't get a grasp on the scale of anything. And everything is all blue. And the smog is so heavy you think you could eat it with a fork.

And you know that the whole thing is completely dead. Nothing lives in New York between the Fuller Dome and the subways, where several thousand subway dwellers stew in their own muck. Nothing can. The air inside the Fuller Dome is some of the worst in the country, almost as bad as that stuff they say you can barely see through that fills the Los Angeles basin. The Space-Agers didn't put up the Dome to atmosphere-seal a piece of the city; they did it to make the city warmer and keep the snow off the ground. The smog was still breathable then. So the inside of the Dome is open to the naked atmosphere, and it actually seems to suck in the worst of the smog, maybe because it's about twenty degrees hotter inside the Dome than it is outside; something about convection currents, the Africans say, but I dunno.

It's creepy, that's what it is. Flying slowly between two lines of skyscrapers, I had the feeling I was tiptoeing very carefully around some giant graveyard in the middle of the night. Not any of that crap about ghosts that I'll bet some of these Africans still believe deep down; this whole city really *was* a graveyard. During the Space Age, millions of people lived in New York; now there was nothing alive here but a couple thousand stinking subway dwellers slowly strangling themselves in their stinking sealed subways.

So I kind of drifted the copter in among the skyscrapers for a while, at about a hundred feet, real slow, almost on hover, and just let the customers suck in the feel of the place, keeping my mouth shut.

After a while, we came to a really wide street, jammed to overflowing with wrecked and rusted cars that even filled the sidewalks, as if the Space-Agers had built one of their crazy car-pyramids right here in the middle of Manhattan, and it had just sort of run like hot wax. I hovered the copter over it for a while.

'Folks,' I told the customers, 'below you, you see some of the wreckage from the Panic of the Century which fills the sidewalks of New York. The Panic of the Century started right here in New York. Imagine, ladies and gentlemen, at the height of the Space Age, there were more than one hundred million cars, trucks, buses and other motor vehicles operating on the freeways and streets of the United States. A car for every two adults! Look below you and try to imagine the magnificence of the sight of all of them on the road all at once!'

Yeah, that would've been something to see, all right! From a helicopter, that is. Man, those Space-Agers sure had guts, driving around down there jammed together on the freeways at copter speeds with only a few feet between them. They must've had fantastic reflexes to be able to handle it. Not for me, pal, I couldn't do it, and I wouldn't want to.

But, God, what this place must've been like, all lit up at night in bright coloured lights, millions of people tearing around in their cars all at once! Hell, what's the population of the United States today? – thirty, forty million, not a city with five hundred thousand people, and nothing in all the world on the scale of this. Damn it, those were the days for a man to have lived!

Now look at it! The power all gone except for whatever keeps the subway electricity going, so the only light above ground is that blue stuff that makes everything seem so still and quiet and weird, like the city's embalmed or something. The buildings are all empty crumbling wrecks, burned out, smashed up by explosions, and the cars are all rusted garbage, and the people are dead, dead, dead.

It's enough to make you cry – if you let it get to you.

We drifted among the ruins of Old New York like some secretive night insect. By now it was afternoon, and the canyons formed by the skyscrapers were filled with deep purple shadows and intermittent avenues of pale blue light. The world under the Fuller Dome was composed of relative darknesses of blue, much as the world under the canopy of a heavy rain forest is a world of varying greens.

We dipped low and drifted for a few moments over a large square where the top of a low building had been removed by an explosion to reveal a series of huge cuts and canyons extending deep in the bowels of the earth, perhaps some kind of underground train terminal, perhaps even a ruined part of the famous New York subways.

'This is a burial ground of magics,' Kulongo said. 'The air is very heavy here.'

'They sure knew how to build,' Koyinka said.

Beside me, Michael Lumumba seemed subdued, perhaps even nervous. 'You know, I never knew it was all so big,' he muttered to me. 'So big, and so strange, and so . . . so . . .'

'*Space Age*, Mr Lumumba?' Ryan suggested over the intercom.

Lumumba's jaw twitched. He was obviously furious at having Ryan supply the precise words he was looking for. 'Inhuman, honkie, inhuman was what I was going to say,' he lied transparently. 'Wasn't there an ancient saying, "New York is a nice place to visit, but I wouldn't want to live there"?'

'Never heard that one, pal,' Ryan said. 'But I can see how your ancestors might've felt that way. New York was always too much for anyone but a *real* Space-Ager.'

There was considerable truth in what they both said, though of course neither was interested in true insight. Here in the blue crystal world under the Fuller Dome, in a helicopter buzzing about noisily in the graveyard silence, reduced by the scale of the buildings to the relative size of an insect, I felt the immensity of what had been Space-Age America all around me. I felt as if I were trespassing in the mansions of my betters. I felt like a bug, an insect. I remembered from history, not from instinct, how totally America had dominated the world during the Space Age – not by armed conquest, but by the sheer overwhelming weight of its very existence. I had never before been quite able to grasp that concept.

I understood it perfectly now.

I gave them the standard helicopter tour of the sidewalks of New York. We floated up Broadway, the street that had been called The Great White Way, at about fifty feet, past crazy rotten networks of light steel girders, crumbled signs, and wiring on a monstrous scale. At a thousand feet, we circled the Empire State Building, one of the oldest of the great skyscrapers, and now one of the best-preserved, a thousand-foot slab of solid concrete, probably just the kind of tombstone the Space-Agers would've put up for themselves if they had thought about it.

Yeah, I gave them all the usual stuff. The ruins of Rockefeller Centre. The UN Plaza Crater.

Of course, they were all sucking it up, even Lumumba, though of course the slime wouldn't admit it. After this, they'd be ripe for a nasty peek at the subway dwellers, and after they got through gaping at the animals, they'd be ready for dinner back in Milford, feeling they had got their money's worth.

Yeah, I can get the same money for a five-hour tour that most guides get for six, because I've got the stomach to take them into a subway station. As usual, it had just the right effect when I told them we were going to end the tour with a visit on foot to an inhabited subway station. Instead of bitching and moaning that the tour was too short, that they weren't getting their money's worth, they were all eager – and maybe a little scared – at actually walking among the *really* primitive natives. Once they'd had their fill of the subway dwellers, a ride home across the Hudson into the sunset would be enough to convince them they'd had a great day.

So we *were* going to see the subway dwellers! Most of the native guides avoided the subways, and the American government for some reason seemed to discourage research by foreigners. A subtle discouragement, perhaps, but discouragement nevertheless. In a paper he published a few years ago, Omgazi had theorized that the modern Americans in the vicinity of New York had a loathing of the subway dwellers that amounted to virtually a superstitious dread. According to him, the subway dwellers, because they were direct descendants of diehard Space-Agers who had atmosphere-sealed the subways and set up a closed ecology inside rather than abandon New York, were identified with their ancestors in the minds of the modern Americans. Hence, the modern Americans shunned the subway dwellers because they considered them shamans on a deep subconscious level.

It had always seemed to me that Omgazi was being rather ethnocentric. He was dealing, after all, with modern Americans, not nineteenth-century Africans. Now I would have a chance to observe some subway dwellers myself. The prospect was most exciting. For, although the subway dwellers were apparently degenerating towards extinction at a rapid rate, in one respect they were unique in all the world – they still lived in an artificial environment that had been constructed during the Space Age. True, it had been a hurried, makeshift environment in the first place, and it and its inhabitants had deteriorated tremendously in two centuries, but, whatever else they were or weren't, the subway dwellers were the only enclave of Space-Age Americans left on the face of the earth.

If it were possible at all for a modern African to truly come to understand the reality of Space-Age America, surely confrontation with the lineal descendants of the Space Age would provide the key.

Ryan set the helicopter down in what seemed to be some kind of large open terrace behind a massive, low, concrete building. The terrace was a patchwork of cracked concrete walkways and expanses of bare grey earth. Once, apparently, it had been a small park, before the smog had become lethal to vegetation. As a denuded ruin in the pale blue light, it seemed like some strange cold corpse as the helicopter kicked up dry clouds of dust from the surface of the dead parkland.

As I stepped out with the others into the blue world of the Fuller Dome, I gasped: I had a momentary impression that I had stepped back to Africa, to Accra or Brazzaville. The air was rich and warm and humid on my skin. An instant later, the visual effect – everything a cool pale blue – jarred me with its arctic-vista contrast. Then I noticed the air itself and I shuddered, and was suddenly hyperconscious of the filters up my nostrils and the goggles over my eyes, for here the air was so heavy with smog that it seemed to sparkle electrically in the crazy blue light. What incredible, beautiful, foul poison!

Except for Ryan, all of us were clearly overcome, each in his own way. Kulongo blinked and stared solemnly for a moment like a great bear; his wife and son seemed to lean into the security of his calm aura. Koyinka seemed to fear that he might strangle; his wife twittered about excitedly, tugging at his hand. The two young men from Luthuliville seemed to be self-consciously making an effort to avoid clutching at each other. Michael Lumumba mumbled something unintelligible under his breath.

'What was that you said, *Mr* Lumumba?' Ryan said a shade gratingly as he led us out of the park down a crumbling set of stone-and-concrete stairs. Something seemed to snap inside Lumumba; he broke stride for a moment, frozen by some inner event while Ryan led the rest of us on to a walkway between a line of huge silent buildings and a street choked with the rusted wreckage of ancient cars, timelessly locked in their death-agony in the sparkly blue light.

'What do you want from me, you damned honkie?' Lumumba shouted shrilly. 'Haven't you done enough to us?'

Ryan broke stride for a moment, smiled back at Lumumba rather cruelly, and said, 'I don't know what you're talking about, pal. I've got your money already. What the hell else could I want from *you*?'

He began to move off down the walkway again, threading his way past and over bits of wrecked cars, fallen masonry and amorphous rubble. Over his shoulder, he noticed that Lumumba was following along haltingly, staring up at the buildings, nibbling at his lower lip.

'What's the matter, Lumumba?' Ryan shouted back at him. 'Aren't these ruins good enough for you to gloat over? You wouldn't be just a little bit afraid, would you?'

'Afraid? Why should I be afraid?'

Ryan continued on for a few more metres; then he stopped and leaned up against the wall of one of the more badly damaged skyscrapers, near a jagged cavelike opening that led into the dark interior. He looked directly at Lumumba. 'Don't get me wrong, pal,' he said, 'I wouldn't blame you if you were a little scared of the subway dwellers. After all, they're the direct descendants of the people that kicked your ancestors out of this country. Maybe you got a right to be nervous.'

'Don't be an idiot, Ryan. Why should a civilized African be afraid of a pack of degenerate savages?' Koyinka said as we all caught up to Ryan.

Ryan shrugged. 'How should I know?' he said. 'Maybe you ought to ask Mr Lumumba.'

And with that, he turned his back on us and stepped through the jagged opening into the ruined skyscraper. Somewhat uneasily, we followed him into what proved to be a large antechamber that seemed to lead back into some even larger cavernous space that could be sensed rather than seen looming in the darkness. But Ryan did not lead us towards this large, open space; instead, he stopped before he had gone more than a dozen steps and waited for us near a crumbling metal-pipe fence that guarded two edges of what looked like a deep pit. One long edge of the pit was flush with the right wall of the antechamber; at the far short edge, a flight of stone stairs began which seemed to go all the way to the shadow-obscured bottom.

Ryan led us along the railing to the top of the stairs, and from this angle I could see that the pit had once been the entrance to the mouth of a large tunnel whose floor had been the floor of the pit at the foot of the stairs. Now an immense and ancient solid slab of steel blocked the tunnel mouth and formed the fourth wall of the pit. But in the centre of this rusted steel slab was a relatively new airlock that seemed of modern design.

'Ladies and gentlemen,' Ryan said, 'we're standing by a sealed entrance to the subways of Old New York. During the Space Age, the subways were the major transportation system of the city and there were hundreds of entrances like this one. Below the ground was a giant network of stations and tunnels through which the Space-Agers could go from any point in the city to any other point. Many of the stations were huge and contained shops and restaurants. Every station had automatic vending machines which sold food and drinks and a lot of other things, too. Even during the Space Age, the subways were a kind of little world.'

He started down the stairs, still talking. 'During the Panic of the Century, some of the New Yorkers chose not to leave the city. Instead, they retreated to the subways, sealed all the entrances, installed space-station life-support machinery – everything from a fusion reactor to hydroponics – and cut themselves off from the outside world. Today, the subway dwellers, direct descendants of those Space-Agers, still inhabit several of the subway stations. And most of the Space-Age life-support machinery is still running. There are probably Space-Age artifacts down here that no modern man has ever seen.'

At the bottom of the pit, Ryan led us to the airlock and opened the outer door. The airlock proved to be surprisingly large. 'This airlock was installed by the government about fifty years ago, soon after the subway dwellers were discovered,' he told us as he jammed us inside and began the cycle. 'It was part of a programme to recivilize the subway dwellers. The idea was to let scientists get inside without contaminating the subway atmosphere with smog. Of course, the whole programme was a flop. Nobody's ever going to get through to the subway dwellers, and there are less of 'em every year. They don't breed much, and in a generation or so they'll be extinct. So you're all in for a really unique experience. Not everyone will be able to tell their grandchildren that they actually saw a live subway dweller!'

The inner airlock door opened into an ancient square-cross-sectioned tunnel made of rotting grey concrete. The air, even through filters, tasted horrible: very thin, somehow crisp without being at all bracing, with a chemical undertone, yet reeking with organic decay odours. Breathing was very difficult; it felt like we were at the fifteen-thousand-foot level.

'I'm not telling you all this for my health,' Ryan said as he moved us out of the airlock. 'I'm telling it to you for *your* health: don't mess with these people. Look and don't touch. Listen, but keep your mouths shut. They may seem harmless, they may be harmless, but no one can be sure. That's why not many guides will take people down here. I hope you *all* have that straight.'

The last remark had obviously been meant for Lumumba, but he didn't seem to react to it; he seemed subdued, drawn up inside himself. Perhaps Ryan was right – perhaps in some unguessable way, Lumumba *was* afraid. It's impossible to really understand these Amero-Africans.

We moved off down the corridor. The overhead lights – at least in this area – were clearly modern, probably installed when the airlock had been installed, but it was possible that the power was actually provided by the fusion reactor that had been installed centuries ago by the Space-Agers themselves. The air we were breathing was produced by a Space-Age atmosphere plant that had been designed for actual space stations! It was a frightening and, at the same time, a thrilling feeling: our lives were dependent on actual functioning Space-Age equipment. It was almost like stepping back in time.

The corridor made a right-angle turn and became a downward-sloping ramp. The ramp levelled off after a few dozen feet, passed some crumbling ruins inset into one of the walls – apparently a ruined shop of some strange sort with massive chairs bolted to the floor and pieces of mirror still clinging to patches of its walls – and suddenly opened out into a wide, low, cavelike space lit dimly and erratically by ancient Space-Age perma-bulbs which still functioned in many places along the grime-encrusted ceiling.

It was the strangest room – if you could call it that – that I had ever been in. The ceiling seemed horribly low, lower even than it actually was, because the room seemed to go on under it indefinitely, in all sorts of seemingly random directions. Its boundaries faded off into shadows and dim lights and gloom; I couldn't see any of the far walls. It was impossible to feel exactly claustrophobic in a place like that, but it gave me an analogous sensation without a name, as if the ceiling and the floor might somehow come together and squash me.

Strange figures shuffled around in the gloom, moving about slowly and aimlessly. Other figures sat singly or in small groups on the bare filthy floor. Most of the subway dwellers were well under five feet tall. Their shoulders were deeply hunched, making them seem even shorter, and their bodies were thin, rickety and emaciated under the tattered and filthy scraps of multicoloured rags which they wore. I was deeply shocked. I don't really know what I had expected, but I certainly had not been prepared for the unmistakable aura of diminished humanity which these pitiful creatures exuded even at a distant first glance.

Immediately before us was a kind of concrete hut. It was pitted with what looked like bullet scars, and parts of it were burned black. It had tiny windows, one of which still held some rotten metal grillework. Apparently it had been a kind of sentry-box, perhaps during the Panic of the Century itself. A complex barrier cut off the section where we stood from the main area of the subway station. It consisted of a ceiling-to-floor metal grillework fence on either side of a line of turnstiles. On either side of the line of turnstiles, gates in the fence clearly marked EXIT in peeling white-and-black enamel had been crudely welded shut; by the look of the weld, perhaps more than a century ago.

On the other side of the barrier stood a male subway dweller wearing a kind of long shirt patched together out of every conceivable type and colour of cloth and rotting away at the edges and in random patches. He stood staring at us, or at least with his deeply squinted expressionless eyes turned in our direction, rocking back and forth slightly from the waist, but otherwise not moving. His face was unusually pallid even for an American, and every inch of his skin and clothing was caked with an incredible layer of filth.

Ignoring the subway dweller as thoroughly as that stooped figure was ignoring us, Ryan led us to the line of turnstiles and extracted a handful of small greenish-yellow coins from a pocket.

'These are subway tokens,' he told us, dropping ten of the coins into a small slot atop one of the turnstiles. 'Space-Age money that was only used down here. It's good in all the vending machines, and in these turnstiles. The subway dwellers still use the tokens to get food and water from the machines. When I want more of these things, all I have to do is break open a vending machine, so don't worry, admission isn't costing us anything. Just push your way through the turnstiles like this . . .'

He demonstrated by walking straight through the turnstile. The turnstile barrier rotated a notch to let him through when he applied his body against it.

One by one we passed through the turnstile. Michael Lumumba passed through immediately ahead of me, then paused at the other side to study the subway dweller, who had drifted up to the barrier. Lumumba looked down at the subway dweller's face for a long moment; then a sardonic smile grew slowly on his face, and he said, 'Hallo, honkie, how are things in the subway?'

The subway dweller turned his eyes in Lumumba's direction. He did nothing else.

'Hey, just what *are* you, some kind of cretin?' Lumumba said as Ryan, his face flushed red behind his pallor, turned in his tracks and started back towards Lumumba. The subway dweller's face did not change expression; in fact, it could hardly have been said to have had an expression in the first place. 'I think you're a brain-damage case, honkie.'

'I told you not to talk to the subway dwellers!' Ryan said, shoving his way between Lumumba and the subway dweller.

'So you did,' Lumumba said coolly. 'And I'm beginning to wonder why.'

'They can be dangerous.'

'*Dangerous?* These little moronic slugs? The only thing these brainless white worms can be dangerous to is your pride. Isn't that it, Ryan? Behold the remnants of the great Space-Age honkies! See how they haven't the brains left to wipe the drool off their chins –'

'Be silent!' Kulongo suddenly bellowed with the authority

of a chief in his voice. Lumumba was indeed silenced, and even Ryan backed off as Kulongo moved near them. But the self-satisfied look that Lumumba continued to give Ryan was a weapon that he was wielding, a weapon that the American obviously felt keenly.

Through it all, the subway dweller continued to rock back and forth, gently and silently, without a sign of human sentience.


Goddamn that black brother Lumumba and goddamn the stinking subway dwellers! Oh, how I hate taking these Africans down there. Sometimes I wonder why the hell I do it. Sometimes I feel there's something unclean about it all, something rotten. Not just the subway dwellers, though those horrible animals are rotten enough, but taking a bunch of stinking African tourists in there to look at them, and me making money off of it. It's a great selling point for the day-tour. Those black brothers eat it up, especially the cruds like Lumumba, but if I didn't need the money so bad, I wouldn't do it. Call it patriotism, maybe. I'm not patriotic enough not to take my tours to see the subway dwellers, but I'm patriotic enough not to feel too happy with myself about it.

Of course, I know what it is that gets to me. The subway dwellers are the last direct descendants of the Space-Agers, in a way the only piece of the Space Age still alive, and what they are is what Lumumba said they are: slugs, morons and cretins. And physical wrecks on top of it. Lousy eyesight, rubbery bones, rotten teeth, and if you find one more than five feet tall, it's a giant. They're lucky to live to thirty. There's no smog in the recirculated chemical crap they breathe, but there's not enough oxygen in the long run, either, and after two centuries of sucking in its own gunk, God only knows exactly what's missing and what there's too much of in the air that the subway life-support system puts out. The subway dwellers have just about enough brains left to keep the air plant and the hydroponics and stuff going without really knowing what the hell they're doing. Every one of them is a born brain-damage case, and year by year the air keeps getting crummier and crummier and the crap they eat gets lousier and lousier, and there are fewer and fewer subway dwellers, and they're getting stupider and stupider. They say in another fifty years they'll be extinct. They're all that's left of the Space-Agers, and they're slowly strangling their brains in their own crap.

Like I keep telling Karen, the tourist business is a rotten way to earn a living. Every time I come down into this stinking hole in the ground, I have to keep reminding myself that I'm a day closer to owning a piece of that Amazon swampland. It helps settle my stomach.

I led my collection of Africans farther out into the upper level of the station. It's hard to figure out just what this level was during the Space Age – there's nothing up here but a lot of old vending machines and ruined stalls and garbage. This level goes on and on in all directions; there are more old subway entrances leading into it than I've counted. I've been told that during the Space Age thousands of people crowded in here just on their way to the trains below, but that doesn't make sense. Why would they want to hang around in a hole in the ground any longer than they had to?

The subway dwellers, of course, just mostly hung around doing what subway dwellers do – stand and stare into space, or sit on their butts and chew their algae-cake, or maybe even stand and stare and chew at the same time, if they're real enterprising. Beats me why the Africans are so fascinated by them . . .

Then, a few yards ahead of us, I saw a vending machine servicer approaching a water machine. Now, *there* was a piece of luck! I sure didn't get to show every tour what passed for a 'Genuine Subway Dweller Ceremony'. I decided to really play it up. I held the tourists off about ten feet from the water machine so they wouldn't mess things up, and I started to give them a fancy pitch.

'You're about to witness an authentic water machine servicing by a subway dweller vending machine servicer,' I told them as a crummy subway dweller slowly inched up to a peeling red-and-white water machine dragging a small cart which held four metal kegs and a bunch of other old crap. 'During the Space Age, this machine dispensed the traditional Space-Age beverage, Coca-Cola – still enjoyed in some parts of the world – as you can see from some of the lettering still on the machine. Of course, the subway dwellers have no Coca-Cola to fill it with now.'

The subway dweller took a ring of keys out of the cart, fitted one of them into a keyhole on the face of the machine after a few tries, and opened a plate on the front of the machine. Tokens came tumbling out on to the floor. The subway dweller got down on its hands and knees, picked up the tokens one by one, and dropped them into a mouldy-

105

looking rubber sack from the cart.

'The servicer has now removed the tokens from the water machine. In order to get a drink of water, a subway dweller drops a token into the slot in the face of the machine, pulls the lever, and cups his hands inside the little opening.'

The subway dweller opened the back of the water machine with another key, struggled with one of the metal kegs, then finally lifted it and poured some pretty green-looking water into the machine's tank.

'The servicers buy the water from the reclamation tenders with the tokens they get from the machines. They also service the food machines with algae-cake they get from the hydroponic tenders the same way.'

The vending machine servicer replaced the back plate of the water machine and dragged its cart slowly off farther on into the shadows of the station towards the next water machine.

'How do they make the tokens?' Koyinka asked.

'Nobody *makes* tokens,' I told him. 'They're all left over from the Space Age.'

'That doesn't make sense. How can they run an economy without a supply of new money? Profits always bring new money into circulation. Even a socialist economy has to print new money each year.'

Huh? What the hell was he talking about? These damned Africans!

'I think I can explain,' the college professor said. 'According to Kusongeri, the subway dwellers do not have a real money economy. The same tokens get passed around continually. For instance, the servicers probably take exactly as many tokens out of a water machine as they have to give to the reclamation tenders for the water in the first place. No concept of profit exists here.'

'But then why do they bother with tokens in the first place?'

The professor shrugged. 'Ritual, perhaps, or –'

'Why does a bee build honeycombs?' Lumumba sneered. 'Why does a magpie steal bright objects? Because they think about it – or because it's just the nature of the animal? Don't you see, Koyinka, these white slugs aren't people, they're *animals*! They don't *think*. They don't have *reasons* for doing anything. *Animals!* Stupid pale white animals! The last descendants of the Space-Age honkies, and they're nothing but *animals*! That's what honkies end up like when they don't have black men to think for them, how –'

Red sparks went off in my head. 'They were good enough to ride your crummy ancestors back to Africa on a rail, you black brother!'

'You watch your mouth when you're talking to your betters, honkie!'

'Mr Lumumba!' the professor shouted. Koyinka looked ready to take a swing at me. Kulongo had moved towards Lumumba and looked disgusted. The Luthuliville fruits were wrinkling their dainty noses. Christ, we were all a hair away from a brawl. A thing like that could kill business for a month, or even cost me my licence. I thought of that Amazon swampland, blue skies and green trees and brown earth as far as the eye could see . . .

I kept thinking of the Amazon as I unballed my fists and swallowed my pride, and turned my back on Lumumba and led the whole lousy lot of them deeper into the upper level of the station.

Man, I just better give them about another twenty minutes down here and get the hell out before I tear that Lumumba to pieces. I had half a mind to take him back in there to that electric people-trap and jam one of those helmets on his head and leave him there. Then we'd see how much laughing he'd do at the Space-Agers!

The tension kept building between Ryan and Lumumba as we continued to move among the subway dwellers; it was so painfully obvious that it was only a matter of time before the next outburst that one might have almost expected the wretched creatures who inhabited the subways to notice it.

But it was also rather obvious that the subway dwellers had only a limited perception of their environment and an even more limited conceptualization of interpersonal relationships. It would be difficult to say whether or not they were capable of comprehending anything so complex as human emotion. It would be almost as difficult to say whether or not they were human.

The vending machine servicer had performed a complicated task, a task somewhat too complex for even an intelligent chimpanzee, though conceivably a dolphin might have the mental capacity to master it if it had the physical equipment. But no one has been able to say clearly whether or not a dolphin should be considered sapient; it seems to be a borderline situation.

Lumumba had obviously made up his mind that the subway dwellers were truly subhuman animals. As Ryan led us past a motley group of subway dwellers who squatted on the bare floor mechanically eating small slabs of some green substance, Lumumba kept up a loud babble, ostensibly to me, but actually for Ryan's benefit.

'Look at the dirty animals chewing their cud like cows! Look what's left of the great Space-Agers who went to the moon – a few thousand brainless white slugs rotting in a sealed coffin!'

'Even the greatest civilization falls some time,' I mumbled somewhat inanely, trying to soften the situation, for Ryan was clearly engaged in a fierce struggle for control of his temper. I could understand why Ryan and Lumumba hated each other, but why did Lumumba's remarks about the subway dwellers hurt Ryan so deeply?

As we walked farther on in among the rusting steel pillars and scattered groups of ruminating subway dwellers, I happened to pass close to a female subway dweller, perhaps four and a half feet tall, stooped and leathery with stringy grey hair, and dressed in the usual filthy rags. She was inserting a token into the slot of a vending machine. She dropped the coin and pulled a lever under one of the small broken windows that formed a row above the trough of the machine. A green slab dropped down into the trough. The female subway dweller picked it up and began chewing on it.

A sense of excitement came over me. I was determined to actually speak with a subway dweller. 'What is your name?' I said slowly and distinctly.

The female subway dweller turned her pale expressionless little eyes in my direction. A bit of green drool escaped from her lips. Other than that, she made no discernible response.

I tried again. 'What is your name?'

The creature stared at me blankly. 'Whu . . . ee . . . na . . .' she finally managed to stammer in a flat, dull monotone.

'I told you people not to talk to the damned subway dwellers!'

Ryan had apparently noticed what I was doing; he was rushing towards me past Michael Lumumba. Lumumba grabbed him by the elbow. 'What's the matter, Ryan?' he said. 'Do the animals bite?'

'Get your slimy hand off me, you black brother!' Ryan roared, ripping his arm out of Lumumba's grasp.

'I'll bet you bite, too, honkie,' Lumumba said. 'After all, you're the same breed of animal they are.'

Ryan lunged at Lumumba, but Kulongo was on him in three huge strides, and hugged him from behind with a powerful grip. 'Please do not be as foolish as that man, Mr Ryan,' he said softly. 'He dishonours us all. You have been a good guide. Do not let that man goad you into doing something that will allow him to disgrace your name with the authorities.'

Kulongo held on to Ryan as the redness in his face slowly faded. The female subway dweller began to wander away. Lumumba backed off a few paces, then turned his back, walked a bit farther away, and pretended to study a group of seated subway dwellers.

Finally, Kulongo released his grip on Ryan. 'Yeah, you're right, pal,' Ryan said. 'That crud would like nothing better than to be able to report that I bashed his face in. I guess I should apologize to the rest of you folks . . .'

'I think Mr Lumumba should apologize as well,' I said.

'I don't apologize to animals,' Lumumba muttered. Really, the man was disgusting!

God, what I really wanted to do was to bury that Lumumba right there, knock him senseless and let him try to get back to Milford by himself, or, better yet, take him back to that crazy 'Cosmic-All' thing, jam a helmet on his head, and find out how the thing kills in the pleasantest way possible.

But of course I couldn't kill him or maroon him in front of eight witnesses. So instead of giving that black brother what he deserved, I decided to just let them all walk around for about another ten minutes, gawking at the animals, and then call it a day. Seemed to me that all of them but Lumumba and maybe the professor had had their fill of the subway dwellers anyway. Mostly, the subway dwellers just sit around chewing algae-cake. Some of them just stare at nothing for hours. Let's face it, the subway dwellers *are* animals. They've degenerated all the way. I figured just about now the Africans would've had their nasty thrill . . .

But I figured without that stinking Lumumba. Just when the whole bunch of them were standing around in a mob looking thoroughly bored and disgusted, he started another 'conversation' with the professor, real loud. Real subtle, that black brother.

'You're a professor of American history, aren't you, Dr Balewa?'

Got to give Balewa credit. He didn't seem to want any part

of Lumumba's little game. 'Uh . . . Space-Age history is my major field,' he muttered, and then tried to turn away.

But Lumumba would just as soon have run his mouth at a subway dweller; he didn't care if Balewa was really listening to him as long as I was.

'Well, then maybe you can tell me whether or not the honkies could really have built all that Space-Age technology on their own. After all, look at these brainless animals, the direct descendants of the Space-Age honkies. Sure, they've degenerated since the first of them locked themselves up down here, but degenerated from *what*? Didn't they have to be pretty stupid to seal themselves up in a tomb like this in the first place? And they did have twenty or thirty million black men to do their thinking for them before the Panic. Take a look around you, Professor – did these slugs *really* have ancestors capable of creating the Space Age on their own?'

He stared dead at me, and I saw his slimy game. If I didn't cream him, I'd be a coward, and if I did, I'd lose my licence. 'Take a look at the modern example of the race, Professor,' he said. 'Could a nation of *Ryans* have built anything more than a few junk heaps on their own? With captive blacks to do the thinking for them, they went to the moon, and then they choked themselves in their own waste. Hardly the mark of a great civilized race.'

'Your kind quaked in their boots every time one of my ancestors walked by them, and you know it,' I told the crud.

Lumumba would've gone white if he could have. In more ways than one, I'll bet. 'You calling me a coward, honkie?'

'I'm calling you a yellow coward, *boy*.'

'No honkie calls me a coward.'

'This honkie does . . . *nigger*.'

Ah, that got him! There're one or two words these Amero-Africans just can't take, brings up frightening memories. Lumumba went for me, the professor tried to grab him and missed, and then that big ape Kulongo had him in one of those bear-hugs of his. And suddenly I had an idea to fix Mr Michael Lumumba real good, without laying a finger on him, without giving him anything he could complain to the government about.

'You ever hear about a machine that's supposed to "merge you with the Cosmic All", Professor?' I said.

'Why . . . that would be the ECA – the Electronic Consciousness Augmenter. It was never clear whether more than a few prototypes were built or not. The device was developed shortly before the Panic. Some sort of scientific religion built the ECA – the Brotherhood of the Cosmic All, or some such group. The claim was that the machine produced a transcendental experience of some sort electronically. No one has ever proved whether or not there was any truth to it, since none of the devices has ever been found . . .'

Kulongo relaxed his grip on Lumumba. I had them now. I had Mr Michael Lumumba real good. 'Well, I think I found one of them, right here in this station, a couple of years ago. It's still working. Maybe the subway dwellers kept it going – probably it was built to keep itself going; it looks like real Space-Age stuff. I could take you all to it.'

I gave Lumumba a nice smile. 'How about it, pal?' I said. 'Let's see if you're a coward or not. Let's see you walk in there and put a working Space-Age gizmo on your head and "merge with the Cosmic All".'

'Have you ever done it, Ryan?' Lumumba sneered.

'Sure, pal,' I lied. 'I do it all the time. It's fun.'

'I think you're a liar.'

'I *know* you're a coward.'

Lumumba gave me a look like a snake. 'All right, honkie,' he said. 'I'll try it if you try it with me.'

Christ, what was I getting myself into? That thing killed people, all those bones . . . Yeah, but I knew that and Lumumba didn't. When he saw the bones, he wouldn't dare put a helmet on his head. Yeah, I knew that he wouldn't, and he didn't, so that still put me one up on him.

'You're afraid, aren't you, Ryan? You've never really done it yourself. You're afraid to do it, and I'm not. Who does that make the coward?'

Oh, you crud, I got you right where I want you! 'Okay, boy,' I said, 'you're on. You do it and I'll do it. We'll see who's the coward. The rest of you folks can come along for the ride. A free extra added attraction, courtesy of Little Old New York Tours.'


Ryan led us deeper into a more shadowed part of the station, where the still-functioning bulbs in the ceiling were farther and farther apart, and where, perhaps because of the darkness, the subway dwellers were fewer and fewer. As we went farther and farther into the deepening darkness, the floor of the subway station was filled with small bits of rubble, then larger and larger pieces, till finally, dimly outlined by a single bulb a few yards ahead of us, we could see a place where

111

the ceiling had fallen in. A huge dam of rubble which filled the station from floor to ceiling cut off a corner much like the one into which we had originally come from the rest of the station.

Ryan led us out of the pool of light and into the blackness. 'In here,' he called back. 'Everyone touch the one ahead of you.'

I touched Michael Lumumba's back with some distaste, but also with a kind of gratitude. Because of him, I was getting to see a working wonder of the Space Age, a device whose very existence was a matter of academic dispute. My reputation would be made!

I felt Kulongo's somehow reassuring hand on my shoulder as we groped our way through the darkness. Then I felt Lumumba stoop, and I was passing through a narrow opening in the pile of rubble, where two broken girders wedged against each other held up the crumbled fragments of ceiling.

Beyond, I could see by a strange flickering light just around a bend that we had emerged in a place very much like the subway entrance. The ceiling had fallen on a set of turnstiles and grillework barriers, crushing them, but clearing a way for us. We picked our way past the ruined barriers and entered a side tunnel, which was filled with the strange flickering light, a light which seemed to cut each moment off from the next, like a faulty piece of antique motion-picture film, such as the specimens of Chaplin I've seen in Nairobi. It made me feel as if I were moving inside such a film. Time seemed to be composed of separate discrete bursts of duration.

Ryan led us up the tunnel, both sides of which were composed of the ruins of recessed shops, like some underground market arcade. Then I saw that one shop in the arcade was not ruined. It stood out from the rubble, a gleaming anachronism. Even a layman would've recognized it as a specimen of very late Space-Age technology. And it was a working specimen.

It had that classic late Space-Age style. The entire front of the shop was made of some plastic substance that flickered luminescently, that was the source of the strange pale light. There has been some literature on this material, but a specimen had never been examined, as far as I knew. The substance itself is woven of fibres called light guides – modern science has been able to produce such fibres, but to weave a kind of cloth of them by known methods would be hideously expensive. But Space-Age light guide cloth, however it was made, enabled a single light source to cast its illumination evenly over a very wide area. So the flickering was probably produced simply by using a stroboscope as a light source for the wall. Very minor Space-Age wizardry, but very effective: it made the entire shopfront a psychologically powerful attention-getting device, such as the Spage-Agers commonly employed in their incredibly sophisticated science of advertising.

A small doorless portal big enough for one man at a time was all that marred the flickering luminescence of the wall of shopfront. Above the shop a smaller strobe panel – but this one composed of blue-and-red fibres which flashed independently – proclaimed MERGE WITH THE COSMIC ALL red on blue for half of every second, a powerful hypnotic that drew me towards the shop despite my abstract knowledge of its workings.

That the device was working at all in this area of the station where all other power seemed cut off was proof enough of its very late Space-Age dating: only in the decade before the Panic had the Space-Agers developed a miniaturized isotopic power source cheap enough to warrant installation of self-contained five-hundred-year generators in something like this.

The very fact that we were staring into the flickering light of a Space-Age device whose self-contained power source had kept it going totally untended for centuries was enough to overwhelm us. I'm sure the rest of them felt what I felt; even Lumumba just stood there and gaped. On Ryan's face, even beneath the tight lines of his anger, was something akin to awe. Or was it some kind of superstitious dread?

'Well, here it is, Lumumba,' Ryan said softly, the strobe-wall making the movements of his mouth appear to be mechanical. 'Shall we step inside?'

'After you, Ryan. You're the... *native guide*.' Fear flickered in the strobe flashes off Lumumba's eyes, but, like all of us, he found it impossible to look away from the entrance for long. There seemed to be subtle and complex waves in the strobe flashes drawing us to the doorway; perhaps there were several stroboscopes activating the wall in a psychologically calculated sequence. In this area, the Space-Age Americans had been capable of any subtlety a modern mind could imagine, and infinitely more.

'And you're the . . . *tourist*,' Ryan said softly. 'A tourist who thinks he knows what the Space-Agers were all about. Step inside, sucker!'

And with a grim, knowing grin, Ryan stepped through the

doorway. Without hesitation, Lumumba followed after him. And without hesitation, drawn by the flickering light and so much more, I entered the chamber behind them.

The inside of the chamber was a cube of some incredible hyper-real desert night as seen through the eyes of a prophet or a madman. The walls and ceiling of the room were light: mosaics of millions of tiny deep-blue twinkling pinpoints of brilliance, here and there leavened with intermittent prickles of red and green and yellow, all flashing in seemingly random sequences of a tenth of a second or so each. Beneath this preternatural electronic sky, we stood transfixed. The dazzling universe of winking light filled our brains; before it we were as subway dwellers chewing their cud.

Behind me, I dimly heard Kulongo's deep voice saying, 'There are demons in there that would drink a man's soul. We will not go in there.' How foolish those far-away words sounded . . .

'There's nothing to be afraid of . . .' I heard my own voice saying. The sound of my own voice broke my light trance almost as I realized that I had been in a trance. Then I saw the bones.

The chamber was filled with six rows of strange chairs, six of them to a row. They were like giant red eggs standing on end, hollowed out, and fitted inside were reclining padded seats. Inside the red eggs, metal helmets designed to fit over the entire head dangled from cables at head-level. Most of the eggs contained human skeletons. The floor was littered with bones.

Ryan and Lumumba seemed to have been somewhat deeper in trance; it took them a few seconds longer to come out of it. Lumumba's eyes flashed sudden fear as he saw the bones. But Ryan grinned knowingly as he saw the fear on Lumumba's face.

'Scares you a bit, doesn't it, boy?' Ryan said. 'Still game to put on one of those helmets?' The wall seemed to pick up the sparkle of his laugh.

'What killed them?' was all Lumumba said.

'How should I know?'

'But you said you'd tried it!'

'So, I'm a liar. And you're a coward.'

I walked forward as they argued, and read a small metal plaque that was affixed to the outer shell of each red egg:

Two tokens – MERGE WITH THE COSMIC ALL – Two tokens.

Drop tokens in slot. Place helmet over head. Pull lever and experience MERGER WITH THE COSMIC ALL. Automatic timer will limit all MERGERS to two-minute duration, in compliance with federal law.

'I'm no more a coward than you are, Ryan. You had no intention of putting on one of those things.'

'I'd do it if you'd do it,' Ryan insisted.

'No, you wouldn't! You're not that crazy and neither am I. Why would you risk your life for something as stupid as that?'

'Because I'd be willing to bet my life any day that a black brother like you would never have the guts to put on a helmet.'

'You stinking honkie!'

'Why don't we end this crap, Lumumba? You're not going to put on one of these helmets and neither am I. The big difference between us is that I won't have to because you *can't*.'

Lumumba seemed like a carven idol of rage in that fantastic cube of light. 'Just a minute, honkie,' he said. 'Professor, you have any idea why they died when they put the helmets on?'

It was starting to make sense to me. What if the claims made for the device were true? What if two tokens could buy a man total transcendental bliss? 'I don't think they died when they put the helmets on,' I said. 'I think they starved to death days later. According to this plaque, whatever happens is supposed to last no longer than two minutes before an automatic circuit shuts it off. What if this device involves electronic stimulation of the pleasure centre? No one has yet unearthed such a device, but the Space-Age literature was full of it. Pleasure-centre stimulation was supposed to be harmless in itself, but what if the timer circuit went out? A man could be paralysed in total bliss while he starved to death. I think that's what happened here.'

'Let me get this straight,' Lumumba said, his rage seeming to collapse in upon itself, becoming a manic shrewdness. 'The helmets themselves are harmless? Even if we couldn't take them off ourselves, one of the others could take them off . . . We wouldn't be in any real danger?'

'I don't think so,' I told him. 'According to the inscription, one paid two tokens for the experience. I doubt that even the Space-Agers would've been willing to pay money for something that would harm them, certainly not *en masse*. And the Space-

Agers were very conscious of profit.'

'Would you be willing to stake your life on it, Dr Balewa? Would you be willing to try it, too?'

Try it? Actually put on a helmet, give myself over to a piece of Space-Age wizardry, an electronic device that was supposed to produce a mystical experience at the flick of a switch? A less stable man might say that if it really worked, there was a god inside the helmets, a god that the Space-Agers had created out of electronic components. If this were actually true, it surely must represent the very pinnacle of Space-Age civilization – who but the Space-Agers would even contemplate the fabrication of an actual god?

Yes, of course I would try it! I *had* to try it; what kind of scholar would I be if I passed by an opportunity to understand the Space-Agers as no modern man has understood them before? Neither Ryan nor Lumumba had the background to make the most of such an experience. It was my duty to put on a helmet as well as my pleasure.

'Yes, Mr Lumumba,' I said. 'I intend to try it, too.'

'Then we'll all try it,' Lumumba said. 'Or will we, Mr Ryan? I'm ready to put on a helmet and so is the professor; are you?'

They were both nuts, Lumumba and the professor! Those helmets had killed people. How the hell could Balewa know what had happened from reading some silly plaque? These goddamned Africans always think they can understand the Space-Agers from crap other Africans have put in books. What the hell do they know? What do they really know?

'Well, Ryan, what about it? Are you going to admit you don't have the guts to do it, so we can all forget it and go home?'

'All right, pal, you're on!' I heard myself telling him. Damn, what was I getting myself into? But I couldn't let that slime Lumumba call my bluff; no African's gonna bluff down an *American*! Besides, Balewa was probably right; what he said made sense. Sure, it had to make sense. That stinking black brother!

'Mr Kulongo, would you come in here and take the helmets off our heads in two minutes?' I asked. I'd trust that Kulongo further than the rest of the creeps.

'I will not go in there,' Kulongo said. 'There is juju in there, powerful and evil. I am ashamed before you because I say these words, but my fear of what is in this place is greater than my shame.'

'This is ridiculous!' Koyinka said, pushing past Kulongo. 'Evil spirits! Come on, will you, this is the twenty-second century! I'll do it, if you want to go through with this nonsense.'

'All right, pal, let's get on with it.'

I handed out the tokens and the three of us went to the nearest three stalls. I cleared a skeleton out of mine, sent it clattering to the floor, and so what, what's to be scared of in a pile of old dead bones? But I noticed that Lumumba seemed a little green as he cleared the bones out for himself.

I pulled myself up into the hollowed-out egg and sat down on the padded couch inside. Some kind of plastic covering made the thing still clean and comfortable, not even dusty, after hundreds of years. Those Space-Agers were really something. I dropped the tokens into a little slot in the arm of the couch. Next to the slot was a lever. The room sparkled blue all around me; somehow that made me feel real good. The couch was comfortable. Koyinka was standing by. I was actually beginning to enjoy it. What was there to be afraid of? Jeez, the professor thought this gave you pure pleasure or something. If he was right, this was really going to be something. If I lived through it.

I put my right hand on the lever. I saw that the professor and Lumumba were already under their helmets. I fitted the helmet down over my head. Some kind of pad inside it fitted down on my skull all around my head, down to the eyebrows; it seemed almost alive, moulding itself to my head like a second skin. It was very dark inside the helmet. Couldn't see a thing.

I took a deep breath and pulled the lever.

The tips of my fingers began to tingle, throbbing with pleasure, not pain. My feet started to tingle, too, and shapes that had no shape, that were more black inside the black, seemed to be floating around inside my head. The tingling moved up my fingers to my hands, up my feet to my knees. Now my arms were tingling. Oh, man, it felt so good! No woman ever felt this good! This felt better than kicking in Lumumba's face!

The whirling things in my head weren't really in my head, my head was in them, or they were my head, all whirling around some deep dark hole that wasn't a hole but was something to whirl off into, fall off into, sucking me in and up. My whole body was tingling now. Man, I *was* the tingling now, my body was nothing *but* the tingling now.

And it was getting stronger, getting better all the time; I wasn't a tingle, I was a glow, a warmth, a throbbing, a fire of pure pleasure, a roaring, burning, whirling fire, sucking, spinning up towards a deep black hole inside me blowing up in a blast of pure *feeling so good so good so good —*

Oh, for ever whirling, whirling, a fire *so good so good so good*, and on *through* into the black hole fire I was *burning up in my own orgasm.* I was my own orgasm of body-mind-sex-taste-smell-touch-feel, I went on *for ever for ever for ever for ever* in pure blinding burning *so good so good so good* nothingness blackness dying orgasm *for ever for ever for ever* spurting out of myself in sweet moment of total pain-pleasure *so good so good so good* moment of dying pain burning sex *for ever for ever for ever so good so good for ever so good for ever so good for ever —*

I pulled the lever and waited in my private darkness. The first thing I felt was a tingling of my fingertips, as if with some mild electric charge; not at all an unpleasant feeling. A similar pleasurable tingle began in my feet. Strange vague patterns seemed to swirl around inside my eyes.

My hands began to feel the pleasant sensation now, and the lower portions of my legs. The feeling was getting stronger and stronger as it moved up my limbs. It felt physically pleasurable in a peculiarly abstract way, but there was something frightening about it, something vaguely unclean.

The swirling patterns seemed to be spinning around a bottomless vortex now; they weren't exactly inside my eyes or my head; my head was inside of them, or they *were* me. The experience was somehow visual-yet-non-visual, my being spinning downward and inward in a vertiginous spiral towards a black, black hole that seemed inside my self. And my whole body felt that electric tingling now; I felt nothing *but* the strange, forcefully pleasurable sensation. It filled my entire sensorium, became *me.*

And it kept getting stronger and stronger, no longer a tingle, but a pulsing of cold electric pleasure, stronger and stronger, wilder and wilder, the voltage increasing, the amperage increasing, whirling me down and around and down and around towards that terrible deep black hole inside me burning with hunger to swallow myself up, becoming a pure black fire vortex pain of pleasure down and down and around and around . . .

Sucking myself up through the terrible black vortex of my own pure pleasure-pain, compressed against the interface of my own being, squeezed against the instant of my own *death.* Oh! Oh! *Death death death.* No No pleasure pain death sex orgasm everything that was me popping No! No! *On through!* becoming moment of death senses flashing pure pleasure pain terror black hole *for ever for ever* in this terrible universe was timeless moment of orgasm death total electric pleasure *no! no!* delicious horrible moment of pure *death pain orgasm black hole vortex no! no! no! no* –

Suddenly I was seated on a couch inside a red egg in a room filled with blue sparkles, and I was looking up at Koyinka's silly face.

'You all right?' he said. Now, *there* was a question!

'Yeah, yeah,' I mumbled. Man, those Space-Agers! I wanted to puke. I wanted to jam that helmet back on my head. I wanted to get the hell out of there! I wanted to live for ever in that fantastic perfect feeling until I rotted into the bone pile.

I was scared out of my head.

I mean, what happened inside that helmet was the best and the worst thing in the world. You could stay there with that thing on your head and die in pure pleasure thinking you were living for ever. Man, you talk about *temptation!* Those Space-Agers had put a god or a devil in there, and who could tell which? Did they even know which? Man, that crazy jungle-bunny Kulongo was right, after all: there *were* demons in here that would drink your soul. But maybe the demons were *you.* Sucking up your own soul in pure pleasure till it choked you to death. But wasn't it maybe worth it?

As soon as he saw I was okay, Koyinka ran over to the professor, who was still sitting there with the helmet over his head. That crud Lumumba was out of it already. He was staring at me; he wasn't mad, he wasn't exactly afraid, he was just trying to look into my eyes. I guess because I felt what he felt, too.

I stared back into Lumumba's big eyes as Koyinka took the helmet off the professor's head. I couldn't help myself. I didn't like the black brother one bit more, but there was something between us now, God knows what. The professor looked real green. He didn't seem to notice us much. Lumumba and I just kept staring at each other, nodding a little bit.

Yeah, we had both been some place no living man should go. The Space-Agers had been gods or demons or maybe something that would drive both gods and demons screaming straight up the wall. When we call them men we don't mean the same thing we do when we call us men. When they died off, something we'll never understand went out of the world. I don't know whether to thank God or to cry.

It seemed to me that I could read exactly what was going on inside Lumumba's head; his thoughts were my thoughts.

'They were a great and terrible people,' Lumumba finally said. 'And they were out of their minds.'

'Pal, they were something we can never be. Or want to.'

'You know, honkie, I think for once you've got a point.'

There was a strange feeling hovering in the air between Ryan and Lumumba as we made our way back through the subway station and up into the sparkly blue unreal world of the Fuller Dome. Not comradeship, not even grudging respect, but some subtle change I could not fathom. Their eyes keep meeting, almost furtively. I couldn't understand it. I couldn't understand it at all.

Had they experienced what I had? Coldly, I could now say that it had been nothing but electronic stimulation of some cerebral centres; but the horror of it, the horror of being forced to experience a moment of death and pain and total pleasure all bound up together and extended towards infinity, had been realer than real. It had indeed been a genuine mystical experience, created electronically.

But why would people do a thing like that to themselves? Why would they willingly plunge themselves into a moment of pure horror that went on and on and on?

Yet as we finally boarded the helicopter, I somehow sensed that what Lumumba and Ryan had shared was not what I felt at all.

As I flew the copter through the dead tombstone skyscrapers towards the outer edge of the Fuller Dome, I knew that I had to get out of this damned tourist business, and fast. Now I knew what was really buried here, under the crazy spooky blue light, under all the concrete, under the stinking saturation smog, under a hole inside a hole in the ground: the bones of a people that men like us had better let lie.

Our ancestors were gods or demons or both. If we get too close to the places where what they *really* were is buried, they'll drink our souls yet.

No more tours to the subways anyway; what good is the Amazon if I don't live to get there? If I had me an atom bomb, I'd drop it right smack on top of this place to make sure I never go back.

As we headed into a fantastic blazing orange-and-purple sunset, towards Milford and modern America – a pallid replica of African civilization huddling in the interstices of a continent of incredible ruins – I looked back across the wide river, a flaming sea below and behind us ignited by the setting sun. The Fuller Dome flashed in the sunlight, a giant diamond set in the tombstone of a race that had soared to the moon, that had turned the atmosphere to a beautiful and terrible poison, that had covered a continent with ruins that overawed the modern world, that had conjured up a demon out of electronic circuitry, that had torn themselves to pieces in the end.

A terrible pang of sadness went through me as the rest of my trip turned to ashes in my mouth, as my future career became a cadaver covered with dust. I could crawl over these ruins and exhaust the literature for the rest of my life, and I would never understand what the Space-Age Americans had been. Not a man alive ever would. Whatever they had been, such things lived on the face of the earth no more.

In his simple way, Kulongo had said all that could be said: 'Their souls were not as ours.'


# Heroes Die But Once


The blackness closed in slowly, languidly, almost sensuously, a thick, deadening irresistible tide lapping at the shores of my consciousness. I struggled, tried to move, but my arms and legs were some place else, some place very far away, fading, numbing, sloughing away. I felt myself losing my senses: vision trailing off into blackness, hearing becoming an empty cave, smell, touch, taste becoming fading old memories . . .

I was dying.

I was dying. My consciousness, my awareness, my entire being, all I ever was or might be was collapsing inexorably inward, towards that imaginary point two inches behind my eyes where the essential me had always dwelt. I was dying.

I was a bodyless point of ego in a sea of final nothingness, a mote beating frantically against the night.

I was dying. Never to breathe the air of Earth again, never to feel Loy's body against me, never to know pain, never even to drift in the private world behind my own eyelids. I was dying. This was death, that-than-which-there-*is*-no-fate-worse. I would have borne an eternity of torment, screamed and shrieked in hellfire for ever, gladly, joyously, if it would only mean that I would somehow, in some state, continue to exist.

I was dying, and as all men do when they have time to contemplate the moment, I was dying badly, a crazed whimpering thing crying futilely against the dark. I was me, *me, me.* I was me-ness, and I felt myself fading, losing, slipping, drifting away from myself into the soft, soft arms of night, towards the tenderest of all moments.

I shrieked once in my fading mind, had time to think briefly of Loy, to say goodbye for ever to the image of her in my mind, and I was not.


I was! I lived! *I lived!*

I had gone, I had been *not*, and now I was. For a long moment, I could think of nothing else. To have not existed and then to be! What could be sweeter? What more of heaven could anyone ask?

I opened my eyes, and then I knew that this was not heaven.

It was a cave, a cave whose walls gave off a pale blue light. I was lying on my back on the hard damp rock, and I could not move. In a circle around me were things like bloated naked brains, pulsing and squirming hideously, brains supported by slimy green bodies like dog-sized slugs. This was not heaven. This was the fifth planet of a yellow sun far, far from Earth. I was alive and I began to remember.

The first thing I remembered was Loy. Loy! Where was she? What were they doing to her? Loy! Loy!

'Loy! Loy! Loy!' I found myself screaming.

I felt a pressure in my mind, a presence, cold and clammy, without passion, without malice, without emotion, without mercy. A pressure that was a questioning, a search, a leaching. I began to remember more . . .

Fifth planet of a yellow sun. A fair green world, not like the others Loy and I had found. Loy . . . my love, my woman, my wife. A honeymoon world, a world fit for colonization, hence a world where, by the terms of the contract, we could spend the remaining six months of our Honeymoon Year

122

enjoying the green grass and the blue sky and the fresh clean air. No more weeks in space in the cramped two-place Scout, no more methane worlds, chlorine worlds, jungle worlds, desert worlds.

The Honeymoon World, the Jackpot World, the Bonus World . . .

Death World.

'Loy! Loy! Loy!'

The circle of grey, quivering brains seemed to pulse faster, as if with some not-quite-familiar strain, and I felt the pressure in my mind change, reach for language concepts in my brain, pick, choose, and form words.

*The woman is elsewhere*, the words that were and were not of my mind told me. *Elsewhere.*

The fog began to evaporate from my memory . . .

We had surveyed the planet from orbit, and, finding it fair and habitable, we had landed the Scout in a lush green meadow close by wooded hills.

Loy smiled at me as we stepped out of the airlock and inhaled the fragrant, heady odours of growing things.

'There!' she said, putting her arm around my waist. 'Now, aren't you glad we decided to take a Honeymoon Contract?'

'*We* were so right,' I said with a little laugh. It had been her idea in the first place, and she had talked me into it. My attitude had been that the government was not about to give anyone something for nothing. A Honeymoon Contract sounded like the best of all possible deals: the government provided any couple who could pass the minimal physical and psychological tests with a two-place Scout to roam the stars for a year together. In return, all we had to do was prepare a brief survey of each planet we found. If we were lucky enough to find one suitable for colonization, we could spend the rest of our year on it, and collect a bonus that would set us up for life when we returned to Earth.

Of course, the government did not do this out of sentiment. The human race needed room to expand, and that meant new planets. Perhaps one out of fifty solar systems had a habitable planet. Therefore, the economical way to go about finding them was to send out plenty of cheap two-place Scouts. Under ordinary conditions, two people simply could not stay sane cooped up alone for a year in the vastness of interstellar space. But a man and a woman . . .

Necessity had made a hard governmental policy out of an ancient romantic notion: the stars were for lovers.

Loy did not quite see it that way. To her, all creation was something designed for our particular pleasure and enjoyment, and so it was the most natural thing in her world for the government to be so thoughtful as to provide us with a free honeymoon. The succession of chlorine worlds, dead rocks and gas giants we had discovered in the first six months of our Honeymoon Year had somehow left this attitude largely untouched – after all, we had each other.

The most beautiful thing about Loy was that she could make me see things her way.

So we were like two children together on a summer Sunday in the park. It was that kind of world, a world of low, broad-bladed grass, brilliantly feathered birds, high blue sky, small six-legged rodents, berry bushes, fruit trees . . . A happy, innocent Honeymoon World.

You can see how happy and wrapped up in each other we had become. No world is a park or a garden. The absence of a full spectrum of predators usually means *something*, and usually something sentient, has wiped out the competition – so they told us in our briefings.

Finally, after days of . . . well, I don't know what else to call it but romping in the meadow, we decided to do a little real exploring in the nearby woods.

Loy was all for travelling as lightly as possible, taking only a sleeping-bag and some concentrates to supplement the local fruits and berries, which had proved edible and rather tasty. We had the closest thing to an argument we ever had when I insisted on taking energy rifles along.

'It's just not right, Bill,' she said, pouting and canting her blonde head to one side at an engaging angle. 'This planet has been so nice to us. It trusts us, and it's only right that we trust it. Carrying those ugly guns . . . it just isn't right, it's being, well, you know, *nasty*.'

I tried to win the argument with a kiss, but she turned sulkily away. 'Look, honey,' I said, 'we don't know what's in those woods. There may be things there that are much nastier than us. An energy rifle can stop an elephant in its tracks, and when it gets dark and scary and gloomy at night in those woods, with strange night noises and things scuffling around in the dark, you'll be glad I insisted on bringing the rifles, even if we never have to use them.'

'But, Bill – '

'Look at it this way. If we *don't* have the guns, we'll have to be suspicious and cautious every time we hear a strange sound – we won't be able to trust anything. But if we *do* have the guns, we won't have to be leery at all, because an energy rifle can stop *anything*.'

'Ooooh, masculine logic!' she sighed, but there was a giggle behind it, and I gave her a hug, and we took the rifles.

The woods were dense and dark, with gnarled, thick-trunked trees and tightly interlaced networks of leafy branches. But the undergrowth was very light, there seemed to be no dangerous animals, and we made good time. By nightfall, we had reached the base of the low, rolling hills. Loy cooked a meal of concentrates, topped off with local fruits and berries. We crawled into the sleeping-bag early, and after several hours of enjoying the cool woods and the night sounds and each other, we drifted off into sleep.

At some indeterminable time during the night, half in dream, half awake, I felt an odd pressure in my mind. The feeling was strange, but not really menacing. It was an awareness of an interest not my own, a cold, emotionless questing for knowledge rifling through my mind as if it were some encyclopedia. A questing, a questioning, a knowledge-vacuum, with no form, no flavour, no personality behind it . . .

I lay there motionless, my eyes closed, in that grey borderland between sleep and wakefulness, wondering whether or not I was dreaming and not really caring.

Suddenly, Loy screamed beside me, and I was instantly wide awake, eyes open, and I saw them.

Encircling our sleeping-bag were ten monstrosities, about the size of very large dogs – bodies like great slimy slugs, supporting what appeared to be naked living brains, brains ten times the size of a human brain, wet and pulsating. The things had no arms, no legs, no tentacles, just ghastly brains on slimy slug-bodies.

Loy was clinging to me, shaking and sobbing. I reached instinctively for the energy rifle close by the sleeping-bag. Something froze my arm, then the rest of me. I was paralysed, and now I was aware, dreadfully aware, of the alien presence in my mind.

I felt it grope in my mind for words, memories of concepts, pick, choose, and form words in my mind.

*Who? From where? What?*

Dazed, numb, only partially in control of the inner workings of my own mind, I found myself forming mental answers to the mental questions.

We're humans, from Earth, another world circling another star.

*Other intelligences*, the presence thought into my mind. *Other races. Most interesting. Possibilities of accumulating much new data. Knowledge expansion. Good.*

There was no emotion behind any of it, unless you want to consider an almost obscene lust for knowledge, data, an emotion. A million angry questions tried to form themselves in my mind, but I felt the mental presence bat them away with casual indifference.

*Different*, the presence said, growing ever more facile with the borrowed words. *You and the other are different from each other. Your physical structures are not contributing to the same mental structure. Do separate races share your planet?*

I was in no mood to answer inane questions. Loy had gone quiet in my arms, paralysed as I was, but I knew that she was still terrified, and I had to act, if only mentally, to remove that which was causing her fear. But my mind was not my own. I felt my total mental resources struggling to answer the alien's questions, my entire stock of memories and mental capacities rising to do its bidding, to fill the yawning knowledge-vacuum.

I watched, almost as an outside observer, as my mind marshalled itself and answered. I found myself explaining things I had never even stopped to consider: what it was to be a human being, the difference between men and women, how Earth was inhabited by billions of separate organic systems called human beings, whose mental structures, minds, were distinct and separate from each other, billions of unique and separate mental universes arising from an equal number of physical organisms.

I felt the presence in my mind boggle, almost stagger, unwilling to believe yet unable to disbelieve. In that moment of confusion I felt the thing's control over my mind waver for an instant, and I used that moment to shape my own confusion into a demand, a question: Who, what, are *you*? Then I tried to reach for the energy rifle again, and I felt the presence resume its iron control of my mind.

There seemed to be a hesitation in the thing, and then a sense of somewhat reluctant decision. I felt words forming themselves in my mind:

*There is a possibility that knowledge on your part may facilitate the accumulation of data. I . . . am. I do not think* of my mental structure as 'I'. The presence detected by your mental structure is that of the mental structure of this planet. This planet bears many species of organisms. The organisms you now see are one such species. They are so specialized that their separate physical structures give rise to one unified mental structure, that is, to what you think of as 'me'. These organisms have no other function but the erection of this mental structure. The mental structure thus erected may control the physical structures of all other organisms, including your own. I am the mental structure of this planet, the sentient being, the intelligent race. According to all previously accumulated data, I had hypothesized that I was the only such mental structure that existed, the only centre of awareness in the universe. Now data is made available to the effect that at least one planet exists where billions of organisms give rise to billions of separate mental structures, so that in effect your planet has several billion intelligent races. This promises a vast new area of knowledge, and much data that may now be accumulated.

It was my turn to boggle, to be unwilling to believe yet unable, by the very nature of the contact, to disbelieve. An intelligent race, thousands, perhaps millions of individual organisms giving rise to but one mind! A mind alone, without companionship, without love or hate or jealousy . . . Without, I suddenly realized, the concept of death. Emotions, hopes, fear – which in the last analysis is always the fear of individual death – how could a mind alone know any of these? What could motivate such a mind, impel it to action?

Suddenly, I felt myself virtually unable to think. The alien mind was dampening my thoughts with an almost irresistible power. It seemed to exult, to rejoice, to loll in a kind of obscene anticipation that was almost sensual in its intensity.

*Such knowledge! Such a rich store of new data! Such a wealth of new possibilities to explore, experiments to perform!*

And I realized that there was only one thing which could occupy such a mind: the quest for knowledge itself, but a quest for knowledge that was not abstract, not cold and intellectual, but raised to the level of a basic emotion, *the* basic emotion, a drive virtually sexual in its power and intensity.

I felt Loy tense against me. I felt her fear and I shared it. There was no point of empathy with such a mind. This was an entity asocial, hence amoral, to its very core. And we were totally in its power.

'Let us go,' I said wordlessly to the world-mind. 'Let us go and we'll tell you all you want to know. When we get back to Earth, we'll send back scientists, men who specialize in knowledge. You can learn more from them than you ever can from us.'

*Yes, that will be good. Later. After all possible data has been accumulated from you. There is much to be learned, very much. It will take a long time to exhaust the possibilities. Especially concerning the peculiar states of mental structure you call emotions. And most particularly the emotion you call love. It seems to be the most powerful and the most important. But this other phenomenon, the one you call death . . . That will require much, much experimentation.*

And I remembered, now I remembered it all. How the alien mind had seized control of our bodies, how we had been trotted against our wills unerringly through the night to the system of caves in the hills, surrounded by the brain-slugs . . . How Loy had been separated from me, once we were within the caves . . . How I had been lying on the cave floor for some unknown length of time, somehow needing neither food nor water, feeling neither hunger nor thirst, totally controlled by the world-mind . . .

I remembered the probing, the endless rifling of my mind for things of significance and things trivial until everything I had ever known, every memory I had ever had, things I had thought I had forgotten, things I never knew I knew, had been sucked from me and greedily devoured by the knowledge-crazed mind.

And then it had begun in earnest, the experiments, the endless, horrible experiments. Pain, hunger, ecstasy, fear, lust, the whole spectrum of emotions and drives – the thing made me experience them over and over again, while it hovered in my mind, observing, clucking to itself, recording, evaluating, savouring.

I remember asking again and again what was happening to Loy, and finally, when the world-mind was good and ready, it let me know. Loy was conveyed into the chamber by a bevy of the brain-slugs, her body thin and drawn and not her own. I was forced to watch, immobilized, while the same things that had been done to me were done to her.

I watched the pain and the fear and the lust play over her features, and all the while I could feel the presence in my mind watching my reactions, accumulating the knowledge of how a man feels when he is watching his bride being tortured.

Then the process was reversed and Loy was forced to watch while the world-mind did things to me.

Finally, the thing was satisfied. *Most interesting*, the words in my mind said. *Although your two mental structures are separate entities, there seems to be some interaction between them. If one of you undergoes unpleasant stimuli, both of you seem to react. It is as if your mental structures were partially connected. This seems to be at least the major part of the phenomenon you call love. Most interesting. Love would seem to be one of the two strongest aberrations called emotions to which your mental structures are prone. One may consider it one pole of your emotional spectrum. The other pole seems to be a fear of this phenomenon you call death. That will have to be investigated most thoroughly.*

And Loy had been led out, and I died for the first time.

Now I truly remembered everything. This was not the first time I had died and been reborn! How many times had I died? I had no way of knowing. Each time, it had been truly death, death without memory of the earlier deaths. Each time had somehow been the one and only time, all-obliterating death itself, and—

*Very good*, the presence in my mind said. *You have died one hundred and seventy-three times. Much data has been gathered, much has been understood. This death is the worst possible thing that can happen to you, the permanent destruction of your mental structure. You now understand death totally. You know in detail just what it is to die. There is nothing that you can experience as being more unpleasant. Most interesting. The same reaction was observed in all of the woman's deaths as well.*

'You filthy—'

It cut me off impatiently, the brain-things pulsing and squirming in the pale blue light. *It was necessary that she undergo the same experiences, both as a control and as a condition of the final experiment.*

'Final experiment?'

*Yes. All possible data has been accumulated, except for one final and most interesting experiment. It has been established that one pole of your emotional spectrum is love. The other is the fear of death. It but remains to determine which is stronger. At the conclusion of this experiment, one of you will be permitted to return to your own planet.*

'*One* of us?'

*Of necessity*, the presence said. *The purpose of this final experiment is to determine which is the stronger stimulus: love or death. You will both undergo the experience of death one final time. This time you will be permitted to retain the memories of all your previous deaths as you die. But this time you will really die. You will not awaken from this death. Each of you will have only one way of saving yourself: you must sacrifice the other. You have only to declare in your mind that you wish the other to die in your place and it shall be done. Then you will be allowed to return to your planet. It should be a most informative experiment.*

And once again, I felt the blackness closing in, numbness overwhelming my extremities, my body sloughing away from me. I felt myself sinking slowly but inexorably into the black, black pool of nothingness . . .

But this time the terror was even greater, for now I remembered this happening before, again and again and again. As each tiny fraction of my being, of all in the universe that was me, was chipped away, I was anticipating it, knowing how it would be, fearing it an instant *before* it came, out of my deep, deep knowledge of exactly what it was to really die. And I knew that Loy was feeling it too.

I felt my consciousness collapsing in upon itself, contracting, fading away to a point, and every moment I was anticipating the next, dying a thousand deaths in one . . .

Inward, ever inward, the screaming animal thing that was me contracted, faded, beating hopelessly against that final, infinitely anticipated oblivion. And Loy was dying too . . .

I was reduced to a point of consciousness, a thing in itself, by itself. A thing ever fading, ever shrinking, and all around was the night, the all-consuming, endless night. The end of me-ness, of hope and fear and pain and love. Of all I ever was, ever would be . . .

And Loy was dying too. No amount of bravery could save her. I couldn't save her. Nothing could save her. We were both dying and only one of us could live, the one who . . .

I was no longer a man, no longer a husband, no longer a lover. I was a thing, a mewling, screaming, panicked thing, a thing that had died and died and died and remembered every moment of those multiple deaths . . .

I was a dying thing, an ego hungering for another instant of life, and the black was closing in, in, in . . .

And then there was nothing left of me but a howling,

maddened voice shrieking against the night: no! *No!* NO!

Screaming and begging, holding on to each instant like a man hanging from a cliff by his fingers, each moment a little more of the edge crumbling beneath his fingernails.

NO! NO! NO!

And Loy too was dying. I could not save her, I could only save *me*. And suddenly love was a far-away thing from another world, another plane of existence. There was no love, there was no Loy, only me, *me*, ME, and soon there would be an end to me, and there would be nothing, nothing, nothing, howling and empty and everything lost to me for ever.

And before I had decided anything, before I realized what I was doing, I was screaming: 'Her! Her! Her! Kill her! Not me! Not me! Her! Her! Her!'

A presence, far, far away said simply, *You shall live*, and the blackness closed in, but I was no longer afraid.

I awoke standing in the meadow next to the ship. Two of the brain-slugs stood beside me.

In front of me stood Loy. She was staring intently at the ground.

*Most interesting*, said the world-mind. *The experiment is concluded, and the results are as anticipated. It was of course not necessary that either of you actually die. You are free to leave.*

The two brain-slugs began to wriggle swiftly away towards the hills, leaving twin trails of translucent slime in the grass.

Loy and I stood there, for long moments, not speaking, not able to look at each other. Finally, after what seemed an eternity, our eyes met for the briefest instant.

But I knew from that flicker of a moment that all that had ever been between us was dead and gone for ever. I only needed that momentary glance into her eyes to know with terrible certainty that Loy had made the same choice I had.

# The National Pastime

## The Founding Father

I know you've got to start at the bottom in the television business, but producing sports shows is my idea of cruel and unusual punishment. Some time in the dim past, I had the idea that I wanted to make films, and the way to get to make films seemed to be to run up enough producing and directing credits on television, and the way to do *that* was to take whatever came along, and what came along was an offer to do a series of sports specials on things like kendo, sumo wrestling, jousting, Thai boxing, in short, ritual violence. This was at the height (or the depth) of the anti-violence hysteria, when you couldn't so much as show the bad guy getting an on-camera rap in the mouth from the good guy on a moronic Western. The only way you could give the folks what they really wanted was in the All-American wholesome package of a sporting event. Knowing this up front – unlike the jerks who warm chairs as network executives – I had no trouble producing the kind of sports specials the network executives knew people wanted to see without quite knowing why, and, thus, I achieved the status of boy genius. Which, alas, ended up in my being offered a long-term contract as a producer in the sports department that was simply too rich for me to pass up. I mean, I make no bones about being a crass materialist.

So try to imagine my feelings when Herb Dieter, the network sports programming director, calls me into his inner sanctum and gives me The Word. 'Ed,' he tells me, 'as you know, there's now only one major football league, and the opposition has us frozen out of the picture with long-term contracts with the NFL. As you also know, the major-league football games are clobbering us in the Sunday afternoon ratings, which is prime time as far as sports programming is concerned. And as you know, a sports programming director who can't hold a decent piece of the Sunday afternoon audience is not long for this fancy office. And as you know, there is no sport on God's green earth that can compete with major-league football. Therefore, it would appear that I have been presented with an insoluble problem.

'Therefore, since you are the official boy genius of the sports department, Ed, I've decided that you must be the solution to my problem. If I don't come up with something that will hold its own against pro football by the beginning of next season, my head will roll. Therefore, I've decided to give you the ball and let you run with it. Within ninety days, you will have come up with a solution, or the fine-print boys will be instructed to find a way for me to break your contract.'

I found it very hard to care one way or the other. On the one hand, I liked the bread I was knocking down, but on the other, the job was a real drag and it would probably do me good to get my ass fired. Of course, the whole thing was unfair from my point of view, but who could fault Dieter's logic; he personally had nothing to lose by ordering his best creative talent to produce a miracle or be fired. Unless I came through, he would be fired, and then what would he care about gutting the sports department? It wouldn't be his baby any more. It wasn't very nice, but it was the name of the game we were playing.

'You mean all I'm supposed to do is invent a better sport than football in ninety days, Herb, or do you mean something more impossible?' I couldn't decide whether I was trying to be funny or not.

But Dieter suddenly had a twenty-watt bulb come on behind his eyes (about as bright as he could get). 'I do believe you've hit on it already, Ed,' he said. 'We can't get any pro football, and there's no existing sport that can draw like football, so you're right, you've got to *invent* a sport that will outdraw pro football. Ninety days, Ed. And don't take it too hard; if you bomb out, we'll see each other at the unemployment office.'

So there I was, wherever *that* was. I could easily get Dieter to do for me what I didn't have the willpower to do for myself and get me out of the stinking sports department – all I had to do was *not* invent a game that would outdraw pro football. On the other hand, I liked living the way I did, and I didn't like the idea of losing *anything* because of failure.

So the next Sunday afternoon, I eased out the night before's chick, turned on the football game, smoked two joints of Acapulco Gold, and consulted my muse. It was the ideal set of conditions for a creative mood: I was being challenged, but if I failed, I gained, too, so I had no inhibitions on my creativity. I was stoned to the point where the whole situation was a game without serious consequences; I was hanging loose.

Watching two football teams pushing each other back and forth across my colour television screen, it once again occurred to me how much football was a ritual sublimation of war. This seemed perfectly healthy. Lots of cultures are addicted to sports that are sublimations of the natural human urge to clobber people. Better the sublimation than the clobbering. People dig violence, whether anyone likes the truth or not, so it's a public service to keep it on the level of a spectator sport.

Hmmm . . . that was probably why pro football had replaced baseball as the National Pastime in a time when people, having had their noses well-rubbed in the stupidity of war, needed a war-substitute. How could you beat something that got the American armpit as close to the gut as that?

And then from the blue-grass mountaintops of Mexico, the flash hit me: the only way to beat football was at its own game! Start with football itself, and convert it into something that was an even *closer* metaphor for war, something that could be called –

## ! ! COMBAT FOOTBALL ! !

Yeah, yeah, Combat football, or better, *Combat* football. Two standard football teams, standard football field, standard football rules, except:

Take off all their pads and helmets and jerseys and make it a warm-weather game that they play in shorts and sneakers, like boxing. More meaningful, more intimate violence. Violence is what sells football, so give 'em a bit more violence than football, and you'll draw a bit more than football. The more violent you can make it and get away with it, the better you'll draw.

Yeah . . . and you could get away with punching; after all, boxers belt each other around and they still allow boxing on television; sports have too much All-American Clean for the anti-violence freaks to attack; in fact, where their heads are at, they'd *dig* Combat football. Okay. So in ordinary football, the defensive team tackles the ball-carrier to bring him to his knees and stop the play. So in Combat, the defenders can slug the ball-carrier, kick him, tackle him, why not, anything to bring him to his knees and stop the play. And to make things fair, the ball-carrier can slug the defenders to get them out of his way. If the defence slugs an offensive player who doesn't have possession, it's ten yards and an automatic first down. If anyone but the ball-carrier slugs a defender, it's ten yards and a loss of down.

Presto: Combat football!

And the final touch was that it was a game that any beer-sodden moron who watched football could learn to understand in sixty seconds, and any lout who dug football would have to like Combat better.

The boy genius had done it again! It even made sense after I came down.

# Farewell to the Giants

Jeez, I saw a thing on television last Sunday you wouldn't believe. You really oughta watch it next week; I don't care who the Jets or the Giants are playing. I turned on the TV to watch the Giants game and went to get a beer, and when I came back from the kitchen I had on some guy yelling something about today's professional combat football game, and it's not the NFL announcer, and it's a team called the New York Sharks playing a team called the Chicago Thunderbolts, and they're playing in L.A. or Miami, I didn't catch which, but some place with palm trees anyway, and all the players are bare-ass! Well, not really bare-ass, but all they've got on is sneakers and boxing shorts with numbers across the behind – blue for New York, green for Chicago. No helmets, no pads, no protectors, no jerseys, no nothing!

I check the set and, sure enough, I've got the wrong channel. But I figured I could turn on the Giants game any time. What the hell, you can see the Giants all the time, but what in hell is *this*?

New York kicks off to Chicago. The Chicago kick-returner gets the ball on about the ten – bad kick – and starts upfield. The first New York tackler reaches him and goes for him and the Chicago player just belts him in the mouth and runs by him! I mean, with the ref standing there watching it, and no flag thrown! Two more tacklers come at him on the twenty. One dives at his legs, the other socks him in the gut. He trips and staggers out of the tackle, shoves another tackler away with a punch in the chest, but he's slowed up enough so that three or four New York players get to him at once. A couple of them grab his legs to stop his motion, and the others knock him down at about the twenty-five. Man, what's going on here?

I check my watch. By this time the Giants game has probably started, but New York and Chicago are lined up for the snap on the twenty-five, so I figure what the hell, I gotta see some more of this thing, so at least I'll watch one series of downs.

On first down, the Chicago quarterback drops back and throws a long one way downfield to his flanker on maybe the New York forty-five. It looks good, there's only one player on the Chicago flanker; he beats this one man and catches it, and it's a touchdown, and the pass looks right on the button. Up goes the Chicago flanker, the ball touches his hands – and pow, right in the kisser! The New York defender belts him in the mouth and he drops the pass. Jeez, what a game!

Second and ten. The Chicago quarterback fades back, but it's a fake; he hands off to his fullback, a gorilla who looks like he weighs about two-fifty, and the Chicago line opens up a little hole at left tackle and the fullback hits it holding the ball with one hand and punching with the other. He belts out a tackler, takes a couple of shots in the gut, slugs a second tackler, and then someone has him around the ankles; he drags himself forward another half yard or so, and then he runs into a good solid punch and he's down on the twenty-eight for a three-yard gain.

Man, I mean *action*! What a game! Makes the NFL football look like something for faggots! Third and seven, you gotta figure Chicago for the pass, right? Well, on the snap, the Chicago quarterback just backs up a few steps and pitches a short one to his flanker at about the line of scrimmage. The blitz is on and everyone comes rushing in on the quarterback and, before New York knows what's happening, the Chicago flanker is five yards downfield along the left sideline and picking up speed. Two New York tacklers angle out to stop him at maybe the Chicago forty, but he's got up momentum and one of the New York defenders runs right into his fist – I could hear the thud even on television – and falls back right into the other New York player, and the Chicago flanker is by them, the forty, the forty-five; he angles back towards the centre of the field at midfield, dancing away from one more tackle, then on maybe the New York forty-five a real fast New York defensive back catches up to him from behind, tackles him waist-high, and the Chicago flanker's motion is stopped as two more tacklers come at him. But he squirms around inside the tackle and belts the tackler in the mouth with his free hand, knocks the New York back silly, breaks the tackle, and he's off again downfield with two guys chasing him. Forty, thirty-five, thirty, twenty-five, he's running away from them. Then from way over the right side of the field, I see the New York safety man running flat out across the field at the ball-carrier, angling towards him so it looks like they'll crash like a couple of locomotives on about the fifteen, because the Chicago runner just doesn't see this guy. Ka-boom! The ball-carrier running flat-out runs right into the fist of the flat-out safety at the fifteen and he's knocked about ten feet one way and the football flies ten feet the other way, and the New York safety scoops it up on the thirteen and starts upfield, twenty, twenty-five, thirty, thirty-five, and then, slam, bang, whang, half the Chicago team is all over him, a couple of tackles, a few in the gut, a shot in the head, and he's down. First and ten for New York on their own thirty-seven. And that's just the first series of downs!

Well, let me tell you, after that, you know where they can stick the Giants game, right? This Combat football, that's the real way to play the game; I mean, it's football and boxing all together, with a little wrestling thrown in — it's a game with *balls*. I mean, the *whole game* was like that first series. You oughta take a look at it next week. Damn, if they played the thing in New York, we could even go out to the game together. I'd sure be willing to spend a couple of bucks to see something like that.

## Commissioner Gene Kuhn Addresses the First Annual Owners' Meeting of the National Combat Football League

Gentlemen, I've been thinking about the future of our great sport. We're facing a double challenge to the future of Combat football, boys. First of all, the NFL is going over to Combat rules next season, and since you can't copyright a sport (and if you could, the NFL would have us by the short hairs anyway) there's not a legal thing we can do about it. The only edge we'll have left is that they'll have to at least wear heavy uniforms because they play in regular cities up north. But they'll have the stars, and the stadiums, and the regular hometown fans and fatter television deals.

Which brings me to our second problem, gentlemen, namely,

that the television network which created our great game is getting to be a pain in our sport's neck, meaning that they're shafting us in the crummy percentage of the television revenue they see fit to grant us.

So the great task facing our great National Pastime, boys, is to ace out the network by putting ourselves in a better bargaining position on the television rights while saving our million-dollar asses from the NFL competition, which we just cannot afford.

Fortunately, it just so happens that your commissioner has been on the ball, and I've come up with a couple of new gimmicks that I am confident will insure the posterity and financial success of our great game while stiff-arming the NFL and the TV network nicely in the process.

Number one, we've got to improve our standing as a live spectator sport. We've got to start drawing big crowds on our own if we want some clout in negotiating with the network. Number two, we've got to give the customers something the NFL can't just copy from us next year and clobber us with.

There's no point in changing the rules again because the NFL can always keep up with us there. But one thing the NFL is locked into for keeps is the whole concept of having teams represent cities; they're committed to that for the next twenty years. We've only been in business four years and our teams never play in the damned cities they're named after because it's too cold to play bare-ass Combat in those cities during the football season, so it doesn't have to mean anything to us.

So we make two big moves. First, we change our season to spring and summer so we can play up north where the money is. Second, we throw out the whole dumb idea of teams representing cities; that's old-fashioned stuff. That's crap for the coyotes. Why not six teams with *national* followings? Imagine the clout that'll give us when we renegotiate the TV contract. We can have a flexible schedule so that we can put any game we want into any city in the country any time we think that city's hot and draw a capacity crowd in the biggest stadium in town.

How are we gonna do all this? Well, look, boys, we've got a six-team league, so, instead of six cities, why not match up our teams with six national groups?

I've taken the time to draw up a hypothetical league line-up just to give you an example of the kind of thing I mean. Six teams: the Black Panthers, the Golden Supermen, the

Psychedelic Stompers, the Caballeros, the Gay Bladers, and the Hog Choppers. We do it all up the way they used to do with wrestling; you know, the Black Panthers are all spades with naturals, the Golden Supermen are blond astronaut types in red-white-and-blue bunting, the Psychedelic Stompers have long hair and groupies in mini-skirts up to their navels and take rock bands to their games, the Caballeros dress like gauchos or something, whatever makes Latin types feel feisty, the Gay Bladers and Hog Choppers are mostly all-purpose villains – the Bladers are black-leather-and-chain-mail faggots, and the Hog Choppers we recruit from outlaw motorcycle gangs.

Now is that a *league*, gentlemen? Identification is the thing, boys. You gotta identify your teams with a large enough group of people to draw crowds, but why tie yourself to something local like a city? This way, we got a team for the spades, a team for the frustrated Middle Americans, a team for the hippies and kids, a team for the spics, a team for the faggots, and a team for the motorcycle nuts and violence freaks. And any American who can't identify with any of those teams is an odds-on bet to hate one or more of them enough to come out to the game to see them stomped. I mean, who wouldn't want to see the Hog Choppers and the Panthers go at each other under Combat rules?

Gentlemen, I tell you, it's creative thinking like this that made our country great, and it's creative thinking like this that will make Combat football the greatest goldmine in professional sports.

## Stay Tuned, Sports Fans . . .

Good afternoon, Combat fans, and welcome to today's major-league Combat football game between the Caballeros and the Psychedelic Stompers, brought to you by the World Safety Razor Blade Company, with the sharpest, strongest blade for your razor in the world.

It's ninety-five degrees on this clear New York day in July, and a beautiful day for a Combat football game, and the game here today promises to be a real smasher, as the Caballeros, only a game behind the league-leading Black Panthers, take on the fast-rising, hard-punching Psychedelic Stompers, and perhaps the best running back in the game today, Wolfman Ted. We've got a packed house here today, and the Stompers, who won the toss, are about to receive the kickoff from the Caballeros . . .

139

And there it is, a low bullet into the end zone, taken there by Wolfman Ted. The Wolfman crosses the goal line, he's up to the five, the ten, the fourteen. He brings down Number 71, Pete Lopez, with a right to the windpipe, crosses the fifteen, takes a glancing blow to the head from Number 56, Diaz, is tackled on the eighteen by Porfirio Rubio, Number 94, knocks Rubio away with two quick rights to the head, crosses the twenty, and takes two rapid blows to the mid-section in succession from Beltran and Number 30, Orduna, staggers, and is tackled low from behind by the quick-recovering Rubio, and slammed to the ground under a pile of Caballeros on the twenty-four.

First and ten for the Stompers on their own twenty-four. Stompers quarterback Ronny Seede brings his team to the line of scrimmage in a double flanker formation with Wolfman Ted wide to the right. A long count –

The snap, Seede fades back to –

A quick handoff to the Wolfman charging diagonally across the action towards left tackle, and the Wolfman hits the line on a dead run, windmilling his right fist, belting his way through one, two, three Caballeros, getting two, three yards, then taking three quick ones to the rib cage from Rubio, and staggering right into Number 41, Manuel Cardozo, who brings him down on about the twenty-seven with a hard right cross.

Hold it! A flag on the play! Orduna, Number 30, of the Caballeros, and Dickson, Number 83, of the Stompers, are smashing away at each other on the twenty-six! Dickson takes two hard ones and goes down, but as Orduna kicks him in the ribs, Number 72, Merling, of the Stompers, grabs him from behind, and now there are six or seven assistant referees breaking it up . . .

Something going on in the stands at about the fifty, too – a section of Stompers' rooters mixing it up with the Caballero fans –

But now they've got things sorted out on the field, and it's ten yards against the Caballeros for striking an ineligible player, nullified by a ten-yarder against the Stompers for illegal offensive striking. So now it's second and seven for the Stompers on their own twenty-seven –

It's quieted down a bit there above the fifty-yard line, but there's another little fracas going in the far end zone and a few groups of people milling around in the aisles of the upper grandstand –

There's the snap, and Seede fades back quietly, dances around, looks downfield, and throws one intended for Number 54, Al Viper, the left end, at about the forty. Viper goes up for it, he's got it –

And takes a tremendous shot along the base of his neck from Number 94, Porfirio Rubio! The ball is jarred loose. Rubio dives for it, he's got it, but he takes a hard right in the head from Viper, then a left. Porfirio drops the ball and goes at Viper with both fists! Viper knocks him sprawling and dives on top of the ball, burying it and bringing a whistle from the head referee as Rubio rains blows on his prone body. And here come the assistant referees to pull Porfirio off as half the Stompers come charging downfield towards the action –

They're at it again near the fifty-yard line! About forty rows of fans going at each other. There goes a smoke bomb!

They've got Rubio away from Viper now, but three or four Stompers are trying to hold Wolfman Ted back, and Ted has blood in his eye as he yells at Number 41, Cardozo. Two burly assistant referees are holding Cardozo back . . .

There go about a hundred and fifty special police up into the midfield stands. They've got their Mace and prods out . . .

The head referee is calling an official's time out to get things organized, and we'll be back to live National Combat Football League action after this message . . .

## The Circus Is in Town

'We've got a serious police problem with Combat football,' Commissioner Minelli told me after the game between the Golden Supermen and the Psychedelic Stompers last Sunday, in which the Supermen slaughtered the Stompers, 42–14, and during which there were ten fatalities and one hundred and eighty-nine hospitalizations among the rabble in the stands.

'Every time there's a game, we have a riot, your honour,' Minelli (who had risen through the ranks) said earnestly. 'I recommend that you should think seriously about banning Combat football. I really think you should.'

This city is hard enough to run without free advice from politically ambitious cops. 'Minelli,' I told him, 'you are dead wrong on both counts. First of all, not only has there *never* been a riot in New York during a Combat football game, but the best studies show that the incidences of violent crimes and social violence diminish from a period of three days before a Combat game clear through to a period five days afterwards, not only here but in every major city in which a game is played.'

'But only this Sunday ten people were killed and nearly two hundred injured, including a dozen of my cops –'

'In the *stands*, you nitwit, not in the streets!' Really, the man was too much!

'I don't see the difference –'

'Ye gods, Minelli, can't you see that Combat football keeps a hell of a lot of violence off the streets? It keeps it in the stadium, where it belongs. The Romans understood that two thousand years ago! We can hardly stage gladiator sports in this day and age, so we have to settle for a civilized substitute.'

'But what goes on in there is murder. My cops are taking a beating. And we've got to assign two thousand cops to every game. It's costing the taxpayers a fortune, and you can bet . . . *someone* will be making an issue out of it in the next election.'

I do believe that the lout was actually trying to pressure me. Still, in his oafish way, he had put his finger on the one political disadvantage of Combat football: the cost of policing the games and keeping the fan clubs in the stands from tearing each other to pieces.

And then I had one of those little moments of blind inspiration when the pieces of a problem simply fall into shape as an obvious pattern of solution.

*Why bother keeping them from tearing each other to pieces?*

'I think I have the solution, Minelli,' I said. 'Would it satisfy your sudden sense of fiscal responsibility if you could take all but a couple dozen cops off the Combat football games?'

Minelli looked at me blankly. 'Anything less than two thousand cops in there would be mincemeat by half-time,' he said.

'So why send them in there?'

'Huh?'

'All we really need is enough cops to guard the gates, frisk the fans for weapons, seal up the stadium with the help of riot-doors, and make sure no one gets out till things have simmered down inside.'

'But they'd tear each other to ribbons in there with no cops!'

'So let them. I intend to modify the conditions under which the city licenses Combat football so that anyone who buys a

142

ticket legally waives his right to police protection. Let them fight all they want. Let them really work out their hatreds on each other until they're good and exhausted. Human beings have an incurable urge to commit violence on each other. We try to sublimate that urge out of existence, and we end up with irrational violence on the streets. The Romans had a better idea – give the rabble a socially harmless outlet for violence. We spend billions on welfare to keep things pacified with bread, and where has it got us? Isn't it about time we tried circuses?'

## As American as Apple Pie

Let me tell it to you, brother, we've sure been waiting for the Golden Supermen to play the Panthers in *this* town again, after the way those blond mothers cheated us, 17–10, the last time and wasted three hundred of the brothers! Yeah, man, they had those stands packed with honkies trucked in from as far away as Buffalo – we just weren't ready is why we took the loss.

But this time we planned ahead and got ourselves up for the game even before it was announced. Yeah, instead of waiting for them to announce the date of the next Panther–Supermen game in Chicago and then scrambling with the honkies for tickets, the Panther Fan Club made under-the-table deals with ticket brokers for blocks of tickets for whenever the next game would be, so that by the time today's game was announced, we controlled two-thirds of the seats in Daley Stadium and the honkies had to scrape and scrounge for what was left.

Yeah, man, today we pay them back for that last game! We got two-thirds of the seats in the stadium and Eli Wood is back in action and we gonna just go out and *stomp* those mothers today!

Really, I'm personally quite cynical about Combat; most of us who go out to the Gay Bladers games are. After all, if you look at it straight on, Combat football is rather a grotty business. I mean, look at the sort of people who turn out at Supermen or Panthers or, for God's sake, *Caballero* games: the worst sort of proletarian apes. Aside from us, only the Hogs have any semblance of class, and the Hogs have beauty only because they're so incredibly up-front gross; I mean, all that shiny metal and black leather!

143

And, of course, that's the only real reason to go to the Blader games: for the spectacle. To see it and to be part of it! To see semi-naked groups of men engaging in violence and to be violent yourself – and especially with those black-leather-and-chain-mail Hog Lovers!

Of course, I'm aware of the cynical use the loathsome government makes of Combat. If there's nastiness between the blacks and PR's in New York, they have the league schedule a Panther–Caballero game and let them get it out on each other safely in the stadium. If there's college campus trouble in the Bay area, it's a Stompers–Supermen game in Oakland. And us and the Hogs when just *anyone* anywhere needs to release general hostility. I'm not stupid; I know that Combat football is a tool of the Establishment . . .

But, Lord, it's just so much bloody *fun*!

We gonna have some fun today! The Hogs is playing the Stompers and that's the wildest kind of Combat game there is! Those crazy freaks come to the game stoned out of their minds, and you know that at least Wolfman Ted is playing on something stronger than pot. There are twice as many chicks at Stompers games than with any other team the Hogs play because the Stompers chicks are the only chicks besides ours who aren't scared out of their boxes at the thought of being locked up in a stadium with twenty thousand hot-shot Hogger rape artists like us!

Yeah, we get good and stoned, and the Stompers fans get good and stoned, and the Hogs get stoned, and the Stompers get stoned, and then we all groove on beating the piss out of each other, *whoo-whee*! And when we win in the stands, we drag off the pussy and gang-bang it.

Oh, yeah, Combat is just good clean dirty fun!

It makes you feel good to go out to a Supermen game, makes you feel like a real American is supposed to, like a *man*. All week you've got to take crap from the niggers and the spics and your goddamned crazy doped-up kids and hoods and bums and faggots in the streets, and you're not even supposed to think of them as niggers and spics and crazy doped-up kids and bums and hoods and faggots. But Sunday you can go out to the stadium and watch the Supermen give it to the Panthers, the Caballeros, the Stompers, the Hogs, or the Bladers and maybe kick the crap out of a few people whose faces you yourself don't like.

144

It's a good healthy way to spend a Sunday
in the open air at a good game when the Super
and we've got the opposition in the stands outnu
Combat's a great thing to take your kid to, too!

I don't know, all my friends go to the Caballero games.
We go together and take a couple of six-packs of beer apiece,
and get *muy boracho*, and just have some crazy fun, you
know? Sometimes I come home a little cut up and my wife is
all upset and tries to get me to promise not to go to the
Combat games any more. Sometimes I promise, just to keep
her quiet – she can get on my nerves – but I never really mean
it.

*Hombre*, you know how it is; women don't understand these
things like men do. A man has got to go out with his friends
and feel like a man sometimes. It's not too easy to find ways
to feel *muy macho* in this country, *amigo*. The way it is for
us here, you know. It's not as if we're hurting anyone we
shouldn't hurt. Who goes out to the Caballero games but a
lot of dirty *gringos* who want to pick on us? So it's a question
of honour, in a way, for us to get as many *amigos* as we can
out to the Caballero games and show those *cabrones* that we
can beat them any time, no matter how drunk we are. In fact,
the drunker we are, the better it is, *tu sabes?*

Baby, I don't know what it is, maybe it's just a chance to get
it all out. It's a unique trip, that's all. There's no other way
to get that particular high, that's why I go to Stompers games.
Man, the games don't mean anything to me as games; games
are like *games*, dig. But the whole Combat scene is its own
reality.

You take some stuff – acid is a groovy high, but you're liable
to get wasted; lots of speed and some grass or hash is more
recommended – when you go in, so that by the time the game
starts you're really loaded. And then, man, you just groove
behind the violence. There aren't any cops to bring you down.
What chicks are there are there because they dig it. The people
you're enjoying beating up on are getting the same kicks beating up on you, so there's no guilt hang-up to get between you
and the total experience of violence.

Like I say, it's a unique trip. A pure violence high without
any hang-ups. It makes me feel good and purged and kind of
together just to walk out of that stadium after a Combat
football trip and know I survived; the danger is groovy, too.

...boy, if you can dig it, Combat can be a genuine mystical experience.

## Hogs Win It All, 21–17, 1578(23)–989(14)!

*Anaheim, 8 October.* It was a slam-bang finish to the National Combat Football League Pennant Race, the kind of game Combat fans dream about. The Golden Supermen and the Hog Choppers in a dead-even tie for first place playing each other in the last game of the season, winner take all, before nearly sixty thousand fans. It was a beautiful, sunny ninety-degree Southern California day as the Hogs kicked off to the Supermen before a crowd that seemed evenly divided between Hog lovers, who had motorcycled in all week from all over California, and Supermen fans, whose biggest bastion is here in Orange County.

The Supermen scored first blood mid-way through the first period when quarterback Bill Johnson tossed a little screen pass to his right end, Seth West, on the Hog twenty-three, and West slugged his way through five Hog tacklers, one of whom sustained a mild concussion, to go in for the touchdown. Rudolf's conversion made it 7–0, and the Supermen fans in the stands responded to the action on the field by making a major sortie into the Hog lover section at midfield, taking out about twenty Hog lovers, including a fatality.

The Hog fans responded almost immediately by launching an offensive of their own in the bleacher seats, but didn't do much better than hold their own. The Hogs and the Supermen pushed each other up and down the field for the rest of the period without a score, while the Supermen fans seemed to be getting the better of the Hog lovers, especially in the midfield sections of the grandstand, where at least one hundred and twenty Hog lovers were put out of action.

The Supermen scored a field goal early in the second period to make the score 10–0, but more significantly, the Hog lovers seemed to be dogging it, contenting themselves with driving back continual Supermen fan sorties, while launching almost no attacks of their own.

The Hogs finally pushed in over the goal line in the final minutes of the first half on a long pass from quarterback Spike Horrible to his flanker Greasy Ed Lee to make the score 10–7 as the half ended. But things were not nearly as close as the field score looked, as the Hog lovers in the stands were really taking their lumps from the Supermen fans who

146

had bruised them to the extent of nearly five hundred take-outs including five fatalities, as against only about three hundred casualties and three fatalities chalked up by the Hog fans.

During the half-time intermission, the Hog lovers could be seen marshalling themselves nervously, passing around beer, pot and pills, while the Supermen fans confidently passed the time entertaining themselves with patriotic songs.

The Supermen scored again half-way through the third period, on a handoff from Johnson to his big fullback Tex McGhee on the Hog forty-one. McGhee slugged his way through the left side of the line with his patented windmill attack, and burst out into the Hog secondary swinging and kicking. There was no stopping the Texas Tornado, though half the Hog defence tried, and McGhee went forty-one yards for the touchdown, leaving three Hogs unconscious and three more with minor injuries in his wake. The kick was good, and the Supermen seemed on their way to walking away with the championship, with the score 17–7, and the momentum, in the stands and on the field, going all their way.

But in the closing moments of the third period, Johnson threw a long one downfield intended for his left end, Dick Whitfield. Whitfield got his fingers on the football at the Hog thirty, but Hardly Davidson, the Hog cornerback, was right on him, belted him in the head from behind as he touched the ball, and then managed to catch the football himself before either it or Whitfield had hit the ground. Davidson got back to midfield before three Supermen tacklers took him out of the rest of the game with a closed eye and a concussion.

All at once, as time ran out in the third period, the ten-point Supermen lead didn't seem so big at all as the Hogs advanced to a first down on the Supermen thirty-five and the Hog lovers in the stands beat back Supermen fan attacks on several fronts, inflicting very heavy losses.

Spike Horrible threw a five-yarder to Greasy Ed Lee on the first play of the final period, then a long one into the end zone intended for his left end, Kid Filth, which the Kid dropped as Gordon Jones and John Lawrence slugged him from both sides as soon as he became fair game.

It looked like a sure pass play on third and five, but Horrible surprised everyone by fading back into a draw and handing the ball off to Loser Ludowicki, his fullback, who ploughed around right end like a heavy tank, simply crushing and smashing through tacklers with his body and fists, picked up two

147

key blocks on the twenty and seventeen, knocked Don Barnfield on to the casualty list with a tremendous haymaker on the seven, and went in for the score.

The Hog lovers in the stands went Hog-wild. Even before the successful conversion by Knuckleface Bonner made it 17-14, they began blitzing the Supermen fans on all fronts, letting out everything they had seemed to be holding back during the first three quarters. At least one hundred Supermen fans were taken out in the next three minutes, including two quick fatalities, while the Hog lovers lost no more than a score of their number.

As the Hog lovers continued to punish the Supermen fans, the Hogs kicked off to the Supermen, and stopped them after two first downs, getting the ball back on their own twenty-four. After marching to the Supermen thirty-one on a sustained and bloody ground drive, the Hogs lost the ball again when Greasy Ed Lee was rabbit-punched into a fumble.

But the Hog lovers still sensed the inevitable and pressed their attack during the next two Supermen series of downs, and began to push the Supermen fans towards the bottom of the grandstand.

Buoyed by the success of their fans, the Hogs on the field recovered the ball on their own twenty-nine with less than two minutes to play when Chain-Mail Dixon belted Tex McGhee into a fumble and out of the game.

The Hogs crunched their way upfield yard by yard, punch by punch, against a suddenly shaky Supermen opposition, and, all at once, the whole season came down to one play: with the score 17-14 and twenty seconds left on the clock, time enough for one or possibly two more plays, the Hogs had the ball third and four on the eighteen-yard line of the Golden Supermen.

Spike Horrible took the snap as the Hog lovers in the stands launched a final all-out offensive against the Supermen fans, who by now had been pushed to a last stand against the grandstand railings at fieldside. Horrible took about ten quick steps back as if to pass, and then suddenly ran head down, fist flailing, at the centre of the Supermen line with the football tucked under his arm.

Suddenly Greasy Ed Lee and Loser Ludowicki raced ahead of their quarterback, hitting the line and staggering the tacklers a split-second before Horrible arrived, throwing them just off-balance enough for Horrible to punch his way through with three quick rights, two of them k.o. punches. Virtually

148

the entire Hog team roared through the hole after him, body-blocking, elbowing, and crushing tacklers to the ground. Horrible punched out three more tacklers as the Hog lovers pushed the first contingent of fleeing Supermen fans out on to the field, and went in for the game and championship-winning touchdown with two seconds left on the clock.

When the dust had cleared, not only had the Hog Choppers beaten the Golden Supermen 21–17, but the Hog lovers had driven the Golden Supermen fans from their favourite stadium, and had racked up a commanding advantage in the casualty statistics, 1578 casualties and 23 fatalities inflicted, as against only 989 and 14.

It was a great day for the Hog lovers and a great day in the history of our National Pastime.

## The Voice of Sweet Reason

Go to a Combat football game? Really, do you think I want to risk being injured or possibly killed? Of course, I realize that Combat is a practical social mechanism for preserving law and order, and, to be frank, I find the spectacle rather stimulating. I watch Combat often, almost every Sunday.

On television, of course. After all, everyone who is anyone in this country knows very well that there are basically two kinds of people in the United States: people who go out to Combat games, and people for whom Combat is strictly a television spectator sport.

# In the Eye of the Storm

Doug had changed the points and plugs, boiled out the carb, and tuned his scoot to a razor's edge back in Denver. The engine should've been running as smooth as the black lacquer on the tank and frame, by all the rules of God and man. But every time the lightning flashed over the hulking backbone of the Rockies, the engine broke up for a few beats, as if there were loose crud in the fuel lines (which there damned well was not), or dirt in the jets, or one of those electrical glitches that could take you a week to run down. Though the slope was steep as it wound up towards the high passes, the road was almost empty, and the bends were still gentle, so

Doug was able to try all sorts of engine speeds in every gear, and there was no relationship between engine speed and the weird coughing in the Harley's voice. She broke up at thirty, at forty-five, at sixty, at eighty – every time the lightning flashed.

Doug didn't like it at all. First, because he had never heard of an electrical storm causing an engine to break up, and, second, because of the thing he had about electricity.

Doug Allard felt no fear in the face of things that would turn the knees of the average citizen to lime Jell-o – that came with the colours of the Avengers – but he believed that electricity was out to get him, in ways large and small. Once he and his old partner Ted had been tooling along through a light drizzle in Florida when out of nowhere a power line along the road suddenly snapped, whizzed past Doug's cheek like a cobra spitting sparks, caught Ted across the chest, and fried him where he sat. And almost every time Doug's chopper was laid up with something he couldn't handle himself, it was some electrical gremlin. Doug and electricity just didn't get along. To him, electricity in all of its manifestations was a cold-eyed snake – like the power line that had killed Ted – out to sink its sparky teeth into his hide as often and as deeply as it could.

So the idea that those bolts of lightning flashing across the strangely clear sky were somehow subverting the loyalty of their little brothers in the ignition system of his scoot not only scared him in a way he wouldn't like to admit, it pissed him off.

'Lay off my chop, mother!' he muttered at the approaching electrical storm, feeling foolish for threatening thin air, but feeling better for having done it just the same.

Doug was headed west across the Rockies to join up with the Avengers in Los Angeles after selling off a crummy grocery store his Uncle Bill in St Louis had left him, and the damned electrical storm seemed to be headed east after God-knows-what, so it wasn't long before the storm was directly overhead.

Lightning danced through a slate-grey sky, slamming and cracking like an artillery barrage, as Doug leaned through the turns, taking them as fast as he could, trying to make as much time as possible before the deluge began. The sky got darker and darker, but no rain fell. Sheets of blinding light ripped across the heavens and lit up the heavily wooded mountains like enormous flashbulbs every thirty seconds or so

150

now, and the Harley's engine was coughing more often than not. Doug's head rang from the crack and rumble of the continuous thunder and the throttle hesitations and stops were making the bike harder and harder to control.

One weird mother of a storm!

Up ahead, the road took a gentle left and climbed around the curve of a tree-covered hill. As he started to put the bike over, Doug smelled electricity in the air so thick he almost choked on it. Looking up at the crest, he saw a searing white bolt of lightning kiss the concrete not twenty yards in front of him and actually walk towards him before it disappeared in a clap of thunder.

Then he was cresting the hill leaning into the left turn at fifty-five – and the world suddenly turned a blinding, crazy yellow. Everything seemed to happen at once, and in slow motion. Through the handlebars, he felt a tremendous jar – the whole frame was vibrating as if someone had bonged it with a huge sledgehammer. His body tingled, he choked on ozone, and the engine quit entirely. The chop started to go down, but some sixth sense told him that if he went down in that instant, or even allowed his foot to touch the road, he had had it. Standing up on the pegs still blinded, he threw his body to the right as hard as he could against the bank of the turn, compensating for the sudden drop in speed. The Harley wobbled crazily, there was a tremendous clap of thunder, and his vision began to clear.

He dimly saw that he was careening across the road, thumping and bouncing towards a steep drop into the heavily wooded gully to the right. He downshifted, slammed on the brakes, the wheels kicked up dirt and screamed, the forward momentum was killed, and the scoot gently slid out from under him. As he rolled away from the bike losing a certain amount of skin, he shouted in triumph.

How many riders had been hit by lightning and lived? *Whoo-eee!*

Picking himself off the ground and making sure nothing major was broken, his next thought was for the Harley. The bike was lying on its side in the tall grass by the side of the road about three yards from having rolled into the rugged-looking little canyon. Grunting, he stood it up on its still-functional stand and inspected the damage. The right front peg was bent at a crazy angle, there was a small rip in the black leather of the seat, and a lot of little dings and scratches all over the right side of the bike, where it had skidded along the ground. There was a strange lightning-shaped strip of paint peeled off the tank, and the metal beneath was etched a dark blue, as if the storm had branded the chop with its own mark. But all things considered, the scoot had come through in fine shape; all it seemed to need to be put into good riding shape was to hammer the peg back into position. Some paint, chrome polish, and new leather, and it would be as slick as before it was hit. But he would try to keep that lightning brand on the tank – maybe try some clear lacquer over it – it was unique; it gave the chop a character that no amount of planning, design, or hard work could.

Only when he had finished inspecting the bike did he notice the weirdness of his surroundings. For one thing, the sky was now clear, and for another the sun was about two hours lower than it had been when he was hit, only minutes before. And the surface of the road was cracked, pitted, and full of jagged holes as far as he could see. The fir trees were wrong, too; taller and thinner than they should've been, the needles very sparse on the branches, but almost four inches long and coloured a sickly greyish-green. The air had a kind of chemical aftertaste, not at all the delicious freshness of the high Rockies. Everything seemed old and sick and generally cruddy.

Muttering to himself and continually glancing back over his shoulder for reasons he couldn't figure, Doug hammered the bad peg back into position with his heaviest wrench, checked out his carb and fuel lines, then tromped on the starter.

Nothing happened, not even a cough. He stomped on the starter ten times without raising a peep. He got off the bike, took a deep breath, looked around at the greyish, sickly forest, the ruined road, shuddered, and tried to dope it out. He just *knew* it was something electrical. Hell – of course!

Sure enough, his fuse had blown, and when he got out his little cardboard box of spares, they were blown, too. Electricity had done him again!

But Doug Allard was damned if he was going to sit in that crummy-looking place just because he had no good fuses for his chop. Swearing, he fished out a half-empty cigarette pack, dumped out the smokes, stripped off the tinfoil, wadded it up, and jammed it into the gap in the fuseholder. It might not provide the protection a proper fuse was supposed to, but that was a chance he had to take. It was either that, or sit here in this damned spot until something came along. From the looks of the road, that might be for ever.

When he kicked the starter this time, the engine caught right away. He cautiously started up what was left of the road, skirting huge potholes and jagged breaks every few yards of the way, creeping along at thirty-five, and wishing his scoot were set up for scrambles. And wondering where the hell he was.

According to the map, there was a dinky little town about forty miles up the road; there would no doubt be a gas station and a place to get a hamburger and some beer. Doug had taken off his peanut tank for this run and fitted a fat-bob which was still about three-quarters full, but the same could not be said for his gut, which had a food-sized hole in it. And after half an hour of dodging potholes, cracks and craters on the ruined road, his arms were stiff with tension and his nerves in need of a few cold beers.

The countryside still seemed all wrong. The fir trees were like nothing he had ever seen, like crude cartoons of the real thing, and the ground between them crawled with giant purplish toadstools and raw-looking mushrooms the colour of dried blood. As the sun sank towards the high ridgeline of the mountains, the clear sky took on an ugly steel-blue cast, and Doug could hear the droning whine of insects even over the sound of the Harley's engine. In half an hour of riding through this unnatural landscape, he hadn't seen a car or a truck or a bike. He didn't like it one little bit. The only thing that kept him from brooding on the ominous strangeness of the world in which he found himself and on how the hell he had got there was the total concentration needed to keep the scoot upright on this crappy wreckage of a road.

Finally, with the sun just starting to slide down behind the mountains, he crested a ridgeline and saw a little huddle of buildings off to the right in the next valley. Just a glimpse, and then the road wound down around the slope of the hill, screening the town from his sight until he reached the valley floor on the outskirts of the little burg.

Or what was left of it.

It couldn't have been much more than a wide spot in the road to begin with: a big Philips-66 station next to a café, a few cinderblock stores, a couple of dozen wooden houses. The town was a burned-out shell, a ruin. The houses were charred skeletons. The store windows were shattered, and it looked as if every scrap of anything of value had long since been carried away. The front of the café had been ripped apart by an explosion and the concrete was pitted with craters left by large-calibre ammunition. There were about half a dozen cars scattered along the main drag, old rusted-out hulks, their tyres rotted away, their windows smashed, their body metal so thoroughly corroded that the colours of their paint jobs were now unrecognizable.

Doug pulled up beside one of the old wrecks and felt a sinking sensation in his gut. It took him a moment more to realize what it was about the hulk that made him shudder. The car body had holes rusted right through it, and when Doug punched the front door, the rotten metal crumbled. The whole body was a brittle shell of rust.

But it was unmistakably a Chevrolet Vega, and GM had started building Vegas in 1971. And this wreck had to be at least ten years old.

He had been asking the wrong question: not where the hell am I, but *when*?

Electricity, that son-of-a-bitch, had really done him in this time! Somehow, that lightning had kicked his ass into the future, and, from the look of this place, it was a future whose best days were long since past.

Well, there was no point in whining and snivelling about it. The first order of business was to survive long enough to reach some place where there were people and play it by the seat of his pants from there. In order to keep going, he had to have food and gas. Three-quarters of a tank might or might not get him to somewhere where there was more fuel; it would be stupid to pass up the chance to drain the pumps of the ruined gas station. There must be some jerry-cans around somewhere.

He chugged over to the Philips-66 station and pulled up by the left-hand bank of pumps. The station building itself was riddled with bullet holes, and it looked like the whole place had been stripped clean. Not a tool or a tyre or a can of oil around, and nothing he could use to hold extra gas.

Well, he had a quarter-empty tank, and two one-quart canteens. Water figured to be a lot easier to come by than gas in the Rockies. He unscrewed his gas cap, plugged the nozzle of the nearest hose into the hole, and squeezed the grip.

Nothing. The pump was bone-dry.

He tried every pump in the station with the same results. It figured. If an atomic war or something had caused things to fall apart, gas would be a mighty precious commodity, and looters sure wouldn't leave it sitting in pumps. And from the looks of this burg, it had been gone over by some mighty efficient looters. It looked like he'd have to search and scrabble pretty hard for gas, maybe appropriate some from some citizens, if he could find some that had any. He still had enough gas in his tank to take him well over a hundred miles. A good thing he wasn't running a little peanut tank for the looks!

He remounted, started the engine, put her in gear, and started to move out of the station. That was when he noticed the heap of bones just beyond the pumps. When he got a real close look, he broke into a cold sweat.

The bones were scattered around a burned-out fire. Some of them had been cracked open for the marrow, and all of them were picked pretty clean. But swarms of ants were crawling all over them, gobbling the tiny scraps of meat that still clung to the greasy bones. And there were two human skulls lying close to the fire. Their tops had been smashed open and the brains eaten out.

Doug slammed the Harley into gear and cranked on the throttle, tearing ass and shooting gravel as if the hounds of hell were after him. And from the looks of that bone pile, something even worse might show up at any moment. The sun was just about setting, and this was sure no place to spend the night!

Doug roared out of the gas station making forty-five, which was really moving considering the condition of the surface. He zipped past a couple of gutted stores and a few burned-out houses, and that was just about all there was of the little town.

Then the road bent to the right around a little hill, and when Doug came out of the curve he saw that the road ahead was blocked by three of the skankiest dudes on three of the most ridiculous-looking bikes he had ever heard of.

The bikes looked like they had started as little 125 c.c. Yamahas or something similar. They weren't chopped at all, but every scrap of non-essential metal had been removed from the frames, making them look almost like bicycles. They mounted knobby tyres front and rear, and huge oversized gas tanks. But the craziest things about them were the outriggers that sprouted on both sides behind the single bicycle-type seats. Lengths of pipe about three feet long were pivot-mounted on frame-members, the play restricted both up and down by sets of springs that might have been scavenged from the forks of mopeds. At the ends of these lengths of pipe, each outrigger had a fat-tyred little wheel off a kid's trail bike mounted on bicycle forks. When the bikes were moving in an upright position, the outrigger wheels would ride about a foot off the ground. Now, at rest, the left outrigger wheels were on the ground, doubling as instant stands. The bikes were the second ugliest and the second weirdest things Doug Allard had ever seen.

The ugliest and weirdest things he had ever seen were the three creeps riding them.

They looked like basketball centres that hadn't eaten for a month: about seven feet tall, thin as skeletons, long, awkward arms and legs that made them seem to be perching on the spindly little scoots like praying mantises. They wore greasy leather pants, black sleeveless vests, and long scabbards at their belts. In the deep shadows of the setting sun, their hairless skin seemed to glisten a pale, waxy green.

But it was their faces that made Doug reach behind him and uncoil the length of chain he kept wrapped around a frame-member as he brought up the Harley about ten feet from the things. They were as bald as green apples, and they had weak little chins under wide, almost lipless mouths which hung open stupidly, showing rows of long, yellow, doglike teeth. Their eyes were crazy and bloodshot, sunk deep in their sockets under apelike hairless brows. They did not look like folks you could trust.

Doug let the three-foot length of chain dangle from his left hand, clanging loudly against the frame of the Harley as it snaked to the ground. 'I'd appreciate it if you boys would clear the road,' he said. 'You'd appreciate it, too.'

The creep in the middle sniffed the air. 'Gas!' he hissed. 'I smell much gas in the strange machine.'

'And much meat on his bones!'

They laughed shrilly, and drew long, sharp-looking swords from their scabbards.

'You named it, mothers!' Doug shouted, as the three spindly bikes came wobbling towards him like awkward insects, their gawky riders having some trouble steering and trying to hold on to their swords at the same time. He shifted into first, gave her a little throttle, and veered off to the right, so that the green creep on the left closed with him about two feet from his chain hand, thrusting clumsily with his sword.

Doug whipped the chain through the air and caught him square across the back of the skull as the outrigger buzzed by. Surprisingly, the thing's head burst like a rotten water-melon, spewing thin splinters of bone and grey-green slime. The out-of-control bike slammed into the scoot next to it – the big geek riding it seemed incredibly clumsy as he tried to avoid the collision – and knocked the rider sprawling to the ground.

. Doug was easily by them now, and his hog could surely outrun their silly machines, but his blood was boiling, and he figured the proper thing to do was finish the job. These creeps were lame pushovers – finishing off the two remaining ones shouldn't even raise a decent sweat.

He whipped his chop around and came back at the one on the ground, who seemed to be having trouble getting to his feet. As Doug passed by, bringing the chain down across the creature's back, he screamed but managed to slash Doug harmlessly on his boot. By the time Doug had turned his bike again for another pass, the greenie had managed to scramble shakily to his feet. Eyes rolling, teeth bared, mouth drooling, he stood woozily slashing his sword through the air as Doug bore down on him.

At the last moment, Doug veered slightly to the right, ducked under the whistling sword, and caught him across the kneecaps with the chain. The greenie screamed, buckled, and fell on his face.

Doug saw that the last outrigger bike was high-tailing it up the road away from him. The cowardly bastard was running out on his partners!

'That won't do you no good, you son-of-a-bitch!' he shouted as he cranked on his throttle in pursuit. Boy, that crud had to be *really* stupid to think he could outrun a Harley on a puny little bike like that!

It was getting dark, so Doug turned on his headlight as he chased the greenie over the tortuous surface of the ruined road. About thirty yards ahead, the spindly little outrigger bike with its skeletonlike rider wobbled and bounced crazily in his high beam like a lurching spider. The geek on the out-rigger seemed a piss-poor rider, hitting half the potholes and rocks in the road, as if he had the reflexes of someone's grand-father. Doug saw what those outrigger wheels were for as now the left, now the right, touched ground for a moment as the bike hit a pothole or a rock and heeled over suddenly. They were like the training wheels on a little kid's first bicycle; without them, the incompetent slob on the outrigger bike would've gone down every couple of minutes on a killer road like this.

In fact, it took all of Doug's skill, reflexes and arm-strength to keep from going down himself on this so-called road. He'd been chasing the outrigger for maybe five minutes, he realized, and he wasn't gaining any ground. Imagine, a 125 c.c. mouse of a bike holding its own against a high-balling chopper! But forty or at most forty-five was as fast as Doug could go on this torture-track road without creaming himself out. At that speed, the outrigger bike was probably going flat out while he still had more than half his throttle left. But a lot of good that did him.

He realized that, crazy as it looked, the outrigger bike design made some sense under these conditions. Road condition imposed forty-five as top speed anyway, so all his big engine did for him was use up more gas per mile at the same speed. That son-of-a-bitch up there could pace him all night, and guess who would run out of gas first!

It really burned Doug to think of that creep outrunning his big scoot on that little bug of his! Man, what would the Avengers say, if he ever got to see their beautiful ugly faces again? The lip-action would be murder!

Up ahead, the outrigger bike disappeared for a moment around a right-hand curve . . .

Suddenly, Doug heard a high-pitched roar, shouts from more or less human throats, a long shrill scream. Then the outrigger bike reappeared, weaving crazily all over the road in his general direction. The rider was missing his left arm, and quarts of green goo were gushing out of the stump. The outrigger slid off the road entirely and shattered against a tree, sending the dying rider flying off into the underbrush.

And then, rushing straight at him, Doug saw the headlights of something over a dozen motorcycles. An instant later, he made them out sharp and clear: over a dozen of the outrigger bikes, each one ridden by one of the tall green skeletons, eyes glowing and swords flashing in the gleam of the headlights.

Doug didn't have time to do any heavy thinking. He cranked on all the throttle he had, hunched his body as low over the tank as he could, prayed he wouldn't hit a hole or a rock in the next thirty feet, and tried to steer for the empty spaces in the crowd of devil-bikes bearing down on him.

Still accelerating, he zipped in between two bikes, taking an outrigger wheel on his left thigh as sharp steel passed over his head, caught his front wheel in a crack in the road, felt his rear wheel going out as he fought for control. He skidded sideways a foot or two, glancing off the front wheel of an outrigger bike, regained control as the outrigger bounced into the bike next to it, ducked another sword stroke that was way off the mark, and then he was through, hauling ass up the dark winding road while all was confusion and shouting behind him.

Doug felt as if he had been riding for days, though it couldn't have been more than an hour or two. Ahead of him, everything was inky black except for the cone of light that his headlamp cut out of the darkness. The road, as full of cracks and potholes as ever, climbed higher into the Rockies, and it was all he could do to keep his scoot upright at forty. Both arms ached from the prolonged effort and tension, and his left leg hurt like hell where the outrigger wheel had caught it. He was starting to see things that weren't there, and not see things that were. A couple of times he started to lean into left turns that were really rights, as the trees and the bouncing beam of the headlight played tricks with his eyes. He longed to stop, if only to take five.

But all he had to do was glance back over his shoulder and see those fourteen headlights about a hundred yards behind to know that a five-minute rest would be the last five minutes he'd ever see. One hundred yards. He had opened up the gap in the confusion of his dash through them, and he hadn't been able to gain any more ground since, though at least they hadn't been able to close in on him.

It was the damnedest bike race he had ever heard of. A couple of miles of straight road, or even a few miles of decently paved bends, and his big chop would leave the mothers in the dust. But on this cow-track, it didn't matter that he had three times the bike they did, that he was three times the rider they were; with all his skill and power, all he could average was about forty, and those little Mickey Mouse machines just buzzed along flat out, flopping around on their outriggers, matching his speed on half the gas consumption.

And that was what really scared him.

With those king-sized tanks and pint-sized engines, those monsters had at least twice his range. Unless they had started this chase more than half empty, he'd run out of gas first, and then it would be his chain against fourteen of those swords. Four or five of the mothers wouldn't have scared him, but *fourteen*? They'd suck the marrow from his bones and eat the brains out of his skull.

Doug took another glance behind, and, as he did, a bolt of lightning lit up the scene like a strobe. Down in the hollow behind him, he saw the fourteen outrigger bikes hopping and jouncing in pursuit like army ants, the flesh of their mantislike riders gleaming with a sickly green wetness. Darkness and a roll of thunder, then another flash of lightning.

Oh, no! Not another goddamned electrical storm. And as he thought it, three quick sheets of lightning pealed across the sky one after the other, as if electricity, his old enemy, had shown up to gloat over his bones. A long, slow rumble of thunder shook his guts.

'Not yet, you mother, not yet!' he shouted at the sky.

Feeling fury surge through him, he cranked on more throttle, hit a little rock, slid sideways, and had to use his pained left leg to keep from going down. He winced, cursed, and saw that the slip had cost him a few yards on his pursuers. Lightning touched a ridge off to his right.

And his engine broke up for a few beats.

Another bolt of lightning hit off to his left, closer this time. Again his engine coughed and hesitated. Man, all he had to do was stall out now! He saw that he had lost another yard or two.

Slam! Bang! He was bracketed on both sides by bolts of lightning, deafened by the thunder. The chop's engine coughed, sputtered, and died.

He could hear the scream of those fourteen flat-out little engines coming up behind him like a swarm of giant wasps. Howling wordlessly, he craned his neck around to see the green demons on their outrigger bikes outlined in another flash of lightning not ten yards behind as he tromped down on the starter with all of his might. The engine caught; he slammed the chopper into gear and cranked it on.

He opened the gap up to twenty yards before he skidded over a crack in the road, sliding sideways just enough to lose back the distance he had gained.

He crested a hill and came roaring down into a little valley around a mild left turn with the devil-bikes thirty feet behind him and lightning cracking through the sky overhead. His engine broke up again, hesitated, almost died, but recaught. The green creeps gained another few feet in the process. They were so close now that he could hear the bloodcurdling cries coming from their throats as they sensed the kill,

Another bolt of lightning, another cough from his engine, and a sword whistled over his head, burying its point three inches deep in a tree beside the road. A second sword clanged off his sissybar, looped high in the air, and just missed his back on the way down. A third sword sent a thin sting through his left shoulder as it sliced through his colours.

Doug Allard knew he had had it. He was beyond fear, beyond despair, beyond knowing what the hell he was doing except on an instinctive level. He was all rage – rage at the monstrosities that would be eating his flesh in a few more minutes, rage at the sparky dragon in the sky who had thrown him into this hell-world in the first place.

Lightning blinded him as one more sword whistled past his head. In one final, defiant gesture, he ripped the headlight wire loose, and held the naked end aloft shouting at the sky: 'Come and get me, you yellow mother-fucker! I dare you! I d–'

The world turned a blinding, crazy yellow. Everything seemed to happen at once and in slow motion. His body tingled, he choked on ozone, and the engine quit entirely. The chop started to go down, but he knew that if he went down in the next instant or even allowed his foot to touch the road, he had had it. Standing up on the pegs, still blinded, he threw his body to the right as hard as he could against the bank of the turn, compensating for the sudden drop in speed. The Harley wobbled crazily, there was a tremendous clap of thunder, and his vision began to clear.

He dimly saw that he was careening across the road, thumping and bouncing towards a steep drop into a heavily wooded gully to the right. He downshifted, slammed on the brakes, the forward momentum was killed, and the scoot gently slid out from under him. He rolled away from the bike, losing a certain amount of skin in the process.

Picking himself off the ground, he saw that the Harley was lying on its side in the tall grass by the side of the road, about three yards from having rolled into a rugged-looking little canyon. It was daylight, the trees were ordinary fir trees, the road was in good repair, there were no green demons on outrigger bikes coming up it, and the electrical storm was retreating across the sky to the east.

Slowly, it got through to him. This was the same place he had been hit by lightning the first time, and about the same time, too, by the look of the sky. None of that crazy stuff had really happened. The lightning must've knocked him out of his head for a few minutes and into a crazy electricity nightmare.

Only then did he notice the thin pain in his left shoulder, the slash in his colours, the blood underneath.

And when he checked out the bike, he found the headlight wire hanging loose and a wad of tinfoil in the fuse-clip.

# All the Sounds of the Rainbow

Harry Krell sprawled in a black vinyl beanbag chair near the railing of the rough-hewn porch. Five yards below, the sea crashed and rumbled against convoluted black rocks that looked like a fallen shower of meteors half-buried in the warm Pacific sand. He was naked from the waist up; a white sarong fell to his shins, and he wore custom-made horsehide sandals. He was well-muscled in a fortyish way, deeply tanned, and had the long, neat, straight yellow hair of a beach bum. His blue eyes almost went with the beach bum image: clear, empty, but shattered-looking like marbles that had been carefully cracked with a ball-peen hammer.

As phony as a Southern California guru, Bill Marvin thought as he stepped out on to the sunlit porch. Which he is. Nevertheless, Marvin shuddered as those strange eyes swept across him like radar antennae, cold, expressionless instruments gathering their private spectrum of data. 'Sit down,' Krell said. 'You sound awful over there.'

Marvin gingerly lowered the seat of his brown suede pants to the edge of an aluminium-and-plastic beach chair, and stared at Krell with cold grey eyes set in a smooth angular face perfectly framed by medium-length, razor-cut, artfully styled brown hair. He had no intention of wasting any more time on this oily con-man than was absolutely necessary. 'I'll come right to the point, Krell,' he said. 'You detach yourself from Karen your way, or I'll get it done my way.'

'Karen's her own chick,' Krell said. 'She's not even your wife any more.' A jet from Vandenburg suddenly roared overhead; Krell winced and rubbed at his eyes.

'But I'm still paying her a thousand a month in alimony, and I'll play pretty dirty before I'll stand by and watch half of that go into your pockets.'

162

Krell smiled, and a piece of chalk seemed to scratch down a blackboard in Marvin's hand. 'You can't do a thing about it,' he said.

'I can stop paying.'

'And get dragged into court.'

'And tell the judge I'm putting the money in escrow pending the outcome of a sanity hearing, seeing as how I believe that Karen is now mentally incompetent.'

'It won't work. Karen's at least as sane as you are.'

'But I'll drag you into court in the process, Krell. I'll expose you for the phony you are.'

Harry Krell laughed a strange bitter laugh and multi-coloured diamonds of stained glass seemed to flash and shimmer in the sun. 'Shall I show you what a phony I am, Marvin?' he said. 'Shall I really show you?'

Waves of thick velvet poured over Bill Marvin's body. In Krell's direction, he felt a radiant fire in a bitter cold night. He heard a chord that seemed to be composed of the chiming of a million microscopic bells. Far away, he saw a streak of hard blue metal against a field of loamy brown.

All in an instant, and then it passed. He saw the sunlight, heard the breakers, then the sound of a high-performance engine accelerating up in the hills that loomed above the beach house. Krell was smiling and staring emptily off into space.

A tremor went through Marvin's body. I've been a little tense lately, he thought. Can this be the beginning of a break-down? 'What the hell was that?' he muttered.

'What was what?' said Krell. 'I'm a phony, so nothing could've happened, now could it, Marvin?' His voice seemed both bitter and smug.

Marvin blotted out the whole thing by forcing his attention back to the matter at hand. 'I don't care what little tricks you can pull; I'm not going to let you suck up my money through Karen.'

'You've got a one-track mind, Mr Marvin, what we call a frozen sensorium here at Golden Groves. You're super-uptight. You know, I could help you. I could open up your head and let in all the sounds of the rainbow.'

'You're not selling *me* any used car, Krell!'

'Well, maybe Karen can,' Krell said. Marvin followed Krell's line of sight, and there she was, walking through the glass doors in a paisley muumuu that the sea breeze pressed and fluttered against the soft firmness of her body.

163

A ball of nausea instantly formed in Marvin's gut, compounded of empty nights, cat-fights in court, soured love, dead hopes, and the treachery of his body which still sent ghosts of lust coursing to his loins at the sight of the dyed coppery hair that fell a foot past her shoulders, that elfin face with carbon-steel behind it, that perfect body which she pampered and honed like the weapon it was.

'Hallo, Bill,' she said in a neutral voice. 'How's the smut business?'

'I haven't had to do any porn for four months,' Marvin lied. 'I'm into commercials.' And then hating himself for trying to justify his existence to her again, even now, when there was nothing to gain or lose.

Karen walked slowly to the railing of the porch, turned, leaned her back against it, seemed to quiver in some kind of ecstasy. Her green eyes, always so bright with shrewdness, seemed vague and uncharacteristically soft, as if she were good and stoned.

'Your voice feels so ugly when you're trying not to whine,' she said.

'Bill's threatening to cut off your alimony unless you leave Golden Groves,' Krell said. 'He wants to force a sanity hearing and prove that you're a nut and I'm a crook.'

'Go ahead and pull your greasy little legal stunts, Bill,' Karen said. 'I'm sane and Harry is exactly what he claims to be, and we'd both be delighted to prove it in court, wouldn't we, Harry?'

'I don't want to get involved in any legal hassles,' Krell said coldly. 'It's not worth it, especially since you won't have a dime to pay towards your residency fee with all your alimony in escrow.'

'Harry!'

Her eyes snapped back into hard focus like steel shutters, and the desperation turned her face into the kind of ugly mask you see around swimming pools in Las Vegas. Marvin smiled, easily choking back his pity. 'How do you like your little tin guru now?' he said.

'Harry, you can't do this to me, you can't just turn me off like a lamp over a few hundred dollars!'

Harry Krell climbed out of his beanbag chair. There was no expression on his face at all; except for those strange, shattered-looking eyes, he could've been any ageing beach bum telling the facts of life to an old divorcée whose money had run out. 'I'm no saint,' he said. 'I had an accident that

164

scrambled my brains and gave me a power to give people something they want and fixed it so that's the only way I can make a living – a good living.'

He smiled, and broken glass seemed to jangle inside Bill Marvin's skull. 'I'm in it for the money,' said Harry Krell. 'So you better clean up your own mess, Karen.'

'You're such a rotten swine!' Karen snarled, her face suddenly looking ten years older, every subtle wrinkle a prophet of disaster to come.

'But I'm the real thing,' said Harry Krell. 'I deliver.' Slowly and haltingly he began walking towards the doors that led to his living-room, like someone moving underwater.

'Bill –'

It was all there in his name on her lips two octaves lower than her normal tone of voice, the slight hunch forward of her shoulders, the lost, scared look in her eyes. It was a trick, and it was where she really lived, both at the same time. He wanted to punch her in the guts and cradle her in his arms.

'If you're crazy enough to think you're going to talk me –'

'Just let me walk you to your car. Please.'

Marvin got up, brushed off his pants, sighed, and, suddenly drained of anything like emotion, said tiredly, 'If you think you need the exercise that bad, lady.'

They walked silently through a slick California-rustic living-room, where Krell sat on a green synthetic-fur-covered couch stroking a Siamese cat as if it were a musical instrument. On either side of him were a young male hippie in carefully cut shoulder-length hair and a well-tailored embroidered jeans suit, and a minor middle-aged television actor whose name Marvin could not recall.

Marvin kept walking across the black rug without exchanging a look or a word with Krell, but he noticed that there was quick eye contact between Krell and Karen, and at that moment he felt the fleeting taste of cinnamon in his mouth.

Krell's private house fronted on a rich, rolling green plateau across the highway from the Pacific end of the Santa Monica Mountains. Rustic bungalows were scattered randomly about the property, along with clumps of trees, paths, benches, a tennis court, a large swimming pool, a sauna, a stable, the usual sensitivity-resort paraphernalia. The parking lot was tucked nicely away behind a screen of trees at the edge of the highway, so as not to spoil the bucolic scene. But the whole business was surrounded by a ten-foot chain-link fence topped by three strands of barbed wire, and the only entrance was a remotely controlled electric gate. As far as Marvin was concerned, that pretty well summed up Golden Groves. This area north of Los Angeles was full of this kind of guru-farm; the only thing that varied was the basic gimmick.

'All right, Karen, what's Krell's number?' he said as they walked towards the parking lot. 'Let me guess . . . organic mescaline combined with acupuncture . . . tantric yoga and yak-butter massage . . . Ye gods, what else *is* there that you haven't been hung up on already?'

'Synesthesia,' she said in deadly earnest, 'and it works. You've felt it yourself; I could tell.'

Uneasily, Marvin remembered the strange moments of sensory hallucination he had been getting ever since he met Krell, like short LSD flashbacks. Was Krell really responsible? he wondered. Better than turning out to be the results of too much acid, or the beginning of a nervous breakdown . . .

'Harry had some kind of serious head injury three years ago – '

'Probably fell off his surfboard.'

'He was in a coma for three weeks, and when he came out of it, the lines between his senses and his brain were all crossed. He saw sound, heard colour, tasted temperature . . . synesthesia, they call it.'

'Yeah . . . now I remember. I read about that kind of thing in *Time* or somewhere . . .'

'Not like Harry, you didn't. Because with Harry the connections *keep* changing from minute to minute. His world is always fresh and new . . . like being high all the time . . . like . . . it's like nothing else in the world.'

She brought him up short with a touch of her hand, and a flash from her eyes, perhaps deliberate, reminded him of what she had been, what they had been, when they first drove across the San Fernando Valley in the old Dodge, with the Hollywood Hills spread out before them, a golden world they were sure to conquer.

'I feel alive again, Bill,' she said. 'Please don't take it away from me.'

'I don't see – '

Overwhelming warmth enveloped his body. He tasted the wine of her hand on his arm. He heard the symphony of the spheres, tone within tone within tone, without end. He saw the dark of inky night punctuated with fountains of green, red, violet, yellow, fantastic flowers of light, celestial fireworks. He felt his knees go weak, his head reel; he was falling. The fountains of light exploded faster, became larger. He put out his hands to break his fall, smelled burning pine, heard the whisper of an unfelt wind.

He was crouched on the grass supporting his bodyweight on his hands, staring down at the green blades. 'Are you okay? Are you all right?' Karen shouted.

He looked up at her, blinked, nodded.

'What Harry never let the doctors find out was that he could project it,' she said.

Marvin got shakily to his feet. 'All right,' he said. 'So I believe that greasy creep Krell can get inside your brain and scramble it around! But what the hell for? What dumb spiel does he throw you to make you want it, that you're experiencing the essence of Buddha's rectum or something?'

'Harry's no mental giant,' she said. 'He doesn't know why it opens you up – oh, he's got some stupid line for the real idiots – all he really knows is how to do it, and how to make money at it. But, Bill, all I can tell you is that this seems to be opening me up at last. It's the answer I've been looking for for five years.'

'What the hell's the *question*?' Marvin said, an old line that brought back a whole marriage's worth of bad memories, like a foul-tasting burp recalling an undigested bad meal. Acid trips that went nowhere, two months of the Synanon game learning how to stick the knife in better, swinging, threesomes both ways, trial separations and trial reconciliations, savage sex, battle sex, dull sex, and no sex. Always searching for something that had been lost somewhere between crossing the continent together in that old Dodge and the skin-flick way of life that meant survival in Los Angeles after it became apparent that he wasn't the next Orson Welles and she wasn't the next Marilyn Monroe.

'What I think is that this synesthesia must be the natural way people are supposed to experience the world. Somewhere along the way our senses got separated from each other, and that's why the human race is such a mess. We can't get our heads together because we experience reality through a lot of narrow windows, like prisoners in a cell. That's why we're all twisted inside.'

'Whereas Harry Krell is the picture of mental health and

karmic perfection!'

They were nearing the parking lot now; Marvin could see his Targa, and he longed to be in it, roaring along the freeway away from Golden Groves and Karen, away from one more expensive last hope.

Once again, she presented him with her flesh, touching both hands to his shoulders, staring full face at him until something inside him ached with yearning. Her face was as soft as it had been when they had been lovers instead of sparring partners, but her eyes were full of an ageing woman's terrors.

'All I know is what I feel,' she said. 'When I'm living in a synesthetic flash, I feel really alive. Everything else is just waiting.'

'Why don't you just try smack?' Marvin said. 'It may not be cheaper than Krell, but at least it's portable.'

'Harry claims that eventually we can learn to do it on our own, that he can retrain our minds, given enough time –'

'And enough money.'

'Oh, Bill, don't make me lose this! Don't let me drown!'

Her hands dug into his shoulders, her body slumped towards him, wrinkles formed in the corners of her mouth, the stench of pathetic desperation –

He saw huge woman's hands knotted in fear raise themselves in prayerful supplication towards him from a forest of sharp metallic edges. He felt her flesh moving over every inch of his body in long-forgotten personal rhythms, and how it had felt to snuggle toasty beside her in bed. He tasted bitter gall and the nausea of panic, smelled musky perfume.

He heard his own tears pealing like church bells as they rolled down his cheeks; he drew the giant hands to him, and they dissolved into an armful of yellow light. Wordless singing filled his ears, and he smelled a long night by the fireside, felt the freshly warm glow of nostalgia's sad contentment.

He was holding Karen in his arms; her cheek was nestled against his neck. She was crooning his name, and he felt five years and more younger. And suddenly scared silly and burning mad.

He thrust her away from him. 'It won't work,' he snarled. 'You're not going to play me for a sucker again, and neither is Krell!'

'You felt –'

'What you and Harry Krell wanted me to feel! Forget it, it won't work again! See you in court.'

He sprinted the rest of the way to his car, tearing little

divots out of the moist turf of Golden Groves.

With four underground films totalling less than ninety minutes to Bill's credit and with Karen having 'starred' in the last two of them, the Marvins had left New York to seek fame and fortune in the Golden West. What they found in Hollywood was that beautiful women with minor acting talent were a dime a dozen (or at best fifty dollars a trick) and that Bill's 'credits' might as well have been Cuban Superman flicks.

What they also found out after four months of starving and scrounging was that Los Angeles was the pornography capital of the world. For every foot of feature film shot in Hollywood, there were miles of split beaver, S&M, and just plain stag films churned out. The town was swarming with film makers' living off porn while waiting for The Big Break and 'actresses' whose footage could be seen to best advantage in Rotary smokers or the string of skin-flick houses along Santa Monica Boulevard known as Beaver Valley. Porn was such a booming industry that most of the film makers knew less about handling a camera than Bill. So when the inevitable occurred, he had plenty of work and the Marvins had an abundance of money.

Seven years later, Bill Marvin was left with his excellent connections in the porn industry, a three-year-old Porsche Targa, a six-room house in Laurel Canyon which he would own outright in another fifteen years, enough cameras and equipment to live well off pornography for ever, and no more illusions about Making It Big.

He was set for life. Sex, both instant and long-term, was certainly no problem in his line of work; four months of screwing around between serious relationships that averaged about six months in duration seemed to be his natural pattern. In the porn business, you connect up with a good lawyer and a tricky accountant early if you know what's good for you, so he had come out of the divorce pretty damn well: fifteen grand in lieu of her share of the house and one thousand dollars a month, which he could pay without feeling too much pain.

He had felt that he could breeze along like this for ever, happy as a clam, until that scene last week at Golden Groves. Now he was rattling around the house as if it were the dead shell of some enormous creature that he was inhabiting like an overambitious hermit crab. He couldn't get his head into a new project, sex didn't turn him on, drugs bored him. He could think of only one thing: Harry Krell's head on a silver platter. And the fact that his lawyer had told him that the sanity-hearing ploy probably wouldn't work certainly hadn't improved his disposition.

What possible difference can it make to me that Karen is throwing my money away on Krell? he wondered as he paced the flagstone walk of his deeply shadowed overgrown garden. If it wasn't Krell, it'd be some other transcendental con-man. The hills are full of them.

If this were a Universal TV movie, I'd still be carrying a subconscious torch for Karen, which is why Krell would be getting under my skin – guru-envy, a shrink might call it. But I wouldn't have Karen back on her hands and knees. No, it's got to be something about that crazy creep, Krell –

*That crazy Krell!*

Bill Marvin did a classic slow-take. Then he double-timed through the ferns and cacti of his hillside garden, trotted around the edge of his pool, through his living-room, and two stairs at a time up to his second-floor office, where he called Wally Bruner, his hotshot lawyer.

'Look, Wally, about this con-artist my wife is –'

'I told you, you miss one alimony payment, and she'll have *you* in court as defendant, and unless you succeed in getting her committed –'

'Yeah, yeah, I know I probably can't have her declared incompetent. But what about Krell?'

'Krell?' Wally's voice had slowed down about twenty miles per hour. Marvin could picture him leaning back in his chair, raising his eyebrows, rolling the word around in his mouth, tasting it out. '*Krell?*'

'Sure. This guy had a head injury so serious he was in a coma for weeks, and when he came out of it he claimed he could see sound, hear light, feel taste, and then he goes into business claiming he can scramble other people's brains the same way. What would that sound like in court?'

'Who swears out the complaint?' Bruner said slowly.

'Huh?'

'The only way to get Krell into court is on a fraud charge, claiming that he can't really project this synesthesia effect, and that he's swindling the marks. That puts him in the position of having to defend himself against criminal fraud by proving he's got this strange psychic power, which, let me tell you, is not a position *I'd* care to defend. If I was his lawyer, I think I'd have to plead insanity to try to beat the felony rap.

If he wins, he spends a few months in the booby hatch and this Golden Groves thing is broken up, which is what you want. If he loses he goes to jail, which you'd like even better. If he tries to convince a Los Angeles judge that he's got psychic powers, he won't get to first base, and, if he tries it before a jury, I'll get him *and* his lawyer thrown in the funny-farm.'

'Well, hey, that's great!' Marvin shouted. 'We got him coming and going!'

'Like I say, Bill,' Bruner said tiredly, 'who's the complainant?'

'In English, please, Wally.'

'In order to get Krell into court on a fraud charge, someone has to file a complaint. Someone who can claim that Krell has defrauded him. Therefore, it must be someone who has paid Krell money for his hypothetical services. Who's that, Bill? Certainly not Karen –'

'What about me?' Marvin blurted.

'You?'

'Sure. I go up there, pay Krell for a month's worth, stay a few days, then come out screaming fraud.'

'But according to you, he really delivers what he claims to . . .'

'As of now, I never told you that, right?'

'You'd have to testify under oath . . .'

'I'll keep my fingers crossed.'

'You really think Krell will take a chance on letting you in?'

Bill Marvin smiled. 'He's a greedy pig and an egomaniac,' he said. 'He tried to get Karen to help convince me he was Malibu's answer to Buddha, and he's more than jerk enough to convince himself that he succeeded. Will it work, Wally?'

'Will what work?' Bruner said ingenuously. 'As of now, this phone conversation never took place. Do you read me loud and clear?'

'Five by five,' Marvin said. He hung up on Bruner and dialled the number of Golden Groves.

Sprawled across his green couch, Harry Krell's body contradicted the lines of tense shrewdness in his face as his eyes for once focused sharply on Marvin. 'Maybe I'm making a mistake trusting you,' he said. 'You made it pretty clear what you think of me.'

Marvin leaned back in his chair, emulating Krell's casualness. 'Trust's got nothing to do with it,' he said. 'You don't have to trust me and I don't have to trust you. You show me that you can give *me* my money's worth; that should convince me that Karen is getting my money's worth, too. Turn me down, and it's one thousand dollars a month you stand to lose.'

Harry Krell laughed and microscopic pinpricks seemed to tickle every inch of Marvin's body. Beside Krell on the sofa, Karen's body quivered once. 'We don't like each other,' Krell said, 'but we understand each other.' There was something patronizing in his tone that grated on Marvin, an arrogant overconfidence that was somehow insulting. Well, the greedy swine would soon get his!

'Then it's a deal?'

'Sure,' Krell said. 'Come back tomorrow with your clothes and a five-hundred-dollar cheque that won't bounce. You get a cabin, three meals a day here in the house, free use of the sauna, the tennis courts, and the pool, at least two synesthesia groups a day, and whatever special events might go on. The horses are five dollars an hour extra.'

'I'm paying for the two of us,' Marvin said. 'I should get some kind of discount.'

Krell grinned. 'If you want to share a cabin with Karen, I'll knock two hundred and fifty dollars a month off the bill,' he said. There was something teasing in his voice.

Involuntarily, Marvin's eyes were drawn to Karen's. There was an emotional flash between them that brought back long-dead memories of what that kind of eye-contact had once meant, of what they had been together before it all fell apart. He found himself almost wishing he was what he pretended to be: a pilgrim seeking to clean the stale cobwebs out of his soul. He had the feeling that she just might agree to shack up with him. But the glow in her eyes was forced by desperate need. Los Angeles was full of faces like that, and the Harry Krells sucked them dry and let them shrivel like old prunes when the money ran out. He had to admit that his body still felt something for Karen's, but he was long past the point where he'd let sex drag him where his head did not want to be; the going up was just not worth the coming down.

'Pass,' he said. Karen's expression did not change at all.

Krell shrugged, got up, and walked out on to the porch in that strange uncertain gait of his, inhaling sharply as he crossed the shadow-line into sunlight.

'I know you're up to something cheap and tricky,' Karen said.

'Then why did you agree to warm Krell up for me?'

'You wouldn't believe me.'

'Try me.'

She sighed. 'Because I still care a little for you, Bill,' she said. 'You're so frozen, so tied up in knots inside, and who should know what that's like better than me? Harry has what you need. Once you've been here a while, you'll see that, and it won't matter why you originally came.'

'Saving your alimony had nothing to do with it, of course.'

'Not really,' she said. And as the words emerged from her mouth, they became brightly-coloured tropical butterflies, and she became a lush greenness from which they flew. There was a soft musical trilling, and the smell of lilacs and orchids filled the air. In that moment, he felt a pang of regret for what he had said, saw the feeling she still bore for him, heard the simple clarity of her body's animal love.

In the next moment, they were staring at each other, and tension hung in the air between them. Karen broke it with a small, smug madonna-smile. Marvin found himself sweating at the palms, and somewhat leery of what he was getting himself into.

The cabin was sure a dump for five hundred dollars a month: a bed, a dresser, a couch, a bathroom, two electric heaters, and a noisy old motel-type air conditioner. Breakfast had been granola (sixty-nine cents a pound), milk, and coffee, and Marvin figured that Krell would use the same health-food excuse to dish out cheap lunches and dinners. The only thing that required expensive upkeep was the riding stable, and that ran at a profit as a separate operation. Krell must be pocketing something like half the residency fee as clear profit. Fifteen cabins, some of them double-occupancy . . . that would be seven grand a month at least!

There's no business like the guru business, Marvin thought as he followed Krell and three of his fellow residents out on to the porch above the rumbling sea.

Four large, plush cushions had been placed on the bare wood in a circle around an even larger zebra-striped pillow. Krell, in his white sarong, lowered himself to the central position in a semblance of the lotus position, looking like the Maharishi as played by a decaying Tab Hunter. Marvin and the other three residents dropped to their cushions in imitation of Krell. On Marvin's left was Tish Connally, a well-preserved thirty-fiveish ex-Las Vegas 'showgirl' who had managed to hold on to a decent portion of the drunk money that had swirled around her for ten years, and who had eyed him a couple of times over the granola. On his right, Mike Warren, the longhair he had seen the first day, who turned out to be an ex-speedfreak guitarist, and, on the far cushion, a balding TV producer named Marty Klein, whose last two series had been cancelled after thirteen weeks each.

'Okay,' said Krell, 'you all know Bill Marvin, so I guess we're ready to charge up for the morning. Bill, what this is all about is that I unfreeze everybody's senses together for a bit, and then you'll have synesthetic flashes on your own off it for a few hours. The more of these sessions you have, the longer your own free-flashing will last, and finally your senses will be re-educated enough so you won't need me.'

'How many people have . . . uh, graduated so far?' Marvin asked sweetly.

To his credit, Krell managed not to crack a scowl. 'No one's felt they've gotten all I've got to give them yet,' he said. 'But some are far along the way. Okay, are we ready now?'

The morning sun had just about burned away most of the early coastal fog, but traces of mist still lingered around the porch, freshened by the spray churned up by the ocean as it broke against the rocks below. 'Here we go,' said Harry Krell.

There was light: a soft, all-enveloping radiance that pulsed from sunshine yellow to sea green with the tidal rhythm of breakers crashing against a rocky shore. Marvin tasted a salty tang, now minty-cool, now chowder-hot. To his right, he heard a thin, throbbing, blues-like chord, something like a keening amplified guitar stretching and clawing for some spiritual stratosphere, higher, higher, higher, but never quite getting there, never resolving the dynamic discord into a bearable harmony. To his left, a sound like the easy ricky-tick of a funky old piano that had been out of tune for ten years, and had mellowed into that strange old groove. Across from him, a frantic syncopated ticking, like a time-bomb running down as it was running out, a toss-up as to whether entropy would outrace the explosion.

And dominating it all, the central theme: a surging, blaring brassy wailing that seemed a shell of plastic around a central motif of sadness – a gypsy violinist playing hot jazz on a

174

uba – that Marvin knew was Harry Krell.

Marvin was knocked back on his mental heels by the flood of transmogrified emotions pouring in on him from unexpected sensual directions. He sensed that in some way, Mike Warren *was* that screaming non-chord that was the aural transformation of his visual persona, that Tish Connally was the funky ricky-tick, and Klein's running-down rhythm, a has-been wondering whether he would fall apart or freak out first. And Krell, phony brass within sad confusion within cheap pseudo-sincerity within mournful regret within inner emptiness like a Muzak version of himself – a man whose existence was in the unresolvable tension between his grubby phoniness and the overwhelming, rich strangeness of the unique consciousness a random hit on the head had given him, grandeur poured by fate into the tawdriest available vessel.

Marvin had never felt pressed so close to human beings in his life. He was both fascinated and repelled by the intimacy. And wondered what they were experiencing as him.

Then the universe of his senses went through another transformation. His mouth was filled with a spectrum of tastes that somehow spread themselves out along spatial dimensions: acrid spiciness like smoked chili peppers to the right, soft furriness of flat highballs to the left, off aways something like garlic and peptic gall, and everywhere the overwhelming taste of peppermint and melancholy red wine. He could hear the pounding of the surf now, but what he saw was a field of orange-red across which drifted occasional wisps of cool blue.

'Now join hands in a circle and feel outsides with your insides,' said the plastic peppermint and musky red wine.

Marvin reached out with both hands. The right half of his body immediately became knotted with severe muscular tension, every nerve twanging to the breaking point like snarled and taut wire. But the left half of his body went slack, soft, and quietly burned-out as four a.m. in bed beside someone you picked up a little after midnight at a heavy boozing and loping party.

'Okay, now relax and drift on back through the changes,' said peppermint and red wine.

Sight became a flickering sequence: blue mists drifting across a field of orange-red, sunshine yellow pulsing through sea green in a tidal rhythm, four people seated in a circle around Harry Krell on a sunlit porch. Back and forth, in and out, the visions chased each other through every possible variation of the sequence, while Marvin heard the pounding

175

of the surf, the symphony for four souls; tasted minty-cool, chowder-hot, smoked chili peppers, flat highballs, peppermint and red wine. The sensual images crossed and recrossed, blending, clashing, melding, bouncing off each other, until concepts like taste, sight, hearing, smell, feel, became totally meaningless.

Finally (time had no referents in this state) Marvin's sensorium stabilized. He saw Tish Connally, Mike Warren, Marty Klein and himself seated on cushions in a circle around Harry Krell on a sunlit wooden porch. He heard the crashing of the surf on the rocks below, felt the softness of the cushion on which he sat, smelled a mixture of sea breeze and his own sweat.

Krell was bathed in sweat, looked drained, but managed to smile smugly in his direction. The others appeared not quite as dazed as Marvin felt. His mind was completely empty in that moment, whited-out, overwhelmed, nothing more than the brain centre where his sensory input merged to form his sensorium, that constellation of sight, smell, sound, taste, touch and feel which is the essential and basic ground of human consciousness.

'I hope you weren't disappointed, Mr Marvin,' Krell said. 'Or would you like your money back?'

Bill Marvin had nothing to say; he felt that he hardly had enough self-consciousness to perceive words as more than abstract sequences of sound.

The bright afternoon sun turned the surface of the pool into a rippling sheet of glare which seemed to dissolve into glass chiming and smashing for a moment as Marvin stared at the incandescent waters. Even his normal senses seemed unusually acute – he could clearly smell the sea and the stables, even here at poolside, feel the grainy texture of the plastic cloth of the beach chair against his bare back – perhaps because he could no longer take any sensory dimension for granted, with the synesthetic flashes he was getting every few minutes. There was no getting around the fact that what he had experienced that morning had been a profound experience and one that still sent echoes rippling through his brain.

Karen pulled herself out of the pool with a shake and a shudder that flashed droplets in the sun, threw a towel around herself, and plopped down in the beach chair next to his. She was wearing a minimal blue bikini, but Marvin found himself noticing the full curves of her body only as an abstract design, glistening arcs of water-sheened skin.

'I can see you've really had a moving session,' she said.

'Huh?'

He saw that her eyes were looking straight at him, but in a glazed, unfocused manner. 'I'm flashing right now,' she said. 'I hear you as a low hum, without the usual grinding noises in the way you sit, and . . .'

She ran her hand along his chest. 'Cool green and blue, no hard silvers and greys . . .' She sighed, removed her hand, refocused her eyes. 'It's gone now,' she said. 'All I get unless Harry is really projecting is little bits and pieces I can't hold on to . . . But some day . . .'

'Some day you'll be able to stay high all the time, or so Krell claims.'

'You know Harry's no fraud now.'

Marvin winced inwardly at the word 'fraud', thinking what it could be like testifying against Krell. *Lord, he might drop me into a synesthetic trance in the middle of the courtroom! But . . . but I could fake my way through if I was really ready for it, if I have enough experience functioning in that state. Krell seems to be able to function, and he's like that all the time . . .*

'What's the matter, Bill?'

'Does my body sound funny or something?' he snapped.

'No, you just had a plain, old-fashioned frightened look on your face for a minute there.'

'I was just thinking what it would be like if Krell really could condition you to be like him all the time,' Marvin said. 'Walking around in a fog like that, sure I can see how it might make things interesting, but how could you function, even keep from walking into trees? . . .'

'Harry *is* like that all the time, and he's functioning. You don't exactly see him starving in the street.'

'I'll bet you don't see him in the street, period,' Marvin said. 'I'll bet Krell never leaves this place. The way you see him walking around like a zombie, he probably goes on memory half the time, like a blind man in his house.' *Yeah,* he thought, *people, food, money – he makes it all come to him. He probably couldn't drive a mile on the freeway or even walk across a street without getting killed.* Suddenly Marvin found himself considering Harry Krell's inner reality, the strange parameters of his life, with a certain sympathy. What would it really be like to be Krell? To be wide open to all that fantastic experience, but unable to function in the

177

real world except by somehow making it come to you?

Making it come to you through a greasy con-game, he told himself angrily, annoyed at the softness towards Krell that had sneaked into his consciousness, at the momentary blunting of the keen edge of his determination.

Rising, he said, 'I'm going to take a dip and wash some of those cobwebs out of my head.'

He took four running steps and dived off the concrete lip of the pool.

When he hit the water, the world exploded for a moment in a dazzling auroral rainbow of light.


'How long have you been here?'

'Six weeks,' said Tish Connally, lighting a cigarette with a match that momentarily split the darkness of her cabin with a ringing gong in Bill Marvin's head. Another synesthetic flash! He had been at Golden Groves for only three days now, and the last session with Krell had been at least five hours ago, yet he was still getting two or three flashes an hour.

He leaned back against the headboard of the bed, felt Tish's body exhale against him, saw the glow of her cigarette flare brightly, then subside. 'How long do you think you'll stay?' he asked.

'Till I have to go make some money somehow,' she said. 'This isn't the cheapest joint I've ever seen.'

'Not until you graduate, become another Harry Krell?'

She laughed; he could feel her loose flesh ripple, almost see pink gelatin shaking in the dark. A flash – or just overactive imagination?

'That's a con,' she said. 'Take it from an expert. For one thing, there are people who have been in and out of here for months, and they still need their boosters from Harry to keep flashing. For another, Krell wouldn't turn you on permanently if he could. We wouldn't need him any more then; where would his money come from?'

'Knowing that, you still stick around?'

'Billy-boy, I've kicked around for ten years, I've been taken every way there is to be taken, took men every way there was for me to take 'em. Before I came here, I'd felt everything there was to feel fifty thousand times, so no matter what I did to get off, I was just going through the motions. At least here I feel alive in bits and pieces. So I'm paying Krell a pretty penny for getting me off once in a while. I've made

178

most of my money on the other end of the same game, so what the hell, it keeps the money in circulation, right?'

'You're a mean old broad,' Marvin said, with a certain affection.

She snubbed out her cigarette, kissed him lightly on the lips, rolled towards him.

'One more for the road, Billy-boy?'

Diffidently, he took her tired flesh in his arms. 'Oh, you're golden!' she sighed as she moved against him. And he realized that she had been hoping for a synesthetic flash to give her a bit of the sharp pleasure that he alone could not.

But he could hardly feel anger or disgust, since he had been looking for something more spectacular than a soft human body in the darkness, too.

Strolling towards his cabin near the sea cliffs in the full moon-light, Bill Marvin saw Harry Krell emerge from Lisa Scott's cabin and walk down the path towards him, more rapidly and surely than he usually seemed to move in broad daylight. They met in a small grove of trees, where the moonlight filtered through the branches in tiger-stripes of silver and black that shattered visual images into jigsaw patterns.

'Hallo, Marvin,' Krell said. 'Been doing some visiting?'

'Just walking,' Marvin said neutrally, surprising himself with his own desire to have a civil conversation with Krell. But, after all, strictly as a curiosity, Krell had to be one of the most interesting men on earth.

Krell must have sensed something of this, because he stopped, leaned up against a tree, and said, 'You've been here a week now, Marvin. Tell me the truth, do you still hate my guts? Are you still out to get me?'

Glad to have his reaction masked by the camouflage-pattern of moonlight and darkness, Marvin caught his breath and said, 'What makes you think I'm out to get you?'

Krell laughed, and for a moment Marvin saw a bright blue cataract smashing off a sheet of glass in brilliant sunlight. 'I heard the look on your face,' Krell said. 'Besides, what makes you think you're the first person that's come here trying to nail me?'

'So why'd you let me come here?'

'Because half the Golden Groves regulars come here the first time to get the goods on that phony Harry Krell. If I worried about that, I'd lose half my trade.'

'I just can't figure where your head's at, Krell. What do

179

you think you're doing here?'

'What am I doing?' Krell said, an edge of whining bitterness coming into his voice. 'What do you think I'm doing? I'm surviving as best I can, same as you. You think I asked for this? Sure, a lot of nuts come through here and convince themselves they're getting religious visions off of me, a big ecstasy trip. Great for them! But for Harry Krell, synesthesia's no ecstasy trip, let me tell you! I can't drive a car or walk across a street or go anywhere or do anything. All I can do is hear the pretty colours, smell the music, see the taste of whatever crap I'm eating. After three years, I got enough experience to guess pretty well what's happening around me most of the time as long as I stay on familiar ground, but I'm just *guessing*, man! I'm trapped inside my own head. Like now, I see something blue-green off to the left – probably the sea I'm smelling – and pink-violet stuff around us – trees, probably eucalyptus. And I hear some kind of gong. There's a moon out, right? If you're saying something now, I can't make it out until I start hearing sound again. Man, I'm so alone here inside this light-show!'

Bill Marvin fought against his own feelings, and lost. He couldn't stop himself from feeling sympathy for Harry Krell, locked inside his weird private reality, an ordinary slob cut off from any ordinary life. Yet Krell was entirely willing to put other people into the same place.

'Feeling like that, you still don't mind making your bread by sucking other people in with you . . .' he said.

'Jesus, Marvin, you're a pornographer! You give people a kick they want, and you make your living off of it. But does it turn *you* on? How'd you like your whole life to be a pornographic movie?'

Bill Marvin choked on a wisecrack which never came out, because the deadening quality of what his life had become slammed him in the gut. What *is* the difference between me and Krell? he thought. He gives the suckers synesthetic flashes and I give 'em porn. What he's putting out doesn't turn him on any more than what I put out turns me on. We're both alone inside our heads and faking it. He got hit on the head by a surfboard and got stuck in the synesthesia trip, and I got hit on the head by Hollywood and got stuck in the porn trip.

'Sorry to put you on such a bummer, Marvin,' Krell said. 'I can smell it on you. Now I can hear your face. What? . . .'

'We're both alike, Krell,' Marvin said. 'And we both stink.'

'We're just doing what we gotta do. You gotta play the cards you've been dealt, because you're not going to get any others.'

'Sometimes you deal yourself your own lousy hand,' Marvin said.

'I'll show you lousy!' said Krell. 'I'll show you how lousy it can be to walk just from here to your cabin – the way I have to do it. You got the guts?'

'That's what I'm paying my money for,' Marvin said quietly. He began walking back up the path. Krell turned and walked beside him.

Abruptly, the darkness dissolved into a glowing gingerbread fairyland of light. To Marvin's left, where he knew the sea was crashing against the base of the cliffs, he saw a bright green-yellow bank of brilliance that sent out pulses of radiance which struck invisible objects all around him, haloing them in all the subtle shades of the spectrum, forming an infinitely complex lattice-work of ever-changing, intersecting wavefronts that transformed itself with every pulse from the aural sun that was the sea. Beside him, Harry Krell was a shape of darkness outlined in a shimmering aurora. He heard a far-away gong chiming pleasantly in the velvet quiet. He tasted salt and smelled a rapidly changing sequence of floral odours that might have been Krell speaking. The beauty of it all drenched his soul through every pore.

He walked slowly along, orienting himself by the supposition that the green-yellow brilliance was the breaking surf, that the areas of darkness outlined by the living lattice-work of coloured wavefronts were solid objects to be avoided. It wasn't easy, but it was somehow enchanting, picking his way through a familiar scene that had transformed itself into a universe of wonder.

Then the world changed again. He could hear the crashing of the sea. On his left, he saw a thick blue-green spongy mass, huge and towering; on the ground, the path was a ribbon of blackness through a field of pinkish-grey; here and there fountains grew out of the pinkish-grey, with greyish stems and vivid maroon crests, tree-high. He smelled clear coldness. Krell was a doughy mass of colours, dominantly washed-out brown. Marvin guessed that he was seeing smell.

It was easy enough to follow the path of dead earth through the fragrant grass. After a while there was another, subtler transformation. He could see that he and Krell were walking up the path towards his cabin, no more than twenty yards away in the silvery moonlight. But his mouth was filled with a now-winey, now-nutty flavour that ebbed and flowed with an oceanic rhythm, here and there broken by quick wisps of spiciness as bird-shapes flapped from tree to darkened tree. The only sound was a soft, almost subliminal hiss.

Dazed, transported, Marvin covered the last few yards to his cabin open-mouthed and wide-eyed. When they reached the door, the strange tastes in his mouth evaporated, and he could hear the muffled grumble of the pounding surf. He laughed, exhilarated, refreshed in every atom of his being, alive to every subtle sensory nuance of the night.

'How do you like living where I live?' Krell said sourly.

'It's beautiful . . . it's . . .'

Krell scowled, snickered, smiled ruefully. 'So the big wise-guy turns out to be a sucker just like everyone else,' he said, almost regretfully.

Marvin laughed again. In fact, he realized, he had been laughing for the first time in over a week. 'Who knows, Krell,' he said, 'you might enjoy living in one of my pornographic movies.'

He laughed one more time, then went into his cabin, leaving Krell standing there in the night with a dumb expression on his face.

Later, when he got into bed, the cool sheets and the soft pillow were a clear night full of pinpoint-bright multicoloured stars, and the darkness smelled like a woman's perfume.

The world went livid red, and the wooden slats beneath his naked body became a smoky tang in his mouth. Marvin felt himself glowing in the centre of his being like a roaring winter fireplace, heard Dave Andrews's voice say, 'Really sweats the tension out of you.'

The flash passed, and he was lying on the wooden bench of the sauna shack, bathed in his own luxuriant sweat, baking in the heat given off by the hot stones on their cast-iron rack. The fat towel-wrapped man on the bench across from him stared sightlessly at the ceiling and sighed.

'Phew!' Andrews said as his eyes came back into focus. 'I could really hear my muscles uncoil. *Twooong!*'

Marvin lay there just sucking up the heat, going with it, and entirely ignoring Andrews, who was some kind of land speculator and a crashing bore. He closed his eyes and concentrated on the waves of heat which he could all but feel breaking against his body, the relief of the grain of the wood against his skin, the subtle odour of hot stone. He had learned to bask in the world of his senses and let everything else drift by .

'I tell you, old Krell may be charging a pretty penny, but it sure cleans out the old tubes and charges up the old batteries . . .' Andrews babbled on and on like a radio commercial, but Marvin found little trouble in pushing the idiot voice far into the sensory background; it was easy, when each sense could become a universe entire, when your sensorium was no longer conditioned to sight-sound dominance.

Suddenly Andrews's voice was gone, and Marvin heard a whistling hurricane wind. Opening his eyes, he saw wispy white billows of ethereal steam punctuated by the multicoloured static of Andrews's words. He tasted something like curry and smelled a piney, convoluted odour.

When the flash passed, he got up, slipped on a bathing suit, dashed out of the sauna, ran across the rich green grass in the high blue sunlight, and dived straight into the swimming pool. The cool water hit his superheated body with an orgasmic shock. He floated to the surface and let the little wavelets cradle him on his back as he paddled over to the lip of the pool, where Karen sat dangling her feet in the water.

'You're sure a different man than when you came here,' she said.

Looking up, Marvin saw her bikinied form as a fuzzy vagueness against a blinding blue sky. 'Well, okay, so Krell's got something going for him,' he said. 'But at these prices, he's still a crook, and, the funny thing is, *he* thinks he's even a *bigger* crook than he really is . . .'

She didn't answer for a long moment, but stared into the depths of the pool to one side of him, lost in the universe of her own synesthetic flash.

When she finally spoke, it came out as a gusher of glistening green-black oil emerging from soft lavender clouds, while Marvin tasted icy cotton-candy. Judging from the discord of her face jarring the soothing melody of the sunlit sky, it was probably just as well.

Marvin luxuriated in a shower of blood-warm rain, saw a sheen of light that pulsed from sunshine-yellow to sea-green; then the flash passed. He was sitting on his cushion on Harry Krell's sunny porch, in a circle around Krell, along with Tish, Andrews . . . and Karen.

Strange, he thought, I've been here nearly three weeks, and

183

I haven't had a booster group with Karen yet. Stranger still was the realization that this hadn't seemed peculiar or even significant until this moment. Like the rest of the outside world, his former relationship with Karen seemed so long ago and far away. The woman to his right seemed no closer to him emotionally than any of the other residents of Golden Groves, who drifted through each other's private universes like phantom ships passing in the night.

Harry Krell took a deep breath, and the vault of the sky became a sheet of gleaming brass; below, the sea was a rolling cauldron of ebony. The porch itself was outlined in dull blue, and the people around him were throbbing shapes of yellowish pink. To his left, the odour of fading incense; across the way, rich Havana smoke, and the powerful tinge of ozone pervaded all. But the smell that riveted Marvin's attention was the one on his right: an overwhelming feminine musk that seemed compounded of (or partially masked by) unsubtle perfume, drying nail polish, beauty cream, shampoo, deodorants – the full spectrum of chemical enhancers which he now realized had been the characteristic odours of living with Karen. Waves of nostalgia and disgust formed inside him, crested, broke, and merged in a single emotional tone for which there was no word. It simply *was* the space that Karen occupied in his mind, the total image through which he experienced her.

Another change, and he saw light pulsing from yellow to green once more, tasted a salty tang. From his left, he heard the ricky-tick of a funky old piano; across the way, a staccato metallic blatting; over it all, the brassy, hollow, melancholy wailing of Harry Krell. But once again, it was the theme on his right that vibrated a nerve that went straight from his senses through his brain and into the pit of his gut. It was as if a gong were striking within an enclosure that rudely dampened its vibrations, slamming the echoing notes back on each other, abruptly amputating the long, slow vibrations, creating a sound that was a hysterical hammering at invisible walls, the sound of an animal caught in some invisible trap. Ironically, the smell of a woodland field in high summer was heavy in Marvin's nostrils.

After a few more slow changes, Krell brought them flickering back through the sequences: blood-warm rain, a sheet of gleaming brass over an ebony sea, the smell of feminine musk and body chemicals, light pulsing from yellow to green, rich Havana smoke, peppermint and red wine, high summer in

a woodland field, flat highballs, melancholy wailing, ricky-
tick . . .

Then Marvin was seated on his cushion next to Karen's,
while the sea grumbled to itself below, and Harry Krell
breathed heavily and wiped sweat out of his eyes.

Marvin and Karen simultaneously turned to look at each
other. Their eyes met, or at least their focal planes intersected.
For Marvin, it was like staring straight at two cold green
marbles set in the alabaster face of a statue, for all the
emotion that the eye-contact contained. Judging from the
ghost of a grimace that quivered across her lips, she was
seeing no less of a stranger. For an instant, he was blinded by
yellow light, sickened by the odour of her chemical musk.

When the flash passed, he saw that she was in the throes
of one of her own; her eyes staring sightlessly out to sea, her
lips twitching, her nostrils flaring. For a moment, he was
overcome with curiosity as to how she was experiencing him;
then, with a small effort, he put this distasteful thought from
his mind, knowing that this was the moment of true divorce,
that the alimony was now the only bond that remained
between them.

A moment later, without a word to each other, they both
got up and went their separate ways. As Karen walked through
the glass doors into the house, Marvin saw a billowing spongy
green mass, and heard her hysterical trapped hammering beat
time for her march out of his life for ever.

And time became the flickering procession of sheets of flashing
images. The sun set over the cliffs into the Pacific, now a
globe of orange fire dipping into the glassy waters and painting the sky with smears of purple and scarlet, now the smoky
tang of autumn fading into the sharply crystal bite of winter
light, now a slow-motion clap of enormous thunder dying
slowly into the velvet stillness. The morning light on the porch
of the beach house was a shower of blood-warm rain, a field
of orange radiance shot with mists of cool blue, a humming
symphony of vibrating energy.

For Bill Marvin, these had become the natural poles of
existence, the only time-referents in a world in which night
might be the toasty woman-smell of his bedroom darkness,
the brilliant starry night of cool sheets against his body, or
the golden light of anonymous female flesh against his, in
which day was the coruscating fireworks of food crunching

between his teeth, the celestial chime of his hot body hitting the cool water of the pool after the curry flavour of the sauna, the billowing green clouds of the surf breaking against the foot of the cliffs.

People floated through this quicksilver wonderland as shifting, illusive constellations of sensory images. Ricky-tick piano. Chemical female musk. Cloud of Havana smoke. The wail of an electric guitar. Peppermint and red wine. Hysterical confined gonging. Smoked chili peppers. Garlic-and-peptic gall. The melancholy wail of a gypsy violinist playing hot jazz on a tuba. The sights and sounds and tastes and smells and feels that were the sensory images of the residents of Golden Groves interpenetrated the images of the inanimate world, blending and melding with them, until people and things became indistinguishable aspects of the chaotic whole.

Marvin's mind, except in isolated moments, consisted entirely of the combination of sensory impulses getting through to his brain at any given time. He existed as the confluence of these sensory images; in a sense, he *became* his sensory experience, no longer time-bound to memory and expectation, no longer a detached point of view sardonically bouncing around inside his own skull. Only in isolated stretches when his synesthetic flashes were at momentary ebbs did he step outside his own immediate experience, wonder at the strangeness in his own mind, watch himself moving through the trees and cabins and people of Golden Groves like some kind of automaton. At these times, he felt a certain vague sense of loss. He could not tell whether it was sadness at his temporary fall from a more sublime mental state, or whether his ordinary everyday consciousness was mourning its own demise.

One morning, when the granola in his mouth had scattered jewelled images of sparkling beads as he crunched it against a coffee backdrop of brown velvet, Harry Krell held him back as he started to walk out on to the porch for his morning booster session.

'This is day thirty for you, Marvin,' Krell said.

Marvin stared back at him dumbly, hearing a hollow brassy wail, seeing a rectangle of bright orange outlined against deep blue.

'I said this is the last day you've paid for. Either pony up another five hundred dollars, or send for someone to take you back to L.A. You won't be in any shape to drive for about a week.'

Marvin's sensorium had changed again. He was standing

in the cool living-room near the open glass doors, through which sunlight seemed to extend in a solid chunk. 'Thirty days?' he said dazedly. 'Has it been *thirty days*? I've lost count.' Lord, he thought, I was only supposed to be here a week or two! I haven't done any work in a month! I must be nearly broke, and the alimony payment is past due. My God, thirty days, and I can hardly remember them at all!

'Well, I've kept good count,' said Krell. 'You've used up your five hundred dollars, and this is no charity operation . . .'

Marvin found his mind racing madly like some runaway machine trying futilely to catch up with a world that had passed it by, desperately trying to sync itself back in gear with the real world of bank statements, alimony courts, four-day shooting schedules, rubber cheques, vice-squad hassles, recalcitrant actresses, greasy backers. If I can cast something in three or four days, maybe I can use the same cast to shoot three quickies back-to-back, but I'll have to scout three different locations or it won't work. That should give me enough money to cover the monthly nut and keep Karen's lawyers off my back if I get all the money up front, pay them first and kite cheques until –

'Well, Marvin, you want to write out another five-hundred-dollar cheque or – '

'What?' Marvin grunted. 'Another five hundred dollars? No, no, hell, I'm broke, I've already been here too . . . I mean, I've got to get back to L.A. immediately.'

'Well, maybe I'll see you around again some time,' said Harry Krell. He walked into the brilliant mass of sunlight, leaving Marvin standing alone in the shadowed living-room, and, as he did, Marvin saw a brilliant pulse of sunshine yellow, heard an enormous chime, felt a terrible pang of paradise lost.

But there was no time to sort his head out. He had to call Earl Day, his regular cameraman, and get him to come out and drive him back to Los Angeles in the Targa. They could put together three concepts on the way in, start casting tomorrow, and have some money in four or five days. Gotta make up for lost time fast, fast, fast!

For the barest moment, Bill Marvin was enveloped in rainbow fire which sputtered and crackled like colour-TV snow, and he heard the zipping, syncopated whooshing of metal birds soaring past his ears, igniting phantom traces of memories almost forgotten after the frantic madness of grinding out three pornies in less than a month, slowing his racing

187

metabolism, catching for a fleeting instant his psychic breath.

Then he was back stiff-spined in the driver's seat of his Porsche, his hands gripping the wheel like spastic claws, the engine growling at his back, barrelling down the left lane of the Ventura Freeway at seventy-five miles per hour in moderate traffic. The flash had come and gone so quickly that he hadn't even had time to feel any sense of danger, unlike the first time he had tried to drive, only five days out of Golden Groves, when he nearly creamed out as the road became a sharp melody through rumbling drums in the twisty Hollywood Hills. Now the synesthetic flashes were few – one or two a day – and so transient that they weren't much more dangerous behind the wheel than a strong sneeze. Each one slipped through his mind like a ghost, leaving only a peculiar echo of vague sadness.

The first couple of weeks of production, on the other hand, had been a real nightmare. Up until maybe ten days ago, he had been flashing every half-hour or so, and strongly enough so that he hadn't been able to do his own driving, so that takes had been ruined when he tripped out in the middle of them, so that the actors and crew sometimes thought he was stoned or flipping out and tried to take advantage of it. Fortunately, he had made so many pornies by now that he could just about do it in his sleep. The worse of it had been that making the films was so boring that he found himself actually waiting for the synesthetic flashes, concentrating on them when they came, even trying to anticipate them, and experiencing the actual work as something unreal, as marking time. He was never much interested in sex when he was shooting porn – after treating female bodies like meat all day it was pretty hard to get turned on by them at night – and the only time he had really felt alive was when he was flashing or involved in one of the hundreds of horrible hassles.

He made an abrupt three-lane jump and pulled off the freeway at Laurel Canyon Boulevard, drove across the ticky-tacky of the San Fernando Valley, began climbing up into the Hollywood Hills. The Valley side of the Hills was just more flatland-style suburban plastic, but once across Mulholland Drive, which ran along the major ridgeline, Laurel Canyon Boulevard curved and wound down towards the Sunset Strip, following an old dry stream bed through a deep gorge that cut through overgrown and twisted hills festooned with weird and half-hidden houses, a scene from some Disney Black Forest elf cartoon.

Usually, Marvin got a big lift out of leaving the dead plastic landscape of lowland Los Angeles for the shadowy, urbanized-yet-countrified world of the Canyon. Usually, he got a tremendous emotional surge out of having finished one film – let alone three – driving away from it all on the last day of cutting, with any one of a dozen readily available girls already waiting at the house for him to start a week-long lost weekend, his reward for a job well done.

But this time, the drive home did nothing for him, the end of the final cutting only left him empty and stale, and he hadn't even bothered to have a girl waiting for him at the house. He felt tapped out, bugged, emotionally flat, and the worst of it was that he didn't know why.

He pulled into his carport and walked around the side of his house into the seclusion of the unkempt, overgrown garden. Even the wild, lush vegetation of his private hillside seemed washed out, pallid, and somehow unreal. The bird sounds in the trees and underbrush seemed like so much Muzak.

He kicked irritably at a rock, then heard the phone ringing in the house. He went inside, plopped down in the black leather director's chair by the phone stand, picked up the living-room extension, and grunted, 'Yeah?'

It was Wally Bruner.

'What's going on, Bill? I haven't heard from you in nearly two months, ever since you started in on that matter we discussed. I heard you'd started shooting three weeks ago, so I knew you weren't dead, but why haven't you got in touch with me? Did you get what you went there for?'

Marvin stared out of the picture window into the garden, where the late afternoon sunlight cast shadows across scraggly patches of lawn under two big eucalyptus trees. Two dun-coloured morning doves had ventured out of their wooded seclusion to nibble at seeds in the grass and gobble moodily to themselves like dowager aunts.

'What are you talking about, Wally?' Marvin said vacantly.

'Damn it, you know! Golden Groves. Harry Krell. Are we ready to proceed?'

Suddenly glowing bubbles of pastel shimmer were drifting languidly up through a viscous wine-coloured liquid, and Marvin smelled the sweet aroma of perfect sunset; just for the tantalizing fraction of a moment, and then it was gone.

Marvin sighed, blinked, smiled.

'Forget it, Wally,' he said. 'I'm dropping the whole thing.'

'What? Why on earth –'

'Let's just say that I went up on a mountain, came down and want to make sure it's still there.'

'What the hell are you talking about, Bill?'

'What the vintners buy,' said Marvin.

'Bill, you sound like you've flipped.'

'I'm okay,' Marvin said. 'Let's just say I don't give a damn what Karen spends her alimony on as long as I have to pay it, and leave it at that. Okay?'

'Okay, Bill. That's the advice I gave you in the first place.'

After he hung up on Bruner, Marvin sat there looking out into his garden where ordinary dun-coloured birds were pecking at a scruffy lawn, and the subtle grey tinge of smog was barely apparent in the waning light.

He sighed once, shuddered, shrugged, sighed again. Then he picked up the phone and dialled the number of Golden Groves.

# We Can Build You Philip K. Dick

We started out making electronic organs and spinets – the Frauenzimmer Piano Company, that was us. Then the bottom dropped out of the market, so we turned over to simulacra – exact reconstructions of famous personalities. We made an Abraham Lincoln, for instance – stupid, because he had *all* Lincoln's characteristics, and he wasn't about to be anybody's puppet.

That was when things really started going wrong. First off, we got tangled up with Sam K. Barrows – American's most enterprising young multi-millionaire – and a plan to settle the moon with our own creations. Then we got tangled up with our own identities, and reality started falling apart.

And from there on in, things just got worse . . .

Another masterpiece of bizarre invention from the Hugo-winning author of *The Man in the High Castle.*

# Rings of Ice Piers Anthony

The government had tried to alter the world's climate by surrounding Earth with a vast canopy of ice. Things went horribly wrong – which was why Gus and Thatch were desperately trying to get their big mobile home up into the mountains, high above the floods which were rapidly drowning out the rest of the world.

They even had some crazy notion about saving civilization from the waters – which was why they took along uptight Zena – who knew far more than she was telling about those rings of ice – and voluptuous Gloria – who turned out to be sometimes a man and sometimes a woman as well. And then they picked up Karen and Floy, and Dust Devil, and Foundling – two latterday Noahs in a motorized ark.

The only trouble was, their little community wasn't the only one which was frantically trying to find dry land, food and fuel. And seeing robbery, looting, murder and cannibalism were now regarded as legitimate means of survival, the struggle for life was apt to become a little vicious at times.